Emily -
Thank you for the support :

LEGENDS
— IN —
TIME
EXILES

LEGENDS IN TIME

EXILES

VINCENT HOBBES
JORDAN BENOIT

Hobbes End Publishing, LLC

Legends in Time: Exiles
Published by Hobbes End Publishing, LLC, a division of Hobbes End Entertainment, LLC.

First Edition, First Printing
Hobbes End Publishing: trade paperback, 2008
Printed in the United States of America

ISBN:
978-0-9763510-2-3

Cover illustration and design: Jordan Benoit
Map: courtesy of Jordan Benoit
All other internal graphics and design: Jordan Benoit
Editing: Carol Gates
Additional production: Nathan Palmer

For information, contact:
Hobbes End Entertainment, LLC
PO Box 193
Aubrey, TX 76227
www.hobbesendpublishing.com

To the faithful and true—our families, friends, and fans—for the support you have given us, and for your constant encouragement that has kept us sitting at our computers for hours on end to make this project possible . . .

This book is dedicated to Todd Reddy

Ellsa Mountain Range
(White Mountains)

Isthor

Whelmore

The
Endlands

Chybum

Cosh

Nador

Gyrih

The Sharaidon Coast

Ellsar

Aronia

Denok Forest

Fairmeadow

Stalkwood

Crevail   Narkhet
           Maat

Merriton

Ogata

The

Kellorian Sea

N
W   E
S

PART 2: EXILES

The barbarian roamed the eastern shoreline of the Empire of Nador. He walked aimlessly, without direction or cause. He traversed the coastline, making his way south along the barren beach. On his right side, to the west, were massive bluffs that loomed overhead. To his left, east, was the powerful Kellorian Sea.

The man's boots carved through the wet sand, the water washing up and then back away again, leaving his path unrecognizable in its wake, rinsing away his presence. After some time, the large man stopped and took a moment to gaze upon the expansive and brutal Kellorian Sea. It seemed to go on forever. As far as the man's eyes could see, the raging sea splashed and swirled on the horizon. The ocean was intense. The man took a few deep breaths, taking in the grandeur and vastness.

After his pause he began walking again.

The man had broad shoulders and was healthy, with brown hair and a beard that was unkempt. His hair fell past his shoulders and was matted and dirty. The man walked with a swagger of both confidence and contemplation. He had walked for many days—too many to count. The man headed south at an aggressive rate; there was purpose in his step. He was unrelenting in his pace, his long stride constant as he walked. The man was weary and tired, but that did not slow him as he pushed on, stepping over fallen logs and overgrown coastal shrubbery.

The area he walked was located on the southeastern outskirts of the empire. It had once been a major Ungoran town, which was a stone's throw from the bordering kingdom of old Serona.

Finally, when the sun was directly above in the sky, the barbarian stopped. He sighed. A rush of relief, of old comforts, came across the man. He stood on the beach, this time the churning Kellorian Sea to his back and the lands of Nador in front of him. He grinned. The barbarian ran his fingers through his full beard, thinking. His pants and tunic were muddied. The sword at his side and the pack slung over his shoulder, which had weighed him down for many years, suddenly were not such the burden. With a flicker of life in his eyes, the man continued to stare inland. A strong gust of cold wind swept past him, rekindling his spirit and determination.

The barbarian stood at the edge of Narkhet Maat, the beach whose corridor led to the town of Crevail, and the rest of the known world of Men. The empire's ruler, Makheb, had named the beach after the Barbarian Wars. No one was quite sure as to why, but the emperor did not explain himself and his subjects did not question him. If their god-like ruler felt the need to name a beach, that was fine with Nador's citizens.

Towering bluffs that lined its expanse protected the eastern coastline of Nador. They acted as buffers to the Kellorian Sea. Below these cliffs were broken beaches and pounding waves. It was different at Narkhet Maat, though. The beach was wide and the swells less brutal. Instead of a sheer wall of jagged rock, this particular beachhead had an opening that led to the mainland on top.

This corridor opened to the beach, on which the barbarian stood, from a wide gap at the top of the cliff, all the way down. The strip was broad, the width of five hundred men, and angled sharply down towards him. The corridor of Narkhet Maat was a crevasse in the towering rock face, a passageway into the lands of Nador.

The man stared at the incline and its magnitude. The passage to the top beckoned him and he began making his way up.

Ahead of him were strange fortifications.

There were hundreds of them. Pieces of wood and iron and other strange objects were strewn haphazardly up the corridor. From afar, they had no detail, no recognizable representation. The man knew this was a new addition to the beach. He had traveled these lands in the past, and had never seen these objects that littered Narkhet Maat. He kept walking, upward, until he reached the first one. It was a large piece of twisted and mangled iron, ten times the height of a man. There were strange symbols etched in the metal.

He walked past it.

The barbarian passed more of these oddities. He saw hundreds of wide spears as he hiked. They pointed at an angle, down towards the beach.

Huge piles of tree trunks and boulders were scattered within the pieces of metal, colossal spikes and rods that jutted from every angle of the corridor. The intention of this mess was simple—defense.

As the man continued walking, he pondered the need for such an elaborate defense system. Certainly, Narkhet Maat would be the best place to construct such defenses—if such a threat existed. Yet it was beyond the man's comprehension as to the purpose behind a powerful empire such as Nador needing them. Since the recorded history of mankind, nothing but ravenous waters and endless openness lay to the east. Of course, the intentions of a ruler, whose face had never been revealed, were probably not meant to be understood. The barbarian shrugged his shoulders and continued up. He ultimately did not care.

He walked on, taking some time until he finally reached the top of the bluffs, where the corridor ended. A few hundred paces away, stood the town of Crevail. It had once belonged to the former Kingdom of Ungora, but now, like all regions south of Denok Forest, was under Nadorian occupation. Civility had entered the old lands of the barbarians under Emperor Makheb's control.

After the Ungorans had been driven from their lands, into the depths of the forest, their villages and cities were ransacked and burned by pursuing Valeecian and Seronan troops. The soldiers were allowed to pillage at will, and were ordered to burn down every town they came across. Perhaps trying to rid the world of Ungoran history, Makheb was insistent that Ungora would no longer be recognizable.

All towns were torched, except one—Crevail.

Although over the years Crevail had become modernized, the town still stood as if a monument to the days when the barbarians were powerful— when life and death hung on the balance, and a time when heroes challenged the mighty war machine of the Ungorans under King Alarik. The new ruler of Men, having defeated the Ungorans, spared only Crevail. The town still flurried with life, although with a different people than the past. Nadorian residents occupied her. Seronans mostly, but many of Valeecian and Umite backgrounds resided within her streets, too. Ungorans no longer lived in what was once a major city of the old kingdom. The town had been completely assimilated into a new Nadorian culture.

A culture brought on by the mysterious Makheb.

From Crevail the sea was visible. It was alone, solitary amongst the surrounding flat lands. The storms of the southern empire had not reached Crevail, but could be seen in the distance, threatening to overtake her shortly. In the emerging presence of the most massive storm mankind had ever seen, the residents of the coastal town stayed busy, preparing for the worst. In addition, masses of formakha, as well as humans, worked steadily. Building and remodeling had been underway for the past few years, the project of fortifying the city continuing under order from Makheb.

The citizens of Nador strived to satisfy their emperor, and it was no different in Crevail. What Makheb ordered, his subjects answered dutifully. Like a father, they followed his lead. Since his coming into the lands of Valeecia twenty-five years prior, Makheb had yet to lead his people astray. They trusted Makheb. They honored him by doing his bidding. They loved their emperor, and feared him, as well. He was their god-ruler, and the trade-off was fair.

For many generations, the people of the known world had answered to kings, so they were used to being submissive. Makheb had thus far been a much better ruler than the previous ones, so bowing to him came easily. With the establishment of Makheb's empire, and the control by a single, omnipotent ruler over all of the lands, the citizens received the fruits of a potent civilization with wealth to be made and glory to be sought. Just as many towns throughout Nador grew in size and population, Crevail was no exception.

The inhabitants of modern Crevail, obviously no longer of Ungoran lineage, made a comfortable home within her. Like other cities, she basked in the now prolific empire. Along with this also came success. The people of Crevail kept their bellies full of food and their heads dizzy with og ale. The people lived in luxury. The town had been remodeled, with only hints of her history left behind. It was as if the world of Men was attempting to receive its retribution from the destruction that had been dealt to it by years of Ungoran brutality. Where once the people of Crevail struggled to survive, their crops having died and the grounds turning sour, now was a town of bliss. If it was vengeance the people sought, then they had attained it, for Crevail no longer resembled any likeness to the old barbarian Kingdom of Ungora. Only the name remained.

The barbarian stood outside the walls of the town, which were also a new addition, and sadness filled him as his eyes became flooded with tears. He could not contain himself. Years of loneliness seemed to be catching up to him. The sight of Crevail, before his eyes once again, was too much.

The magnificence was too much.

The luxuries were too much.

The menacing barbarian stood in the afternoon sun, with the dark outline of the purple storm that approached from the south, and stared at the old town of his homeland. This was not the Crevail that he remembered. These were not the lands of honor, but of gluttony. Ungora was no more, and the barbarian was saddened by the thought.

After some time, the man stood up straight, adjusted his pack across his shoulder, and walked towards the town. Narkhet Maat was at his back, the town in front. His past weighed on his soul—his future unknown. He walked closer, his eyes taking in the new town of Crevail.

And despite it all . . . he was home.

Stride by stride, hoof against frail dirt, the black stallion panted and frothed as it galloped across the wide plains. The sun had risen, and as a new day began Gromulus and Lorylle traveled as far as they could away from the trade city, Cosh, and towards the northern realm of Nador.

The Nadorian exiles were headed northwest, to the border of the great empire, and into uncertainty. Their destination was not yet known, and their trust resided in a sword.

By the urge of Antiok, the pair rode on.

15

She awoke in a struggle. She sat up abruptly, unsure for a moment who she had been fighting. Then, she remembered again. She saw *him*. *He* reached for her. Niralyn began to cry.

The sun was shining through the curtains, foreshadowing yet another brilliant day in the lands of Aronia. The curtains glowed with the incoming sunlight, warming the room. Another beautiful day in Ellsar, and the queen was frightened.

"Kedor . . . Kedor," she spoke softly. Her voice was barely above a whisper as she gently touched his arm.

The king's eyes opened, staring into hers. "Yes, my love?"

She did not say anything at first. Her eyes gazed into her brave king's and the two held the moment. Slowly, Kedor's hand came up and brushed her cheek. He wiped away her tears.

Niralyn finally whispered, "I had a terrible nightmare."

Still lying down, the king put his face close to hers. He kissed her softly on the forehead, giving her the comfort she needed. "My queen, it is only the ramblings of our minds that scare us in our sleep. We are cursed in that we dream of the unthinkable. It was not real, I can assure you."

"*He* was real. *He* was horrific."

King Kedor smiled a little. "And who is this man who eyes my bride? I shall take his head and mount it amongst the many other creatures I have slain." He was trying to calm her through jest, but it was not working.

Niralyn was afraid.

"*He* was watching me. *He* spoke to me . . . but . . . I am afraid I cannot remember what he said. Perhaps I did not even hear his words . . . only saw the words his lips formed. *He* reached for me—" Niralyn trailed off as she remembered.

The King of Aronia held her tighter. She was his pride, and he was highly protective of her. "Does this man have a name?"

"*He* is no man."

Risard awoke just outside the crypt. He sat up and a sharp pain echoed in his head. He lay back down in the soft mud, and then wincing, he sat up again, this time slowly. He rubbed his face, dried blood and muck covering his hand. He looked down and noticed bloodstains on his tunic.

Risard screamed, "GROMULUS!"

After some time he was fully composed and on his feet. Risard looked around, but could not find any weapons. He shook his head and walked out of the cemetery, and into the darkness of the storms that blotted out the sun. They were howling, pushing the raindrops sideways, and stinging Risard's face as he found his horse, climbed atop, and rode back towards Cosh.

He made his way past Veris' estate. At least two-dozen soldiers stood the grounds, searching through the rubble that was once the senator's home. Bodies of the many servants were being pulled out, and the soldiers lined them up in a neat row. Risard passed by the soldiers as they looked at him oddly, no doubt due to his dirty and scathed appearance, and he continued to ride. At the property's front, masses of onlookers stood in small groups. They made way as he galloped past.

Risard worked his way through the streets of Cosh and finally came to the Senate building. He dismounted, crossed the breezeway and climbed the steps. Two legionaries saluted as they held the doors. Risard walked past hastily, not returning the salute. Inside he walked the hallway, turned left, and walked along farther. Finally he came upon a door, which led to Parlock's private chambers. Without knocking, Risard walked into the consul's quarters.

After entering, Risard saw Parlock talking with someone. He stood inside the entrance, observing. Across the room, Parlock spoke to a man dressed in all black. The man's head and face were covered with long scarves. At his side was a thin-bladed sword. Parlock spoke a few words that were inaudible, and Risard saw the other man nod. The man turned and walked towards the doorway, near to where the centurion stood. Risard noticed he looked human, but somehow different. The man was an Osa'har—a dweller of the Endlands. Risard had never seen one before, and could only catch a brief glimpse of him. His hair was dark, his eyes green. They were more angled than those of the Men east of the Endlands. According to the stories, the Osa'har were people who had existed many generations in the arid regions of the Endlands. As he walked near, Risard saw the man's face was darker than his own, rough and scarred like leather. His nose was flatter, less protruding. As the man strode past Risard, his eyes blinked. His eyelids closed from side-to-side. The robed man passed, not paying him the slightest bit of attention, and left the room.

Corbidon had business that needed tending.

Risard stood for a moment, and then held his head high as Parlock walked towards him. The senator eyed him strangely. Purple ash coated Risard's face and his hair was matted with mud and blood.

Parlock approached the soldier and asked, "What happened to you, centurion?"

Risard replied, "I was left for dead—"

Parlock eyed him sharply. The battered and soiled face of Risard made him wary. "Did you take care of our little problem?"

Risard frowned and lowered his head, yet said nothing.

Parlock's voice rose. "Answer me, centurion!"

Risard spoke, "Consul, I have failed. I let the man escape."

Anger was written on Parlock's face. Before he could speak, Risard raised his head and spoke more, "Sir, I have important news to tell you—"

After speaking for some time, Parlock dismissed the centurion back to the ranks. He was to join his legion, which was now camped not far away from the trade city, and remain there, awaiting further orders. Risard bowed and left the senator's chambers, ashamed and angry. Parlock stood alone, his mind racing.

❦❦❦❦❦

Crevail had drastically changed. A tall wall made of tree trunks surrounded the city. The trunks were thick and firm, as tall as five men. Scaling such fortifications would have been nearly impossible, for six archer towers were positioned with a clear view of the town's surroundings. The sentry towers were plated with gold, and colorful cloths wrapped around their makings. Crevail had not only become successful, but boastful, as well. The sun beat down on the man as he walked towards the nearest gate, which seemed busy. As he neared, the barbarian looked up at one of the towers. Six men stood atop, bows in their hands, yet their arrows remained in their quivers. He nodded as they stared at him approaching. They did not respond.

The man reached the entrance, and it was indeed busy. Eight Nadorian legionaries stood guard outside the gate, four on each side. Another twelve men, mostly merchants and traders, stood outside. They were noisy, obviously conducting their usual business. As the stranger approached he saw a burly man with an oil-slicked beard yapping loudly. The man was barking orders at a few workers, while in the middle of a heated discussion with a few local farmers at the same time. Another twenty formakha went about their tasks, carrying the supplies that were being checked at the gates.

The wanderer approached, and the large, burly man stopped in mid-sentence, staring at him. "Hey, you," the foreman started. "What is your business here?"

The barbarian stood, staring back. "My business is ta enter this town." His voice was deep, guttural—distinct.

However, the foreman did not seem to notice. He spat on the ground. "Use the main gate around the corner, this entrance is for formakha."

The barbarian respectfully nodded his head. He did not say anything, and started in the direction the foreman had gestured.

The foreman continued his conversation with the farmers, and then he looked back at the stranger. He asked loudly, "Are you new to these parts?"

The barbarian looked back. He did not answer.

The foreman felt a tingle of fear and got the hint. He spoke, "It matters not. Go on around the corner, follow the wall. It will lead you to the main gate. This one is strictly for slave labor."

The barbarian nodded and turned again to leave. The foreman watched as the stranger rounded the corner. There was something different about the barbarian. Something about the way he looked, the way he spoke. The foreman could not place exactly what, and soon turned back to his duties.

As the barbarian rounded the wall, he bumped into three formakha slaves carrying lumber and pottery. He smacked directly into one and the creature dropped its goods, stepping backwards to regain its balance. The other two simply continued on as the fallen one began quietly picking up the spilled supplies. The barbarian looked at the creature, mostly out of curiosity. He laughed and began to walk past.

Very suddenly the formakha stood up, took a step towards the man, and stood its ground. It was only for a moment. Most would have passed it off as reaction, but the barbarian sensed something else. *Resistance,* he thought to himself. The man stepped even closer, his face near the formakha's own head. He eyed the almost lifeless eyes of the formakha, but found nothing. The creature knelt back down and began picking up the rest of the fallen goods. The barbarian proceeded to the main entrance.

Eventually he rounded a corner of the town's wall system, and came to the main entrance. It, too, was busy. Dozens of people were coming and going through the large, open gates. Massive stone pillars, resembling horns, sat in rows on either side of the gateway. Embedded in each were strange carvings. In front of these were two guard booths on the outside, and two more inside the town's limits. High above were two more archer towers, each with six men alert at their post. The barbarian counted fifteen guards on the outside of the gates, as well as the twelve in the towers above.

Amongst the sentries, people of all ages were pulling carts and carrying bundles of wood on their backs. Pack mules, piled high with skins, pottery, precious metals and blankets from the reaches of the empire, were being unloaded outside. Beasts, such as mules, seemed to be favored over the formakha slaves that he had seen at the last entrance. A woman with a basket of fresh herbs smiled at him as he walked past. The barbarian could smell the fresh basil. It made him salivate, for he had been without a solid meal for quite some time. Being midday, the town was well alive, unlike the eerie lifelessness on the beach. People were so busy with their daily routines, that they hardly paid attention to the stranger as he mixed in with the mob.

It was strange. A strong military presence seemed to scour Crevail, more so than the usual guards. Ordinarily, Nadorian soldiers were only posted to protect the interests of the empire, but here in Crevail, it was different. Soldiers were everywhere. Four more came out from the gates, relieving others of their posts. They were heavily armored, which did not make sense to the traveler. However, they did not carry their spears and shields, but instead had only short swords at their sides and wore full body armor. They wore helmets, each adorned with crimson plumes. Long capes ended at the backs of their knees.

The barbarian stood in line, patiently waiting his turn. He was thinking of a childhood friend when someone stepped on his foot. The barbarian turned and looked at an old man who was carrying a small basket of fruit. The elderly man walked slowly, wearing nothing but a ratty tunic, obviously a man of poverty.

"I . . . I am sorry, young sir. At my age, it is hard to keep one's balance," apologized the man, staring up at the towering barbarian.

"Never mind, old man," he replied. "Let me help ya'h carry that burden."

The old man graciously accepted, and the barbarian grabbed the basket from the man's hands. He sat it on the ground for a moment and un-slung his own burden from his shoulder, the pack thumping on the ground below. He untied the top of his pack and opened it. Then, he put the elderly man's basket of fruit on top of his effects. He lifted his pack and carried the man's belongings and his own, together.

"That is most kind of you, good sir. Good-hearted people are few and far between here as of late. It is nice to see that kindness has not completely vanished."

The barbarian only nodded, returning the smile. They stepped forward a few more paces as they approached the head of the line.

The old man turned once again to the barbarian and said, "*Ah*, I once had your strength. When I was young, as you are, I was very strong. The strongest in my village."

The barbarian, trying to keep pleasant, asked, "Where are ya'h from, old timer?"

The old man smiled. "The old lands of Serona. I only moved here a year ago. My wife passed away and I have family that moved to Crevail. I like it, I suppose."

The barbarian answered politely, "An old friend of mine was Seronan." He thought back to the past, and smiled.

The old man then asked, "Where might you come from? Your accent, it does not sound as if it is of these parts. Perhaps you are . . . southern Valeecian, originally?"

The barbarian smiled at this. "Actually, my home was near here. A half-day walk."

The old man laughed, which led to a coughing fit. After he was done he continued, "Sorry, at my age. . . . Well, it does not matter. You say a half-day, *eh*? You must be mistaken . . . or perhaps I did not hear you correctly. At my age, your hearing goes quickly."

Luck would have it that the barbarian would not have to answer. They were next in line. The old man stepped forward, his head lowering, as a large Nadorian legionary said, "Your business?"

The old man stood still, not answering the soldier. Instead, he seemed to be thinking. He was pondering his new acquaintance's last words. The soldier barked, "Be quick, old man. State your business."

The old man then spoke, "Only to sell my fruit and pick up supplies before these strange storms approach, as everyone else."

The soldier only nodded, and then turned towards the barbarian. "And your business?"

The barbarian answered, "Ta help my grandfather trade these fruits, and get him home soon." The old man looked up at the barbarian strangely, but said nothing, no doubt believing he had not heard the man's words correctly.

The soldier eyed the two. He was relaxed and unmistakably bored by his guard duty. "That is good. You should get him home before long. It seems the fury of the gods will plague us with those storms tonight," he said, looking almost dreamily at the southern skies of darkness. "Move along."

The barbarian held the old man's arm, helping him along his way. They walked only twenty paces when they came across another group of guards, these younger than the last.

"State your business here," one demanded.

The barbarian answered, "I already have."

The other three legionaries laughed at this, and the fourth was quickly angered at the response. "I gave you a direct order. Now answer me or I will have you detained."

The barbarian, usually quick to anger, kept his composure. "My business is the same as everyone else. Does this town not exist for trade any longer?"

The legionary, who was a few years too young to have fought in the Barbarian Wars, eyed him up and down. "I see you carry a sword, stranger."

"As does any able-bodied man. Is the carrying of arms illegal in the empire now?"

The soldier did not like the man's attitude. He snapped at him, "This town is under strict watch by order of the Senate. Times are wary and you are beginning to irritate me."

His comrades stepped a little closer.

The barbarian laughed. "I am no threat, I assure ya'h. My blade is dull and I carry only fruits ta trade at the tables."

The soldier eyed the man's pack across his back, seeing the fruits inside. "And you carry no other weapon?"

"No," the barbarian lied.

After another stare, the soldier noticed the line beginning to grow longer and the impatient faces of the citizens who stood in it. "Then what are you wasting my time for, peasant? Move along!"

The barbarian nodded and moved forward once more, the old man alongside him. Thus, he entered Crevail's main gate and the city within.

Silence.

The air was quiet. The storm had finally calmed in Cosh.

The Walfyre looked upon the rubble that had once been Consul Veris' estate. He was peering from behind a hedgerow that followed the long, dirt road up to the estate. He was at the southern edge of the manor, looking at the burnt home. The creature could not believe what he saw. He thought he had arrived too late, that he had stayed too long tending to his business, and because of this, Consul Veris was most likely dead. He cursed himself. He felt he had failed Emperor Makheb.

Findyk, still dressed in his royal armor and holding the emperor's spear, stepped out from behind the once beautifully manicured shrubbery, which was now coated with purple ash from the storms. The shrubs began to wither and decay underneath the strange ash. He slowly made his way to the disarray. Findyk stopped, looking down at the spear in his hands. He knew he should hide it. It would be recognizable and questions would be raised as to why a Walfyre carried the emperor's spear. He walked back to the hedgerow and hid it underneath some thick underbrush. He cringed at having to place the valued artifact in the filthy ash, but he had no choice.

Findyk then returned his direction to the estate once more. As he got closer, stepping over a grassy hill and bringing the rubble completely into view, he noticed two sentries posted by the front door of the home. The house had been ransacked—that was obvious—and nearly burnt to the foundation. However, the main doorway remained.

The rains poured the previous night and had stopped the fire before it burned down the entire house. The storm still impended overhead, persisting north as if a bad omen. The storm discomforted Findyk.

With his mind on overload, he gathered enough courage to continue his route. He was determined to discover the fate of the young man whom he was sent to look after. He had to find out if his fears were indeed true. The Walfyre pressed through the smog of the smoldering embers of the fire, mindful of his surroundings, and saw the horrors. The lifeless bodies of the servants were everywhere. At a quick count, he saw seventeen men and women who had innocently met their fates, dishonorably slain by the very soldiers whom they believed protected them. Findyk was troubled by the barbarism. The odor of charred bodies sickened him. The men and women had been defenseless, not deserving their outcomes. The Empire of Nador had turned on her own.

Findyk inconspicuously walked on.

He approached the two sentries who stood by the doorway. The fog shielded his approach until he stood only a few paces away. Thunder cracked overhead. Findyk stepped out from the twisting smoke, alarming the men. Their immediate action was to grab their spears and point them his way.

"Halt," shouted one.

"State your business, quickly," said the other.

Findyk spoke, *"Click.* Easy, gentlemen. Rest your weapons," his voice authoritative.

The soldier recognized the emblem on the Walfyre's shoulder. "Sorry, sir. I did not realize your rank." After a brief pause, he continued, "However, this area is closed to all who do not belong here." The two men pulled their spears back upright, acknowledging Findyk's place within the empire. Although not a soldier, the insignia on his shoulder let them know he was an aide to the emperor.

One of the guards spoke, "What brings you to this post, sir?"

Findyk replied flatly, ignoring the question, "What of the consul? *Click.* Did your men apprehend the culprit?"

The soldier spoke, "No, not yet. Consul Veris is nowhere to be found. Our men searched this place, but we found no trace of him."

Findyk concealed a sigh. He was relieved. "Do you know where he might have gone?"

The soldier continued, "A stable boy told us he went west . . . right before we ran him through." The soldier chuckled at this.

Findyk said, "I shall have a look around—"

"No," the other one interrupted. "We are under strict order from the Senate. Nobody is allowed access without permission."

Findyk eyed the two. "Were you under order to kill these innocent servants?" He was disgusted by the legionaries' actions.

The soldier stepped closer. "We were given full liberty to eradicate the enemy by any means necessary."

Findyk did not back down. "Do not disrespect me, soldier. I am under order from Emperor Makheb, himself. I serve only him, as do the armed forces of Nador. *Click.* Step aside, soldiers. . . . Your emperor commands it."

"Sir, I cannot."

The Walfyre was impatient. "I grow tired of your disobedience. What is the name of your commanding officer? *Click. Click.* I shall speak to him at once."

The two guards looked at one another. They did not want trouble. They grumbled and stepped aside, allowing the Walfyre to pass.

Findyk said, "I will forgive you . . . this time. Though, do not ever test me again. *Click.*" He walked past.

Findyk spent some time searching through the once lavish home. It lay in crumbles. He looked for clues. Nothing.

Finally, Findyk walked back to the sentries. They looked at him skeptically. He spoke, "Gentlemen, you stated a stable boy told you he headed west?"

One nodded.

"Where exactly? What is west of here?"

The soldier responded, "Just a grove in the distance. After that, nothing but wide plains, until the Endlands."

The other said, "In that grove is a cemetery, I believe. Old, and in shambles. Our men have already searched there. . . . They found nothing of any significance."

Findyk thought about this. "What do you think has become of him?"

"I do not know, sir. He will be found sooner or later. Word is that no expense shall be spared for his capture. Five hundred nidaki to the man who finds him, I hear. He will be found," the soldier said confidently.

Findyk thanked them for their time and turned to leave.

One of the men added, "Do you mean to investigate the cemetery? If so, I shall have to obtain permission—"

Findyk lied, "No, soldier, that will not be necessary. *Click. Click.* I trust your men have done so thoroughly. I shall report to your superiors . . . and I will inform them . . . that you men are doing a wonderful job." The soldiers smiled and stood up straighter.

Findyk walked away. He went back to the hedgerow, ducked down, and took the emperor's spear. He followed the line of shrubs to the corner of the lot and followed a tree line along the west side of the property. Walfyres were experts at concealment and Findyk was not seen, at least not by any Nadorian guards.

Corbidon watched from the shadows.

Findyk followed the property's edge to the back of the grounds. Once at the western wall, the Walfyre looked around him briefly to make sure there were no guards lurking about. After he told himself the path was clear, he tossed the spear over the top of the large concrete wall, and then with one swift motion, jumped high into the air, landing back down atop the wall's catwalk. He looked to his sides, to the pathways that led beyond in either direction—still not a guard in sight. Findyk then grabbed the spear again and discretely slid over the other side of the wall, and out of Cosh.

He stayed low, traveling through the tall grass until he came to the grove of which the two soldiers spoke. He entered it slowly, spear ready. He found the cemetery gates and footprints the soldiers had made in the mud. The Walfyre walked past the tombstones and down the wet trail. The trees above were coated with the same purple ash that was carving its way from the south. Finally, he came across the large crypt. The soldiers had wandered near, but failed to go inside. Findyk shook his head at their incompetence. He pushed the door open wider, stepped inside, and allowed his eyes to adjust. Then he searched the three rooms.

Findyk saw the overturned caskets. He knew there had been a struggle. He assessed that two people had been inside, and a third had met them outside. There was blood. Findyk then walked back outside, seeing the imprint of where a man had fallen. Two sets of tracks led out of the crypt. He followed them, studying the fight that had taken place. He then realized that two had fled the scene in one direction, and guessed the other had left later, heading back towards the trade city. He followed the pair of tracks. Back at the gates, he saw a faint trail leading north. Horse tracks. He was baffled that no one else had seen them. Findyk hurried his pace, following the trail.

He traveled north, hoping to find Veris before it was too late.

Behind him, Corbidon followed.

16

The trading tables were busy in Crevail. Fruits and vegetables were bartered. People bought a variety of fish and wild game. The chingle changle of gold nidaki coins was persistent as the two walked into the market.

The streets were busy. The people were anxious. As the young barbarian helped the elderly man find an honest trade for his goods, he noticed the citizens seemed to be uneasy. The presence of soldiers had undoubtedly created concern amongst them.

The barbarian asked his companion, "Is it always like this?"

The old man responded, "You mean the soldiers? How long have you been away from Crevail?"

The barbarian once again did not respond, and the old man was not stupid. He was realizing the man did not care to speak about himself. The old man continued, "No, it has been like this for nearly a week, now. You have heard the news, have you not?"

The barbarian looked at him in question. "What news? I have been away for some time."

The old man nodded. "It makes sense. Your surprise, I mean. The reason for the soldiers is simple. About a week ago, although I cannot be sure. . . . At my age, time slows. . . . Anyways, about a week ago, two senators were assassinated right here in Crevail."

"Really?"

"*Oh,* yes. Praetors Wallis and Jacard were very important men of not only Crevail, but also Nador. They were poisoned, I believe. At least that is what the rumors are. Although, none of us know for sure. The empire is keeping quiet about it. However, almost immediately, a hundred more soldiers entered Crevail and took up their posts. It was like . . ." the old man trailed off.

"What was it like?"

"As if, they already knew. . . . The soldiers arrived shortly after the deaths of the two praetors . . . almost too quickly. I guess word travels fast in the empire. Nevertheless, it has been tense in Crevail. And now, with these strange storms approaching—"

The barbarian looked back south. He had seen the storms as he traveled the coastline, bravely marching towards their menacing presence. He un-fearfully saw how they loomed in the distance, as if waiting for him to enter Crevail before they pounced. Fear was settling amongst all of the people of Crevail, and as the storm waited, the barbarian grinned.

I am home.

The floor was closed to all patricians. Only the powerful stood within the Senate chambers. These powerful few were loud and frenzied. They spoke to one another quickly. The many doors of the chambers were guarded on the outside. One of the doors opened, two soldiers standing erect while Parlock entered the room briskly.

The doors shut behind him.

He walked down the steps and onto the floor. All eyes were upon him. "Gentlemen, I have important news to tell you."

In a small semicircle stood seven men, all facing the approaching Parlock. He walked to them, brushed back his grey hair and faced them. General Vesuth, commander of the armed forces of Nador stood next to his long-time comrade, General Thad, who controlled the southern serpenti cavalry. Vesuth was Thad's superior. He only answered to Makheb, who was now missing. This simple fact left Thad and him in a predicament. Rules had been set if the emperor ever went missing or died. The Senate, the politicians, would control the military of Nador. It made sense to have civilians control such a mighty force in their emperor's absence, which was now the case. However, the problem was that the Senate was in full rebellion, whether or not the majority of the members understood that fact. Only a handful of men were overthrowing the empire.

Generals Vesuth and Thad did not know of the takeover, although Vesuth was beginning to figure it out. Thad had already expressed his disloyalty to Makheb. He understood what was happening. He did not care much for the emperor, almost having as much disdain for Makheb as did Vesuth.

It bothered Vesuth, not that he was under Makheb's command, but that Makheb would not use his reputable armies to conquer more lands. The battle at Cosh, the end of the Barbarian Wars, had proven great for the Men who formed Nador. They drove back a powerful force—the Ungorans. They pushed the savages out of their lives and benefited greatly from the occupation of their lands. Nador's northern legions were the perfect force, and backed with accurate archers and the serpenti cavalry of the southern armies, Nador could have marched into any kingdom and conquered it.

Vesuth was still angry at the emperor's inaction. As a general, he thought the emperor should use his armies for greater glory. Instead, they remained silent. Over the past five years, since the wars, Vesuth felt unneeded. He felt a general was made for—born for—war. Indeed, Generals Vesuth and Thad were opposed to the emperor's rule, and would make valuable assets to those who conspired against him.

Next to the two military leaders stood Consuls Ernstyn and Hattock. They were middle aged, wealthy and powerful. They were two of the five consuls in Nador, all of whom only answered to Makheb. They were experienced and popular amongst the people of the empire. Although the governing body would take on a new form, Ernstyn and Hattock were natural leaders. They were diplomatic and would adapt to lead this new government. People would follow them. People trusted them, unlike Parlock, of whom citizens of Nador always seemed weary.

Next to the two senators stood the three kings of old. Rhoaden, the previous king of Valeecia, seemed to gather the most attention. He had longtime grudges against the emperor. He was the most shamed, for Makheb had taken his throne by support of his own subjects many years before. His own people, Valeecians, opted for a mysterious, cloaked ruler over him. Rhoaden wanted revenge the most, it seemed. It was his orchestration from the beginning. Much of his family's gold went to supporting this takeover. He wanted his kingdom back—his throne—his honor.

With him stood the fat king of old Serona, Nyrusus, and the wise Umite king, Briom. They both had their grudges, as well. They were forced with the ultimate of decisions, to let their kingdoms enter slavery and death by the Ungorans, or relinquish their power to a leader who would rule all lands south of Denok Forest. In doing the honorable thing for their people, they were banished from their seats of power. Now, they sought to find that power once more.

Parlock said, "Gentlemen, I have news about Consul Veris. He was last reported to have escaped our attempt at capturing him."

The three old kings shook their heads, and Rhoaden spoke up, "That is careless, Consul Parlock. That man can hurt our plans."

Briom nodded. "Yes, the people of this region like him. They say he is honest and hard working. They seem to favor him over many."

This comment did not sit well with Parlock. He raised his hands slightly, calming the three. His two fellow politicians and two military leaders held their composure much better. "Everything is fine. His escape works out better for our plans. Dead or alive I do not care."

Briom then said, "Yes, but if he gets word to the people, they might just believe him. What is your plan, Parlock? How do you intend to take care of this problem?"

All eyes went to Parlock. "It is simple, gentlemen. We curse Veris' name in public, and glorify Makheb."

This time, General Vesuth spoke. His voice was deep, and commanding. "Makheb's name holds no glory for me. Why shall I speak of him in high regard?"

Parlock answered, remembering Vesuth and Thad had no solid evidence to believe anything but what they were told. The story would be simple. Parlock and the elite would damn Veris' name, make him the traitor of all traitors, and take control. Yet, his words to the generals had to be cautious.

"General Vesuth, it is our duty to honor our leader's name. It *is* true, everyone in these chambers holds the same opinion as you. More facts will reveal themselves, but for now, we are an empire missing its leader. Consul Veris had something to do with that. We have evidence that he was in the emperor's chambers the night our leader went missing. Since then, Veris has been on the run. He confronted Praetors Leydius and Tourous, and myself, only yesterday . . . accusing this very Senate, the one our emperor formed, to be at the heart of his disappearance."

Hattock grumbled, his face seeming sad. "Appalling, it is."

Parlock nodded, then continued, still addressing Vesuth directly, "The man nearly killed a centurion, a brave officer of *your* own armies, and fled north. We think, most likely, he is headed for Denok Forest, although we are not certain."

Briom spoke, "What do we do about him, then? Our borders are secure, and he will never survive outside our lands."

Rhoaden laughed. "Parlock is right, gentleman. Perhaps his escape does work in our favor."

"Let me stress this, gentlemen," Parlock said. "The emperor of Nador is missing and Consul Veris had something to do with it. Our people need us. We will show a united front. Politicians and generals will stand together, side-by-side, to calm the people."

Vesuth understood what was happening, although not the full details, and it appealed to him. "So, Parlock . . . what would you recommend we do?" he asked, committing himself to the plan.

Parlock paused, pleased that the general was showing his loyalty. "We assume control over Nador until we can find Makheb. The Senate will enact emergency powers and our government . . . our empire . . . will be controlled by us."

Every man in the room grinned.

The consul proceeded, "We will loudly proclaim to Nador of Consul Veris' traitorous actions, and offer a bounty on his head. We have had our differences before, but it is time we come together. We remaining four consuls, the praetors, and even popular patricians will join hands with the military leaders to defend our empire from that . . . traitor."

The men nodded their heads. Briom asked, "And if the emperor is missing forever, what then do we do?"

"Sadly, that may be the case. Ogata has informed me that there was a struggle in the emperor's chambers. Three beasts and one man were found dead—much blood. The people will have no problem believing the emperor's untimely death at the hands of Veris."

Nobody asked it. Not a single man in the room asked the question—

was Consul Veris really responsible for the emperor's death? They did not care about truths. Vesuth understood the plot, and chose to accept it. Thad was seeking glory, as well. The three kings wanted their authority back. The politicians wanted riches. All wanted power.

Parlock spoke again, "Gentlemen, it is simple. We in this room, first and foremost, must stay together. We convince the public of this atrocity and our seats will be secured. The people will join in our efforts to expand Nador to her next glory, and cheer when we march our armies . . . wherever we choose."

The men understood. Hattock spoke, "Wanted signs seeking his capture are already being placed in all villages and cities in the empire."

Parlock added, "We will focus our efforts on the northern towns, as that is his most probable direction. He would not travel east or south, for only vast oceans would be found. And he would not travel west. If he does, then he is out of our hands, anyways."

Rhoaden spoke, "How can we be sure he is headed north?"

Parlock replied, "His whereabouts are being taken care of as we speak. Do not worry about that. Veris *is* headed north. Once we find his exact location, we must take him out for good."

General Vesuth pondered all of this, and took a moment before he spoke, for he was a patient man. "Posters are already being placed, you said?" he asked Hattock.

Hattock responded, "Yes, we are addressing the people of Cosh tomorrow. Consul Vasarius is doing the same in Ogata, with other regions to follow. They are especially restless in Ogata."

Ernstyn nodded. "Yes, we could have problems in Ogata. That was where the emperor made his residence, after all."

Vesuth was still curious. "How would you have known *that* early of the emperor's disappearance . . . ?" he trailed off, beginning to realize his question, and the answer.

Parlock looked at Vesuth, "Do you serve your empire, general?"

Vesuth stood taller. "Yes, I do. I fought for the formation of this empire, just as we all did."

"Of course you did. You fought quite valiantly. I ask of you then: do you wish greatness and glory upon this empire, or a slow decay of her le-

34

gions?"

Vesuth stared at Parlock. "Our legions should march once again."

Parlock nodded, looking at Thad, who bowed in respect. "Now, the details. We, too, will address the public soon. Rhoaden, Briom and Nyrusus, you gentlemen will unfortunately stay . . . hidden. We cannot risk your exposure quite yet . . . or the people will be . . . suspicious." He paused, and there were no questions, so he went on, "The senators will convince the public. In the meantime, General Vesuth—"

"Yes?"

"I would recommend, because that is what you asked for, that you increase security in Nador's major towns . . . to keep the peace." Parlock leaned in closer and whispered, "General, amass your armies. Show me legions and I will show you new enemies."

Vesuth answered, "I will."

Parlock smiled sinisterly. "Very good. You will be a wonderful asset to this empire . . . this new empire. As we help the public understand, your job will be to not allow them any choice."

"Understood."

Parlock went on, "We accuse Veris publicly. We call for his capture, his fair trial, and the people will give us his death."

Rhoaden did not understand this logic. "What do you mean 'fair trial?'"

Parlock answered, "Of course, we intend to follow the law. Our duty is to Makheb's law. His law states that any citizen receives a fair trial. We shall support that."

Vesuth then replied, showing the others his willingness to side with them, "A fair trial would only hurt us. He would certainly tell the story in his favor . . . bring up more questions . . . create fear."

Briom added, "We cannot allow him to do so."

Parlock answered, "And we will not. The people will call for the death of a traitor, a murderer, and support the only other option."

Ernstyn continued for Parlock, "Emergency senatorial powers."

Vesuth understood. The three kings did not.

Parlock answered before they could ask, "Complete control is negated to the Senate according to the law. After we enact these powers, by public support, the Senate will control the empire. Immediately, we will follow the citizens' outcry and issue orders for Veris' death. We will make an example out of him. Once he is out of the way, we can further our conquest."

Ernstyn added more, "We will create a reason for the people to answer to us. Once this happens, we will expand."

Vesuth stood quiet, thinking. Finally, he spoke, "Yes, expansion. That is why we are all here, is it not? The borders of Nador must widen."

The others nodded in agreement, though the three kings remained quiet. Vesuth continued, "Our armies are meant for marching. Give me war and I shall give you my loyalty, gentlemen. I will work alongside you to ensure the greater good of the empire."

Thad stepped forward. "Myself, I serve our greatness. We cannot prevail with idle legions. This empire will collapse without them."

Parlock nodded. "You are right, we shall save this empire."

Thad asked, "And my role?"

Parlock was a master politician. His eyes relaxed, his expression humbled. "I would ask of you, great general, a personal favor to this body. A favor that will earn you a seat on the council that will soon rule Nador."

"Ask your favor."

"To set this council at ease, I ask that you see this problem of Consul Veris is dealt with swiftly. Take as many men as you need and find him."

"Why me?"

"So we can guarantee the job is done. Kill the man. Kill Consul Veris and you shall sit inside the inner circle."

Thad looked at his longtime friend, Vesuth, and then looked back. "If my duty to this empire is to kill a traitor, then I know my service is indeed glorious. I shall hunt him down. Will there be any conflicts with the laws concerning—?"

"The laws are our job. Let us handle them," responded Hattock.

Ernstyn chimed in, "You will have full authorization once you find him, as well as full support from the people."

General Thad nodded again. "I shall leave now. We will have to send many men in many directions to find his exact location."

"I have someone who will aid you in finding him," responded Parlock.

"Whom?"

"He will present himself when he finds Veris."

Generals Vesuth and Thad left soon after. They had much work to do. The politicians were the planners, but these two were the ones who would implement. They had already sent soldiers to over a dozen major towns in the empire, although that had been done without them realizing as to why. It was becoming obvious that someone, although Vesuth and Thad did not know whom, had previous knowledge. Someone knew Veris and the emperor would meet. Someone knew Makheb would disappear. They suspected both the senators and the former kings, but they did not question it. They wanted their war, their glory, and soon they would achieve it.

Back inside the senatorial chambers, the three politicians and the three kings spoke more openly.

Rhoaden questioned, "Parlock, is it wise for Vesuth and Thad to know of our involvement? They do control the armies of Nador."

Hattock rebutted, "The Senate controls the military."

"Are you sure? Soldiers generally hate politicians," responded Rhoaden. "They do, however, respect their generals. Especially Vesuth. Any of his men would die for him. How can we be sure they will go along with our plans?"

Parlock was unconcerned. "Vesuth and Thad will not be a problem, I can assure you. They despise Makheb as much as any of us. Makheb used them for his glory, yet never let them achieve their own. When requested, many times, to seek answers to our missing legions, Makheb refused."

He was speaking of five years prior, when the Ungorans had been driven away and two legions of Valeecia's finest were ordered to march west into the wicked Endlands, after the Troxen force that had attacked. General Taius, under whom Vesuth and Thad served, and his men were never heard from again.

Parlock went on, "They despise Makheb for not having sent more legions to the west. Makheb only told them that it was not the right time to do so. It did not make sense. Vesuth thinks Makheb is weak. No, they will be of great help to us."

Nyrusus of old Serona, having remained silent for much of the conversation, finally spoke, "Will Thad succeed in finding Veris? Will that not create suspicion? A general sent to do a lieutenant's work?" It made no logical sense to the kings.

He had a good point. General Thad was the commander over many men. Sending him on an errand's mission to find and assassinate a fleeing senator was excess. Yet, Thad would guarantee Veris' death. He was vicious in his ways. He was brutal.

He would kill Consul Veris without hesitation.

Parlock answered, "We will have to take the risk. General Thad will assure the job is done. His success will prove his loyalty."

Nyrusus shrugged his shoulders. "That is fine. However, I do not believe it is necessary. How dangerous can this one man be?"

Parlock's face tightened. He grew instantly serious. "It is interesting that *you* ask that question, being from Serona, yourself."

"How so?"

"Because the man we seek . . . you know quite well."

Nyrusus shook his head adamantly. "You are mistaken, Parlock. I have never met this Veris. I have heard much of the man, but you remember, I have been in seclusion, as have my fellow kings."

Parlock took a step forward. "You do know him." He paused, the men anxiously awaiting his next words. "I just received word, before this meeting, that Consul Veris had been hiding a great secret from us."

Ernstyn, Hattock, Rhoaden, Briom and Nyrusus leaned forward as Parlock finished, "Consul Veris is not who he claims to be. He is—Gromulus, the great warlord of Serona."

Everyone gasped.

"Yes. The man, who many say helped save the people of this empire, is now an enemy of the state."

17

Deep in the renovating settlement of Crevail, past the shops and markets, was a small, local barbershop. It was a new structure, built only a few years prior. A business practice such as a barber would never have existed in the old Kingdom of Ungora, but in modern Nador, it had potential. People now cut their hair short to fit certain social molds, and only outsiders, the ones who dwelt in small villages, kept their hair long. The local barber was successful. It was one of the many signs that proved a promising growth of a town that was once primitive and crude, which under Makheb's rule, came the promise of a new age of refinement.

The owner of the shop was a man named Armosan. He was bald, middle aged, had a round midsection and a thin, well-manicured mustache. He was proud of his mustache. The man was friendly, which came with the territory of being a barber, and had earned himself an honest name within the walls of Crevail.

Armosan was conversing with a much older man. The two sat in the corner of his shop, gossiping about everything from the deaths of Wallis and Jacard to the rumors of the flooding in the south that now engulfed the horizon. They spoke of curvy women and the horrors of the Barbarian Wars. A barbershop was always a place for men to gossip and chat amongst themselves, and hardly anything surprised Armosan anymore. He sat talking, with his back to the front entrance of his shop, facing the elderly man who was leaning on a rickety stool, his back against the wall.

Armosan was in the process of making a point about the need for more formakha in Crevail when he noticed the old man's eyes grow wide. Clearly, he was not being listened to anymore. Armosan turned slowly towards the front door of his shop and stared.

The large, menacing barbarian stepped through the doorway, for a moment blocking out the sunlight of the clear day in Crevail. The traveler stood still, sizing up the room and allowing his eyes to adjust. The barbarian spoke in a deep and accented voice, "Good day, gentlemen," he said, his dialect strange.

Armosan collected his thoughts quickly. "G . . . good day, sir. H . . . how might I help you this morning?" Although he tried to conceal it, there was a tremble in his voice. The man before him was massive. Armosan did not make eye contact, keeping his head respectfully lowered.

The barbarian swaggered inside the barbershop, his eyes looking around before finally settling back to the shop owner. The traveler seemed preoccupied in his thoughts. His kind was no longer local to Crevail, nor welcomed.

Armosan realized he had never seen this man in town. The man before his eyes looked rugged and wild. It seemed, by the look of him, that he had been traveling for quite some time. He had the look of a warrior written on his face. The man brought a chill of fear into the room. The old man, with whom Armosan had been in discussion, kept his head lowered. No doubt, the old timer wished he could disappear.

The barbarian spoke again, his voice gruff, "Kind sir, I am in need of a trim and a bath."

Armosan replied quickly so as not to offend his customer, "*Ah,* do come in, good sir. You may place your belongings there—" he said, pointing to a shelf, "—and I shall take good care of you. I can get you trimmed up, and behind my shop is a bathhouse. They offer the cleanest water and best women in Crevail. The caretakers there will be happy to tend you."

The stranger unclipped his sword, placing it on the shelf. Slowly, he slipped his pack off his shoulder and laid it down, as well. He walked towards the barber's chair and sat down heavily. Even seated, the man was large. Armosan breathed slowly, keeping his hands from shaking. An accidental nick might result in the man's wrath. Armosan steadied himself as he gathered his cutting tools.

"Now, what would you have me do today?"

After some time, Armosan's work was finished. He held up a mirror and the barbarian viewed the barber's effort. The warrior brushed his fingers through his beard, which was now shorter and no longer tangled. His hair, although still quite long, now looked neat and trimmed.

The barbarian looked at Armosan as he stood back up. In a low, grumbling voice the large man spoke, "Thank ya'h, good sir. It has been years since I have seen my own face. I almost forgot what it looks like."

Politely, yet fearfully, the barber replied, "It was my pleasure, sir."

The barbarian had fully stood up at that point and was towering over Armosan. The barber was intimidated. He struggled to control his trembling. "N . . . now sir th . . . there is the issue of a small fee. A man has to keep his business afloat, you understand?"

The barbarian looked down. He could see the fright in the eyes of the man before him. He had seen that same fear many times before. "And how much did this cost me?"

Armosan thought for a moment. "For you, sir, only three nidaki."

The barbarian reached in a small pouch hidden inside his tunic and pulled out a large handful of nidaki coins, letting them drop into Armosan's sweaty palm. The sum was triple the amount requested. "For ya'h time, my friend. Now, where did ya'h say that bathhouse was?" The long-haired barbarian began gathering his effects.

The expression on Armosan's face was rich. He looked up at the man and said, "Yes, of course. If you go through this door in the back of my shop—" he said, pointing to a nearby door, "—it will lead you directly into the bathhouse. Our buildings are connected."

The barbarian placed his hand on Armosan's shoulder as an expression of gratitude, then slung his pack across his own shoulder, reattached his sword, and walked towards the rear door.

The barber, overwhelmed with curiosity, stumbled through his next words, "S . . . sir, before you go m . . . might I ask a question?"

"Aye," grunted the barbarian.

"What is your name?"

The large man smiled wide. Proudly, he said, "I am Tornach."

Armosan's face grew pale. He had a hunch, a ticking in the back of his head the moment the stranger had entered his shop, and the man had just confirmed it. The traveler, standing in the shadows of the doorway, was indeed Tornach. His accent should have given away the fact that he was Ungoran.

Tornach had a reputation. He was a valiant warrior, having fought alongside the famous Gromulus of Serona during the Barbarian Wars. Tornach, although an Ungoran, fought with the Seronan army against his own people. Legends and myths circulated about the man.

Armosan wiped sweat from his brow. He stepped back a pace. He was realizing that he had just cut the hair of a war hero—the man who had helped change the tide of battle—the man who was feared by many. Armosan began thinking of the numerous fables about Tornach. They were countless and he did not know how true they were. Some told that the man had been baptized in blood in an ancient Ungoran ritual upon birth. Some told that he had spat in the face of the Ungoran king. It was said that Tornach's only joy in life was battle, and by the size of him, Armosan figured that rumor might be true. The Ungoran had fought his own people, and prevailed. He had been a hero of the wars, but now, those legends had surpassed the man. The rumors circled wildly inside Armosan's head as he stared at the great warlord.

Tornach returned the stare until he broke Armosan's trance, instantly causing the older man to avert his eyes. The barbarian chuckled and then turned again, passing through the door at the back of the shop.

Armosan mumbled to himself, "Much blood is on that man's hands."

Tornach passed through the short hallway that connected the two shops. He opened another door and entered the bathhouse. He paused inside the dark room. The walls were inlayed with miniature ceramic tiles that depicted various battle scenes—relics of the past. Battles, rituals, commencement ceremonies and fables were all displayed along the inner walls of the bathhouse. Vivid drapery and ornate candles were neatly placed everywhere. The large barbarian was in awe. He had never seen such eloquence. The man placed his hands on one wall, feeling the hundreds of small tiles, each with its own color and shape—each with its own story. It was beginning to be too much for the stranger. This was not the Crevail he remembered as a child.

Ungora is no more, he thought sadly.

Tornach had been born in a small speck of a village only a half-day walk from Crevail. His father, Riean, had perished in combat shortly after the Barbarian Wars had begun, fighting alongside the bloodthirsty Ungoran raiders. After his father died, the child had been left to be raised by his widowed mother, Marnuit. From time to time, the two would make the

42

trek into Crevail, seeking supplies and conversation. Tornach had always enjoyed that time in life, childhood. Since the death of his mother, he was left to tend to himself. He had not entered Crevail in many years.

Confusion now gripped Tornach. Although large and frightening, the man seemed sad. A hollow look in his eyes spoke clearly the emptiness in his heart. He was lost. Thoughts of the past-—visions of the wars and of his mother—plagued him as he stepped farther into the large open room of the bathhouse. Half a dozen men sat in the giant pool where scantily clad women bathed them. Tall, decorated columns lined the perimeter of the pool, which climbed all the way to the vaulted ceiling overhead. The ceiling had an opening the exact size of the pool itself, which allowed the afternoon sunlight to reach into the room from above. The bathhouse, and its elegance, was fascinating to the barbarian, yet he also felt as if he did not belong. He nearly turned, wanting to omit the bath, but before he could, two beautiful women approached him.

Tornach hardly noticed their presence. The very idea of being in Crevail was numbing to him. Tornach thought to the past, when his mother and he would walk the simple roads of Crevail, passing through the market-place, trading furs and vegetables for other necessities.

Now, things were different. The city had changed. It had morphed into the empire. Although some of the old buildings and Ungoran architec-ture remained, the city had been remodeled to resemble the newly formed Nador. Nearly all remnants of the past city were gone. Crevail was a new place, like a shrine to a dead civilization. Tornach felt a stab of pain. The past had become a burden. He held back his tears.

Tornach felt he was at the end of his existence.

With hardly any control left in his body, the two women led him far-ther into the bathhouse, escorting him gingerly to a small, private bath. He allowed them to lead, his mind in another world.

He daydreamed of his childhood.

The women began scrubbing him. One spoke softly in his ear, "Who are you, anyways? I do not recall seeing you in these parts. Perhaps, a fish-erman?"

The other woman joked, "He is no fisherman. . . . He is much too strong to be a fisherman. . . . Perhaps a lumberjack?" She ran her fingers through his hair.

No response.

"Where are you from, so that I might find more of your kind," flirted the other.

He did not hear them. He was drifting.

"Who are you?" one asked again, leaning in closer.

Tornach was still lost in his own despair. His head was spinning. He took three gulps from a chalice of wine, and the women refilled it for him. Tears welled up in his eyes again. The barbarian swayed, drinking even more wine. Then, as if finally realizing the women were speaking to him, he looked at them.

She repeated herself, "Who are you, dear?"

Tornach looked directly into the woman's eyes, and spoke. His accent was distinct. "My own name spills from the mouth of every man like a legend. Though I am but a mere mortal, unlike ya'h god-king, Makheb. I am no god. I am no legend. Yet, I am ta be feared."

The two women snickered in unison at his retort. One spoke, "Well, I am not afraid of you," she said in an alluring voice.

The barbarian continued drinking, ignoring the women's intentions. His head was growing fuzzy, and calmness was finally reclaiming him. "I have done much. I have spilled blood both on and off the field of battle, all in the name of my own self-preservation. Now, I am lost. Now, I truly seek salvation. . . ."

The two women giggled. One said, "You shall find no salvation here."

Tornach ignored her and continued, nearly drunk, "Many seasons ago I had purpose. I had loyal friends with a common cause. They were good friends. Now, I desire no enemies, but I still have many. I am cursed by the gods. I am a stranger to this new land called Nador. My name, which was once honored, is now profaned." The barbarian took another swig of the wine. "What am I good for if I have no purpose?"

"I can think of a few things," spoke one of the women seductively.

The barbarian looked at them. "Ya'h know not who I am. Where ya'h can handle my body, and do as ya'h may, ya'h cannot handle my name."

The girls were mesmerized, staring into his eyes as he continued.

"For I am Tornach, last of the Ungorans."

* * *

That night, drunk and tired, Tornach slept. His dreams brought him back to the past. He dreamt of the dead.

He dreamt of old friends.

Nearly eight years before, Gromulus was making his way through southern Ungora. He walked cautiously, for the lands of Ungora were deadly at that time. It was hostile territory, and Gromulus traveled alone. He walked slowly.

Gromulus was in layers of dark, leather garments. The material kept him warm. On his back were a bow, quiver, and twenty-five arrows. On each side of his hips rested a sword. Short, and broad at the hilts, they angled sharply to a point. His long, dirty blonde hair fell well past his shoulders. On his face was a large, bushy beard.

A piece of elegant cloth hung to the side of his face. It was purple and woven with what appeared to be small symbols in strings of gold. At the moment, it hung along the left side of his beard, yet one day the man would keep it secured across his face, concealing his identity.

He would become strange about that.

Now, however, he showed his face, exposing it to a light gust of wind that blew through the trees of the grove. Finally, the sun was beginning to set and the evening air chilled him. He continued walking, headed south, nearing the lands of Serona. He had seen a group of marching Ungorans head in the same direction, with cause, into Seronan lands, as well as the lands west, in Ume. He saw their tactics. He saw their flaws.

The Ungorans were massive and brutal. However, what they had in strength and power, they lacked in organization and discipline. Their raids were usually fast and caught villagers off guard and ill prepared. They killed with no mercy, gloating as they ravaged people's lives. There was glory to be had as an Ungoran warrior.

Exhausted, he leaned back at the base of a tree, looking at the dark skies. He could hear birds chirping and the wind whispering. He closed his eyes, listening even more. Underbrush provided concealment for most of his body as he rested. Occasionally he could hear sounds of bigger creatures scurrying about, but nothing seemed to bother the man. He was unafraid.

His eyes grew heavy and his thoughts grew dim.

He had to stop for the night.

Gromulus closed his eyes and began dozing.

Just then, something whizzed overhead.

sssssszzzP!

Gromulus opened his eyes alertly. His instincts brought his right hand to the hilt of one of his swords. He lay silent. He saw nothing. He heard nothing.

Then, the sound came again. This time, it was closer.

sssssszzzP!

Gromulus lay frozen. He was tired, and it took him a moment. He heard another of the sounds, and understood.

Arrows.

In rapid succession, they came.

sssssszzzP! sssssszzzP! sssssszzzP!

Some hit nearby trees, impaling them. Others coasted into shrubbery. One hit nearby, striking a small tree, but instead of sticking, it fell to the ground. Gromulus, staying low, crawled closer. The black- and red-stripped feathers on the arrows gave them away.

Ungoran arrows. Suddenly they came in masses.

Dozens of arrows flew by, now seeming to have real direction. Gromulus was well concealed, and knew he had not been spotted. However, the arrows were too close. Gromulus lowered to a crouching position, trying to look over a mound of dirt. He could not see anything. Then, the young man rose, his right hand still on the hilt of one of his swords.

He saw something. Someone.

Leaves were rustled and twigs snapped as another sound got closer. In a flash, a large man raced over the hill and crashed into Gromulus, sending them both down hard.

Whoever it was, he had been running full speed and had not seen Gromulus, either. Gromulus now shakily stood up, one of his twin blades already drawn. His head was dizzy, and every time he blinked, he saw flashes of light. The man before him was slower to rise. Finally, as if having forgotten his urgency, the large barbarian stood up. His shoulders wider, and his tangled beard and hair more fierce, Gromulus sized up his opponent. Immediately, Gromulus could tell he was Ungoran by the way the man was dressed.

Gromulus' heart raced. He began to perspire nervously. Now, he faced Tornach.

And if the clothing did not give away the man's origins, his dialect soon would. Ungorans were humans, the same as the Men in the other kingdoms; however, they were unusual in some respects. They were typically larger and had more defined features. Their jaws were squared, and their bodies heavy-boned. They wore their hair knotted and tangled. Their clothing was also different, more primitive, much like their weapons, which eventually led to their defeat.

Ungorans also spoke differently. They shared the same language as their fellow Men, but theirs was beginning to change. Their already deep and bellowing voices began to get shorter and more abrupt. Their speech was harsh. It was callous. It was mean.

"If ya'h wish ta live, I suggest ya'h put up ya'h sword and begin running," said the man. His accent was heavy, but he would later learn to disguise his speech, an attempt to hide it from the world.

The barbarian's dirty hair blew across his face, which upon it rested a grin. Then, Tornach laughed, bent down and gathered the large bag he dropped and flung it back across his shoulder. He looked at Gromulus one last time, smiled again, and sprinted away—towards Serona.

Gromulus was puzzled. Everything was a blur. The entire scene took only a few moments, and he quickly realized that arrows were still flying overhead. Instantly, he looked back north, into the woods, and saw them coming, a large group of Ungoran raiders—their faces painted red.

An arrow barely missed his face.

Gromulus ran after the barbarian.

Tornach woke from his dream. The storm had arrived, and the rains fell outside. The ash would soon come. The warrior struggled to go back to sleep.

The elitists were still in full discussion, despite the late hour. They had dined on a great feast, yet still, they did not feel like celebrating. They argued. They grew irritated.

"Parlock," said Rhoaden, "Answer me this—" His voice was beginning to slur from too much wine. "How is it that *nobody* recognized this Veris for who he really is? Out of all the people in Cosh, you say he is the most popular, am I right?"

Parlock nodded, regretfully.

Rhoaden continued, "How is that? Gromulus of Serona, of *all* people?"

Parlock understood their concern. They were angry about the blunder.

It was Consul Hattock who spoke next. "Gentlemen, let me assure you, this is not Parlock's fault. I, myself, have met with the young consul many times. Are we sure this man's identity is what you say it is? Is he *really* Gromulus?"

"Unfortunately, he is. My source would not be mistaken about that fact." For the first time, Parlock was worried. *I should have known. They are all looking at me because I knew him the best. Yet, I did not see it.* Parlock turned and walked a few steps away from the sitting men. He pondered something, but did not say what was on his mind. Then, he turned back and addressed the men, "Has anyone at this table ever spoken to Gromulus—face-to-face?"

They all shook their heads, no.

"Have any of you seen the man up close?"

Some had.

Briom spoke up, "I have never met the man myself. The closest I was to him was during a celebration after we took back the lands of Ume. He rode past me, with many men, but his face was covered."

"I, too, have seen him once," Nyrusus said. "However, it was dark and he wore a helmet, and a mask covered his face. He did not reveal himself. I took it as a sign of disrespect. I only remember the man's long hair, shaggy beard . . . damn, it could have been anyone." He paused. "The stories tell that Gromulus left our lands after the wars."

Parlock chimed in, "Yes . . . some do. Others say he settled in the lands of Serona, starting a farm."

Ernstyn added, "I was led to believe Gromulus of Serona traveled west, into the Endlands, and was never heard from again."

Briom had neither seen, nor spoken to the heroic warrior. "I heard that Makheb had him killed. That made sense to me, because Gromulus, at least at that time, could have challenged the throne."

Parlock looked up and smiled. "Why, old friend, do you say that?"

Briom, all eyes upon him, "Well, Gromulus is a hero in the eyes of every man, woman and child in Nador. I hear they even speak highly of him in Aronia. He was a man who served his people well. He did not ask for anything in return—"

"Why would Makheb want him dead?" interrupted Rhoaden.

Briom went on, "Because he could have been a threat. Unlike Gromulus, Makheb wanted control. He used the Ungoran threat against us, and took our lands. His rise to the throne was one of might."

Rhoaden nodded, "Much like our own."

"Yes, but Makheb was a stranger here. Remember the accounts of everyone's reaction when he arrived in Ogata?" Nyrusus asked, now looking at Rhoaden, the former Valeecian king.

Rhoaden cleared his throat, and then spoke, "Many times I attempted to warn the people, but they were ignorant. They chose to rid me and welcome . . . *him.*"

"Gentlemen, relax," said Parlock in a soothing voice. "None of this matters. Our plans are underway. We will not have to worry about the emperor any longer. We do not serve him, the people do not serve him. Instead, they shall serve us. Let us announce to the public tomorrow, at midday, that our emperor has disappeared. They will call for Veris' head and we shall have it."

Ernstyn nodded, "And by next year, we shall have conquered all the lands of the known world."

Hattock smiled at this, "Yes, I shall walk the halls of Ellsar, drink King Kedorlaomer's wine, and mate with his wife."

The room filled with laughter.

18

A small sliver of light beamed through the cracked window, letting Tornach know another day had started. He squinted his eyes, looking around the room. His head was still fuzzy as he studied his surroundings. Then he remembered where he lay. He looked over at the two women sleeping next to him soundly. Their faces were serene. They were beautiful, both captured in a ray of sunlight that was fast diminishing in the outside world due to the steadily increasing storms.

They will never understand my pain, he thought.

Tornach rose out of bed quietly, so as not to disturb the women's slumber. He pushed back his hair and proceeded to get dressed. Once accomplished, the barbarian leaned down and lifted his bag of effects, heaving it over his shoulder with ease, and headed towards the door. He stopped, looking back at the women, grunted under his breath, and turned and left the room.

Tornach walked through the same hallway as the night before, remembering the small tiles on the wall, but somehow feeling they had changed. He rubbed his head, for it hurt, and entered another door that led back to the barbershop. The barber, Armosan, was sitting in one of his chairs, reading a letter.

"Good day, barber," Tornach grumbled. "How are ya'h this morning?"

Armosan turned, looking up at the man. "My morning is well, young sir. I hope last night went well for you."

"Aye, it did. Many thanks ta ya'h, barber."

Armosan replied his thanks and Tornach walked to the front door, readying himself to leave. He stopped, pondered something, then turned and spoke again. "I do appreciate ya'h kindness, barber. So far, the kindness of people, such as ya'h, has made me feel welcome once again. I have good memories of this town, ya'h understand?"

Armosan could only nod. Tornach turned and walked out. Like so many people in Tornach's life, his meeting with Armosan was short-lived.

Little did Armosan know, Tornach rarely gave thanks to anyone. It was truly a sign of gratitude, however short the acknowledgement may have been.

Tornach entered into the morning air.

Armosan watched as the man exited his shop. He was curious as to why the man was in Crevail. He wondered if it was bravery or stupidity that brought him. He was also curious as to what was inside the barbarian's pack. If Tornach had known Armosan, perhaps he would not have shown his gratitude. If he had remembered the man's profession, maybe he would have been more skeptical.

Armosan was a barber, his business consisting of two things: haircuts and gossip. As Tornach spent the past night indulging himself, Armosan spent his getting drunk and telling everyone near that there was an Ungoran in town. He failed to mention, however, that this specific Ungoran helped save the modern world. He did not mention that this barbarian helped the Seronan clans drive his own people from the lands. He also failed to mention that this stranger fought along the great Gromulus—legendary and mysterious. No, Armosan only gossiped. He embellished, as the men of Crevail grew drunk and angry. Now, the barber sat still in his shop chair, feeling ashamed.

Tornach walked out into the day. There was a break in the storm. The clouds lingered overhead, but he could see the sun was rising from the east, amidst its darkness. Tornach smiled. The town was already busy. People were setting up their shops for the day, making the tables ready for trade. The barbarian brushed his hand through his trimmed beard, rejoicing in the fresh shave and bath and other pleasantries. As he walked away from the barbershop, he turned and looked at the southern and western skies. They were darker. The storms moved slow, eerily creeping their way towards Crevail.

Strangest storms I have ever seen, thought Tornach, looking at the intimidating mauve color as the storms stood sentry, ready to swallow the town.

As Tornach walked the dirt streets of Crevail, memories of his mother rustled in his head. The town brought back these memories. He did not remember his father much, due to his fate in the early years of the Barbarian Wars. Supposedly, a Seronan farmer had killed him. The men of Tornach's village promised their revenge. It had been swift and severe. Tornach remembered hearing the news, and feeling not honor, but shame at the time. His mother, too, had not lived to see her son's eighteenth birthday. He had known her well.

No matter how much he tried, he could not stop the memories from coming back. His mother had been a good woman. She had curly red hair that was always worn in a tight bun. Her eyes were like the clearest of skies, bright blue, with very non-Ungoran features. The people of his village had known it, although they never mentioned it. She had been Seronan by birth. Her features were not as distinct as the Ungoran women in her village. They were soft, gentle.

Tornach's mother had been kind. Unlike Ungoran mothers, his own had taught him that same kindness, and love. She taught him how to question the world around him. Tornach knew that everything good in him was a credit to his mother, Marnuit.

But, that was long ago. That was another time. This place is no longer Ungora, he thought. *This is not what Crevail should have become. It is a mimic and an insult to a great people, despite their faults. No, this is not Crevail. This is not the home I once knew.*

Tornach walked on. He passed stone buildings and even more made of wood. The streets were clean. He watched as children played and merchants began their trading. Nadorian citizens from the local region began entering the town, their arms and backs loaded with goods. Tornach also noticed the presence of many soldiers. *More than there should be.* He remembered the old man from the day before, the one with whom he had spoken upon his arrival. He recalled that the man had told him that two senators were assassinated recently. He figured it plausible. Nador was an empire of the future. Military power and a strong, central government were important to her existence. Therefore, a strong soldier presence in the town of two murdered senators made sense. He walked on, passing two sentries. Tornach exchanged looks with the pair and they looked back suspiciously.

He kept walking.

Tornach eventually walked up to a trading table, where a woman and her daughter were setting up for the day. Atop the table, the barbarian saw baskets filled with haddoi fruit. This fruit only existed in the old lands of Serona. He had not tasted its sweet nectar in years. Tornach pulled a nidaki coin from his tunic, laid it on the table, and sorted through the fruits, finding one that was ripe. He turned it over in his hand, the delicious scent causing him to salivate. It caused him to think of a time many years ago. A time when he lived amongst friends, in the old lands of Serona. The people had always been kind in Serona. They always had a place of honor for him at their tables. It was a time when he could eat and drink and laugh.

Those days are over now.

He took his fruit and looked up at the woman behind the counter. He noticed her staring strangely at him. Others nearby did, as well. However, Tornach did not think much of it; he only wanted the fruit.

"Ladies," he said, bowing his head to the mother and child behind the counter. "I see ya'h have the fruit from the old lands of Serona."

They looked at him oddly.

He continued, "The haddoi—"

They still only stared.

Tornach continued, "It is the sweetest fruit I have ever had the pleasure of tasting. My lips have not touched this fruit in many years. I will take this one."

The lady only stared at him bitterly. She bent down, whispered something in her daughter's ear, and the girl scurried away quickly. Then, the woman looked back at Tornach. This time, her face was harsh with disgust.

She glared at Tornach angrily. "Just take it and leave—barbarian!"

Tornach was in shock. He could not find any words. Finally, his voice soft and humble, he spoke. "My lady . . . I assure ya'h I mean ya'h no harm."

"Take it and leave!" She glared at him. Others at trading tables nearby gave him odd stares. "I said leave—Ungoran!"

Tornach's heart sank. He struggled to maintain his breath.

He was accustomed to this mistreatment. It was why he roamed the lands. It was why he was without a home. Tornach was different. It was not so much his looks, as it was his speech. He could not completely hide his

54

Ungoran accent no matter how hard he tried. The people of Nador hated Ungorans. They had no tolerance. Tornach felt sadness. He looked at the woman and stared into her cold, hateful eyes. He saw the fear. Her eyes showed it.

Tornach dropped the sweet fruit on the table. He no longer wanted it. He shook his head and without a word, or another look back, left the trading tables.

Anger filled his heart.

Tornach walked quickly as the woman behind him began chattering loudly to her fellow traders. The barbarian was ashamed, wanting desperately to find a hole and burrow himself deep within. He walked down a narrow alley, then another. Behind the buildings were bums and drunks, sleeping in the gutters. *Perhaps I belong here, with them.* Life would be simpler for Tornach if he were unrecognizable. But it was easy to spot an Ungoran; their voices gave them away.

He walked. Ahead of him was a tavern. *I need a drink,* he thought to himself.

Tornach entered the building. As it was before midday, the room was nearly empty, only a handful of patrons, most too drunk to notice his presence. Even the barkeep did not seem to care. The tavern smelled rancid, like decayed ethithu, and the air was stale. Tornach wondered when the last time this foul place was cleaned. He moved in farther, taking a seat at the bar. Broken glass crunched under his feet as he positioned himself on the stool. A large rat scampered past him.

My kind of place.

The barkeep turned from his duties and looked at Tornach. "What do you want?" he asked flatly.

Tornach paused, and then said, "Give me the finest og ale ya'h have. Actually, make that two. I have much ta think about."

The barkeep poured three.

Tornach slurped down one, the next, and then the last. He pounded the last mug on the bar counter. "Again," he demanded, his spirits already being lifted. The barkeep obliged.

Tornach swallowed the next three just as quickly. "Again."

* * *

The drinks kept coming and time began to pass. As noon came, he was drunk. A man, perhaps only a few years older, sat by him. His name was Judtheca, but people called him Jud, for short. He was a farmer from the old lands of Ume and had headed east a year prior, seeking a better life. Tornach noticed the bar filling with patrons. He began talking with the stranger, who was well on his way to intoxication, himself.

After some time, Tornach and Jud seemed to be getting along. They conversed as they drank. Tornach even bought the man a few drinks. Then, in a stupor, Tornach asked, "Jud, do ya'h know any good drinking songs?" His speech was becoming slurred. His Ungoran accent became more distinct.

Jud thought for a moment, taking long enough to make Tornach believe he had forgotten the question, but finally responded. "I am afraid, good sir, that I do not. At least, none that I can remember."

Tornach grinned. "No worries, my friend. Jud . . . I know a song . . . an old Ungoran drinking song. . . . I learned it when I was a young man. I shall teach it ta ya'h."

Jud smiled, nodding his approval. Tornach humored him.

Tornach began pounding his half-empty glass of og ale on the wooden bar. A slow, steady beat.

Thump. Thump. Thump.

Tornach kept the pace. "Are ya'h ready, Jud?"

Jud smiled, took his own mug and joined in, "Yes."

Tornach, pounding his glass louder, began to sing:

> *'Ten mighty Troxen dancing in the woods*
> *Ungorans come and steal their goods*
> *We take em ta the village and cut them up*
> *Ten mighty Troxen—spill their blood!*
>
> *'We take them ta the village for all ta eat*
> *Troxen have some damn good meat*
> *We even cut their horns ta hang on walls*
> *Troxen, Troxen—ya'h all will fall!'*

Tornach swallowed the remaining ale in his mug and slammed it on the bar, as was Ungoran tradition. He laughed heartily. Jud did, too, but he was a drunk and did not know better. Tornach laughed again as the many inhabitants looked at him in disgust, yet the barbarian did not care. He was used to the stares. He did not fear their ridicule, nor their fury, which like in many other towns he traveled, was beginning to fester. The people of the bar began quietly whispering amongst one another. Whispers of *"Ungoran"* began to flow through the room. A few patrons even left the bar.

The barkeep, realizing Tornach might cause problems, stared hard at him. Finally, he spoke, "Hey . . . quiet down or I will have to toss you out with the other drunks. You are scaring away my customers."

Sometime later, Tornach sat at the dusty bar, intoxicated. He laughed out loud, and then began singing more Ungoran drinking songs. The patrons, especially those who fought in the wars, began to take more notice. Jud finally stood up and left without saying a word. Tornach sat alone at the bar. A man from across the room shouted an obscenity. Tornach turned in his stool, shouting back to no one in particular.

"Do ya'h fear me?"

Someone yelled, "You are not wanted here."

Another said, "Ungoran!"

Tornach looked in their direction, but he could not make out the faces, everyone was a blur. He said, "Ya'h should fear me. I am Tornach, the last Ungoran ta walk this land. I fear no man!"

A few more obscenities were hollered, but they were careful to not be recognized. None had the courage to stand up to the barbarian. After all, the legends of Tornach were hard to forget. Well respected amongst his men during the wars, the whispers of Tornach's abilities in battle were known to the entire world.

The barbarian now looked back to the barkeep, who had stepped back a few paces. His face was bewildered. Tornach said, "Do ya'h not see? Do ya'h not hear my accent? I am Ungoran!"

The barkeep could only manage a timid, "Yes, sir." He was growing scared.

Tornach continued, "This is why they will not face me. They curse my name, but have not the courage ta stand toe ta toe with me. Do ya'h understand?" He was yelling at this point. Drunk and terrifying, Tornach was angry.

The barkeep could only whimper, "Yes, sir. I have heard of you. You were a great name in the ranks of the Seronans. I, myself . . . kind sir . . . fought with the Umites."

Tornach eyed the man, "Then why do they taunt me?"

The barkeep was without words. He helplessly stood still, wiping his hands obsessively on his apron and wishing the man would just leave. Then, a hand rested gently on Tornach's shoulder.

Without fear, the barbarian turned slowly. "*Aw,* finally. A man ta challenge me." Tornach had committed himself to the possibility of a fight. He had done this many times in his past, especially in local taverns. A warrior must acknowledge that death will one day take him, and care not when. Tornach cared not if he lived or died. He was prepared. Now, like the past five years, Tornach had still not found his place in life. He had wandered before meeting Gromulus, and he was still wandering. His friends had gone their separate ways, on to better things. Yet, Tornach was still lost. If he could not call Crevail his home, then he was convinced he would never have a home within the empire.

I was loved at one point. When I was killing my own people, I was loved. Now, they hate me. Tornach looked at the man standing behind him. He spoke, "They shun me. If ya'h possess a dagger, use it now." Tornach turned back, looking the barkeep in the eyes. The man could tell the barbarian had no fear. He seemed to welcome his death as he closed his eyes and smiled.

The man behind him spoke, his words directed to the barkeep. "Fear not, Tornach and I are friends." Then, he said to the Ungoran, "Let me get us a bottle of wine."

Tornach only nodded. Then, slowly, he looked up at his new companion, completely realizing that this man posed no threat. He actually seemed genuine.

The man said, "Come, let us drink somewhere more quiet." Tornach followed as the man led him to a table in the corner, where a shadow from a torch hid them. At least it somewhat did, but the patrons still knew he was there. They hushed their tones, though. As Tornach walked past the seated patrons, he eyed each and every man. They knew he did not fear them. Although, Tornach realized the outcome, which was the same, over and over again. Usually he was forced to leave any town he entered. Driven to travel forever it seemed. He knew, soon, that the locals in Crevail would take it upon themselves to rid their town of him.

Tornach laughed at the thought as they found their table. In his mind, these men were not Crevailians. They were Nadorians, but Crevail was in the old lands of Ungora.

He thought aloud as he sat down, "They would never last a day amongst Ungorans. The men who once held these lands were strong."

Finally, Tornach took the time to acknowledge the man in front of him. He was probably twice his age, his face wrinkled. A scar rested on the man's chin and his hair was a dark grey, yet still thick. The man looked at him and said bluntly, "You are Tornach, are you not?"

The barbarian nodded.

"*The* Tornach? The Ungoran warrior who fought with the Seronans against his own people?"

Tornach nodded again. He sipped his wine.

The man went on, "You fought with the Seronan militia . . . under the great Gromulus. . . ."

Tornach spat, "I did not fight under that man. . . . I fought *with* him."

The man nodded his understanding. His face was beaming. He smiled, elated, and continued, "I knew it was you, I just knew it. Your features are similar to anyone else, for the most part, although you Ungorans seem to be a little bigger . . . square jawed."

Tornach rubbed his own chin and laughed.

The man went on, "But, it was your accent. It is a dead giveaway, I tell you." He was right. Tornach had always tried to hide his harsh and guttural dialect. Over the years, it had started to fade naturally. However, when he drank, his accent reared its ugly head. The man added, "I have never sat down and spoken to an Ungoran before."

"Because most would have had your head by now," retorted Tornach.

"This is a blessing. I cannot wait to tell my friends that I met the mighty Tornach. They will never believe me. I have heard the legends about you."

Tornach smiled. He liked the praise, and even more, he liked hearing that legends were told about him. "I am sure they are greatly exaggerated."

The man smiled, "Well, yes . . . you are shorter than the stories say . . . but I assure you, most of the tales I hear about you are good ones. Without men such as yourself, Serona would have fallen. How bold it was to face the enemy, especially when the other kingdoms hid in the shadows."

Tornach, having finally calmed down, actually smiled. Humbly, he extended his hand. "What is ya'h name, old man? I would surely like ta know the man who honors mine."

The man shook it with glee, saying, "Excuse me for not doing that sooner. . . . My name is Kelnum."

"How long have ya'h been here in Crevail?"

"I came here shortly after the wars—to seek opportunity."

Tornach asked, "Have ya'h found that . . . opportunity, here in Crevail?"

Kelnum smiled, "I think I have."

Tornach was sipping his wine. He preferred og ale, but the wine was sweet, as it was made from northern Ungoran berries, where the land ended and the dreaded forest of the Denoktorn began. The wine calmed him.

Kelnum then asked, "Tornach, it is none of my business, but I heard your outrage. What ails you, young man? You are youthful . . . capable as any."

Tornach answered, "Kelnum, my life has become nothing. I am shunned everywhere I go. I was a leader, a hero—my name was once cherished. Men spoke my name in high regard. Now, however, my name is feared. It is spat upon. I am disgraced." Tornach's eyes filled with tears, but he held them back. "Everyone looks upon me as if I were a monster, because I am Ungoran. You are right, I look like any other man, but my speech gives away my lineage. I am cursed to walk these lands without talking if I am ta survive."

"But, you are a great warrior. Why would people hate you so?"

"Perhaps it is because I still roam the old lands of Ungora. Perhaps people here cannot shake the past." Tornach took another sip of his wine, nearly emptying the glass. As Kelnum refilled it, Tornach continued sadly, "I was a great warrior, aye. I killed Troxen and I killed my own people. I shall no longer be part of my culture for my deeds, but I did so ta defend those who were . . . good. You ask me what ails me, old man? My answer ta ya'h . . . my answer is that I am lost. I have traveled far, and still not found my place. There is nowhere else ta go. Even the good people of this empire hate me. They do not know who I am, only from where I came. I came here just yesterday, towards those wickedly strange storms, ta the only home I have ever known . . . ta find I am not wanted here, either." This time, the man wept softly.

Kelnum remained quiet, respecting the man. Then, Tornach spoke again. "Look around ya'h, Kelnum. What did the wars truly do? The people live under the threat of an empire now. Crevail never needed guards. Ungora was never suspicious of her own . . . except for perhaps . . . me. No, the people here seem eager ta submit, much like they did before."

"Are you speaking of the Ungorans?"

Tornach laughed. "No. I am talking about people of Ume and Valeecia and Serona. Nadorians. This empire will corrupt itself just like the Ungoran kingdom did. King Alarik led the Ungorans to their doom much like the emperor will now. The people will be slaves . . . they just do not know it yet." He sipped his drink. "Without Gromulus, would the Seronans have fought? Ask yourself that—"

Kelnum pondered it. Finally, he proposed, "Tornach, my new friend, let us leave this tavern. The rains outside seemed to have ceased for the moment," he said, looking out the window. "Let us take a walk through town."

Tornach agreed. He finished the bottle of wine, ordered another, and walked out with the man. The sack was still slung across his back.

Outside the air was still, yet damp. Overhead, the skies were churning, but the rains had stopped for the moment. The light ash had yet to fall on Crevail, but soon would. This would frighten the residents even more. Much like in Ogata, and even Cosh, the insanity of such weather was dumbfounding. The air was muggy as they began walking. Next to him was Kelnum.

They made their way out of the alley and into the hustle of the streets. Tornach kept silent. Kelnum was talking about something, but Tornach was only halfheartedly listening. His mind was elsewhere. They rounded the corner, and outside a bakery stood twelve men. One of them was Armosan. His eyes met Tornach's and he lowered his head. The other eleven, however, did not.

"Ungoran!" one shouted.

"Barbarian!" another shouted.

The flooded streets froze immediately. People fixated their eyes on Tornach. He was their enemy and their stares proved it. He was Ungoran, therefore he was to blame. They blamed him for the wars. They blamed him for all the deaths. *He* was the reason they no longer had brothers or sisters. *He* had killed them in the Barbarian Wars. The people of Crevail wanted the outsider gone.

The pack of men made their way closer. One of the men cast a stone that hit Tornach directly above the eye. A gash opened and blood trickled down his face. Kelnum could only stand next to Tornach, watching. He tried tugging at Tornach's sleeve, urging him to leave. "Tornach, I think we should go." But the Ungoran held his chin high. Kelnum saw there was no fear in the man's eyes. If he did indeed have fear, he did not show it. The barbarian stood his ground as even more men approached. "Tornach!" exclaimed Kelnum again. His words went on deaf ears.

The people of Crevail were now in uproar. Women, even children, were taunting the stranger. Men called for his death.

"Kill him."

"Kill the Ungoran!"

"Make him pay!"

More stones were pelted at Tornach. A few missed and a few found their mark. They hit his face and his chest, but failed to truly injure the man. The stones were more of a humiliation than a threat.

The angry mob continued its assault on the barbarian. They circled in closer, surrounding the pair; there was no way out of this for him. The screams and shouts persisted, and in an act of desperation, Tornach drew his sword.

The crowd immediately stepped back in fear. They stopped their pursuit and silenced their outcries. With blood dripping down his face and welts forming on his body, Tornach glared into their eyes. His stare was powerful, letting the children know he would be in their dreams that night. His breathing was that of a madman, with raspy grunts coming from under his breath.

All was silent now. Tornach held the blade up in the air. The crowd gasped and stepped back a few more paces. He lowered the blade to his chest and pressed it firmly. He then sliced his body across his upper chest. The wound split and spilled blood immediately. Every eye in the crowd went wide, taken aback by the stranger's actions. This was the man's final act of desperation, his cry for help. The people finally understood. He was just another man, not an animal. They lowered their heads in shame, for they had wanted to kill him only a moment before. But now it was as if every man, woman and child understood the barbarian's pain.

Tornach crouched to the ground on one knee, the blood pouring from his body. Just this morning he was in high spirits, the world having seemed new to him. Now, he wept. He cast the sword aside as if giving permission to the people to come and kill him—he was ready.

But they did not.

Kelnum looked at the docile crowd and decided it was time to leave. He reached down and grabbed Tornach's arm and threw it over his shoulder. He heaved the Ungoran to his feet and looked back at the silent crowd. They knew he wanted only to get Tornach out of town. The circle of people split open, letting them through.

Tornach was able to stand on his own two feet, but was having trouble walking. They slowly made their way through the mob. Kelnum looked back to make sure they were not coming after them, but the crowd stood quiet and still, every eye on the two.

The pair stumbled to Kelnum's carriage. He helped Tornach into the back and the barbarian passed out. He murmured words under his breath, which Kelnum could hardly make out. They were names.

"Gromulus . . . Fayorn . . ."

Kelnum took the reins of his horses, smacked the straps and the two left Crevail.

19

The man announced amidst the still thundering storms, "Good people of Ogata, may I have your attention." His voice was loud and he stood atop a plank, looking down upon the crowds. "The Senate would like to convey its appreciation for your patience." He paused, but only for a moment. "I come to you today with tragic news. The rumors that you have heard are indeed true. A great tragedy has befallen our empire. Emperor Makheb is nowhere to be found." The patrician stood at his podium, looking down at the grim faces.

The mob was aghast. The people whispered amongst themselves. The rumors had circulated, but now it was official. The patrician continued, his voice somber yet steady, "I regret to inform you of a travesty, yet the Senate felt it important to release this fact—our emperor is missing. Inside his chambers was a great struggle. A few assailants were found dead—" he paused again, this time for effect. "Our mighty emperor must have fought valiantly." His voice was proud. "The Senate wants the people of this mighty empire to be informed, and secure."

Someone called from the mass of people, "Is our emperor dead?"

The patrician replied, "That, we do not know."

"Was he kidnapped? Where is he?" the questions were being asked openly.

The patrician raised his hands. "Ladies and gentlemen, please . . . the Senate will keep everyone informed. We are doing all we can to find out what happened to our beloved emperor, but I am afraid we have no evidence of his whereabouts thus far."

"What will we do?" the crowd asked. They began to panic.

The patrician then added, "We do, however, have one lead. . . ."

The crowd hushed.

"There is one man who was last known to be in the emperor's presence, before this incident."

"Who?" they shouted.

"We believe this man has something to do with Emperor Makheb's untimely disappearance. The Senate has issued orders to seek out this man, and question him. If he undeniably harmed our emperor, he will be brought up on charges."

"Who is this man?" they shouted. "We shall string him up. Take his head." The crowd was agitated, their anger ran like a fever through the masses.

"I am afraid the identity of this man . . . will be a shock to you all."

"Who?" they demanded.

"Consul Veris."

The crowd went silent.

The patrician continued, "Consul Veris is who we seek for the disappearance of Emperor Makheb. Consul Veris," he said again.

"Consul Veris," repeated the crowd.

The mob went out of control.

*   *   *

The serpenti twisted and stretched from the jagged rocky canyons and into the vast, dried and decayed desert of the Endlands. Makheb sat high atop, riding into the abyss. The emperor of Nador was days past human lands, as well as human reasoning. The mood was strange and the atmosphere was quiet.

Things were different in the Endlands.

Death lurked everywhere and Makheb's colorful serpenti could feel it. Onward the beast pushed, slithering its way across the barren grounds. Its massive body pressed forward, taking Makheb a great distance into the lands of the unknown. The serpenti hissed as Makheb kicked its side, urging it on. It was mostly black and yellow, with shades of green woven amongst its rough scales. The serpenti's tongue flickered, as if seeking reason in a place where reason did not exist. The beast moved forward, leaving a gaping trail in the sand. Had it not been for its rider, the serpenti would have long since turned around. Even a beast as dense as a serpenti feared the Endlands. It trudged forward, afraid.

The emperor sat mounted, his black eyes looking straight ahead, towards his destiny. His mind was void of thought. His expression was flat as he focused on the emptiness of the terrain.

Many creatures and civilizations existed in the Endlands, most completely unknown to Men. The numerous fables and mysteries were indeed true. Past the Walfyre homeland of Gyrih, the Endlands began. The vast sands continued towards the horizon, never ending. Due to the winds, dunes would appear and disappear the same day, only to reappear again somewhere else. The ground moved, shifting and flowing in all directions. Rivers of sand existed in the Endlands, flowing gently towards all regions. Those who resided there used these rivers for travel, on barges.

Makheb had been riding for over a week and had covered much ground. Through the rocky canyons, north of Gyrih, and out into the flat, desert region, Makheb headed northwest—towards Baalek. The ashen clouds that plagued the southern lands of Nador were no longer overhead. It was as if the storm, too, wanted nothing to do with the Endlands. It stopped shy of the border, cautious. Instead of dark clouds, the sun shone brightly, heating the cracked and thirsty ground beneath. The air was dry and arid. Waves of heat rose through the cracks in the brittle earth, flithering on the horizon like apparitions. The clouds, what few there were, were amber and still.

Makheb rode on.

Afternoon approached and the dust from the scratchy sands of the Endlands coated the serpenti. As Makheb continued to ride, the winds began to pick up. By midday, dust storms had aroused. They whipped and churned up sand. Makheb's robes swatted and brushed the stinging shards like a horse's tail, keeping him free of the dust. The wall of debris blinded both serpenti and rider. Makheb, unveiled since his meeting with Consul Veris, reached inside his robes and pulled a new, more elaborate veil out. He attached it across his face, which protected him from the elements and concealed his identity once again.

Makheb continued at the same aggressive pace. He was relentless in his mission. He knew time was of the essence. The emperor rode longer, until he saw *it* in the distance. An object. It was far away and he could only make out its silhouette. The sands were blowing madly at this point, racing across the desert in a fury. Makheb, curious about the object, rode closer. He traveled down a slight decline and across a ridge. As he neared, he began to make out the distinctive shape. It looked like a colossal boulder, but there was something else about it, as well.

It was unnatural.

Makheb stopped his serpenti at the base of the statue. He looked up at the giant monument, which towered over him. It was enormous, towering over both the ruler of Nador and his serpenti. The statue mesmerized Makheb. He steadied the beast as he dismounted, the long strands from his robes aiding him in his descent to the ground. The god-like emperor let a solemn sigh of understanding drift from his mouth.

His muscles tightened—a clear sign of frustration. Makheb's hollow eyes traced their way up the monument, all the way to the top. He stood close to the massive sculpture. He wondered why this sculpture was here and what purpose it served. Was it a monument . . . or a warning?

Makheb himself was at a loss as to these questions, stepping closer as he ran his hand across the features of the sculpture. The winds blew sand across it, but it was still clearly distinguishable. The statue had been constructed out of a strange looking metallic alloy. Makheb was not surprised.

Staring straight into the eyes of a giant face, which jutted from the monument, Makheb pulled his cloak tighter. The face pointed east, towards Nador. He looked farther up and saw it, a crown of sorts portrayed above the face's brow. Inlayed were a series of foreign characters. The emperor nodded his head, as if agreeing.

Soon, Makheb turned back and hoisted himself into the saddle again, loosely holding the reins. He sat atop his beast, his robes flowing in all directions, lashing at the sands. Makheb sat, pondering the future as he gazed into the giant replicated face. A cold gust of wind blew through the arid wasteland as he stared up at the unveiled face of Ramunak.

Finally, Makheb kicked both his heels into the beast, and it slowly began to move on. Around the statue and onwards, he moved, until he dared to look back at the monument one last time. Instantly he pulled back on the reins again, staring in shock.

A sudden shriek of insanity echoed into the atmosphere. The high-pitched howl screamed in thousands of voices, and echoed through the Endlands. Makheb's robes flayed out in perfectly straight jolts as if being shocked from undercurrents of power.

Makheb steadied the serpenti once more, looking at the reverse side of the shrine. It was battered and beaten, vandalized and skewered. The dust, which was kicking up all around, appeared to purposefully clear out of the way. Makheb's view was unobstructed. He saw it clearly, as if something wanted him to.

Unsure of its meaning, Makheb shuddered at the sight of his own unveiled face.

He continued on, towards Baalek.

❧❧❧❧❧

Ten men sat at the Aronian king's table, all listening in silence. As their king spoke they became more anxious. King Kedorlaomer had summoned his top advisors and generals into yet another meeting. He explained the strange burden that had been resting on his shoulders. He was calm while he told them. He let his advisors know everything was fine within the borders of Aronia, and that outside the borders, into other human lands, was what worried him. Questions were plaguing the king, and he shared these questions to his faithful men, who listened carefully.

Kedor told his men about the feelings he had been having. Although a man of reason, he relied heavily on his instincts. Had it not been for these instincts, the Troxen band that invaded during the Siege of Cosh might have withdrawn from the battle victorious. They surely would have caused problems for the Seronan clans and the Valeecian army had Kedor not engaged his White Knights that day. To his men, the king's urgency seemed the same.

None of his advisors and military confidants had heard any dismal news from the south. According to their best knowledge, all was well in Nador. Since trade and communication between Aronia and Nador was scarce, each man accepted that all was well to the south of the forest. However, they trusted their king and made arrangements to find out more.

King Kedor issued orders to his men to post riders along the forest borders and to interview the few merchants who dared brave the dreaded Denok Forest. The doors to the royal parlor opened loudly. Anyone interrupting the king while in a meeting must have solid cause, and every man stood still as a soldier entered. In walked an Aronian knight, a faithful protector of the lands of the righteous. His name was Trenos, well respected and liked by the king. He entered the room, walking the length of the chamber, his posture and step perfect. He never once took his eyes off his king as he approached. The soldier stopped a few paces shy of his ruler and bowed his respects.

"What brings you, Trenos?" asked Kedor, his demeanor still calm.

"I beg your pardon for this intrusion, my king, but I felt this news could not wait," replied the man.

Kedor smiled. "It is fine, old friend. What is the urgency?"

Trenos continued, "Riders from the western edge . . . the border guards have reported a band of Troxen have set camp just outside our lands."

"Troxen? How many?"

"Not many, my king. The reports say a dozen. Sensing the urgency, I have dispatched scouts to search for any signs of an invasion. Thus far, it would seem the encampment is all they consist of. A small band."

If Kedor was shocked, he did not show it. "Tell me, Trenos, do they appear hostile?"

"No, my king. Their numbers are small and they are not dressed for battle. The reports say they are cautious and respectful . . . careful not to cross our border."

The men in the room shifted their eyes from the soldier to their king, anxiously awaiting his response to this. Kedor continued, "They have no threatening manner?"

"No, my king, not that we can see. Border guards did make contact, though. They spoke to one of the Troxen—reportedly their king. He calls himself Trag-lak."

The room filled with murmurs. Everyone had heard that name before. Kedor responded, "What does he want? They would not be so desperate to consider invasion, would they?" He was not seeking an answer, simply thinking aloud.

Trenos responded, "He most humbly requested a meeting with you, my king."

Everyone looked at Kedor. "Is that so?" the king responded.

Trenos only nodded.

Kedor thought to himself, and then spoke, "Trenos, get some rest, you look tired. After you do so, I want you to muster two hundred knights. Have them pack heavy—full armor, and prepare to ride to the western border. I will lead them myself and see what this King Trag-lak wants. Be ready, we shall leave when I give word."

With that, Trenos said, "Yes, my king," bowed again and dismissed himself as rapidly as he entered.

After the doors shut, the king of Aronia eyed his advisors. "Gentlemen, we will proceed on the side of caution. Double the border guards and increase the riders along the forest. Question any merchant and find out what is going on. While you do so, I shall personally ride to the border and find what this cursed Troxen king wants."

One of the advisors asked, "Sire, are they planning an invasion?" He was worried, as was everyone else.

Only the king kept his reserve. "We shall prepare as if there was an invasion coming." He paused, thinking. "Yet, I do not believe so. A dozen Troxen, despite their size, are of no threat. I believe the threat comes from Nador."

The men were confused, but they all nodded their heads. They would increase security and ready themselves if there was a threat to their kingdom.

One then asked, "My king, are two hundred men enough?"

"I shall be fine." King Kedor continued. "If the will of our god so demands, and I do not return, I shall leave instructions with Niralyn. Until then, keep a cautious head about you and rest assured that we are safe from any threat." *Well, almost,* he thought. "In the history of Aronia, many armies have tried marching on our lands. Not one has ever reached the gates of Ellsar. The god of Aronia will protect us. His glory will be handed down to the steel of our horsemen. You are all dismissed. Duty and honor."

"Duty and honor," they repeated.

The men left the room. Kedor sat by himself, pondering.

It has started, the king thought.

King Kedorlaomer entered his chambers. His guards opened the doorway to his private room and he stepped through the entrance. The walls were servium stone, as was the entire city. It glistened even on dreary days, and its brilliance shined on clear ones. Inside he walked and immediately saw Niralyn. She was speaking to Mirra, her handmaiden. Kedor stood aside, respecting her privacy and taking the time to gaze upon his beautiful wife.

She is so innocent, he thought.

Niralyn soon dismissed Mirra, who ushered past the king. She smiled as she passed. The doors closed behind her and immediately Niralyn rushed at Kedor.

"My love," she exclaimed. "I have missed you all day!" She nearly leapt in his arms, hugging him tightly, her hands sensually brushing at his neck as she kissed him three times. She whispered seductively in his ear, "You should not spend so much time away from me." Her firm bosom pressed against him. She continued, "What matters take my king's time?"

"A presence on our western border."

"What presence takes my king from his duties?" She was being playful and flirtatious. Her youth was showing.

"Troxen."

Niralyn pulled back from her husband, her hands on his shoulders. "Troxen? My king, are we being invaded? They would not try that. Did they not learn their lesson when you drove them from our lands?"

"I do not think this is about invasion. My generals are alert, though, so do not worry. The border guards say that their leader, Trag-lak, desires to speak with me."

"Is that safe? What if it is a trap?"

Kedor smiled. "They shall face the wrath of Aronian blades. No, my instincts tell me they bring no hostilities. However, it must be important. We have not had contact with Troxen in quite some time. This is unlike them."

"Why do you say that?"

"Because Troxen are usually not so courteous. Normally, you know when Troxen are on your lands by the thumping of their stride and the beat on their shields. They are destructive, and our scouts would know of an invasion. We would have much time to plan. Instead, this king of our enemies wants to speak with me. It is unlike Troxen, because Troxen usually lack diplomacy."

Niralyn batted her eyes, looked down and asked, "Do the Troxen not maintain diplomacy with Nador?"

"Yes," he acknowledged. "Troxen need their trade, though. It is necessary for them. Regardless, this . . . Trag-lak requests my presence. When we are ready, I shall ride to the western border."

Niralyn looked sad, but she was a queen and despite her youth, she was reserved with her emotions. She had learned long ago that a queen must always appear in control. "What will my king have me do?"

"Have faith that all will be well for Aronia and our people. I have ordered the generals to secure the borders and prepare. The public shall be told of these events." In Aronia, King Kedor was insistent that his people always be privy to the kingdom's future. "The Troxen pose no immediate threat, so I shall be home within ten days time. However, if my journey takes longer, I will send word. As for your duties . . . keep the people calm."

She kissed him again, and then rested her head on his shoulder. Niralyn was much in love. She spoke softly in his ear, "My dreams have worsened. I shudder at having to close my eyes . . . and without you at my side—"

Kedor held her. "It is only a dream. Aronia's queen is protected in Ellsar."

"I know, my dear. I will miss you. Do not worry for me. You are right, they are only dreams and I am Aronian and we fear no wickedness."

This made Kedor smile. His wife was a noble queen. He looked into her with eyes of kindness.

The two embraced, their spirits one.

❦❦❦

Across the empire, the people of Nador's boundaries were being addressed. In Crevail, the most recent victim to the plundering storms, the people called for the death of the traitor, Veris. Their cries were far from peaceful. They even put the blame on Veris for the deaths of Wallis and Jacard. The announcement was conveniently made moments after the lavish funeral for the two assassinated praetors. It had a good effect.

* * *

In the ash-ridden city of Merriton, in the old lands of Serona, crowds were in a frenzy of anger and disgust. The storms had wrecked their towns and they were frightened. They even reasoned that the odd storms were somehow to be blamed on the traitorous senator. They called for Veris' head.

In Cosh, Veris' hometown, people stormed the streets in shock and awe. Those who knew Veris personally were skeptical to his involvement, and chose to keep silent. They were fearful of the Senate's power and terrified to go against public opinion, however rash.

In the northern towns, such as Stalkwood, Fairmeadow and Chybum, the newly informed people were also fearful. As everyone else in the empire, they did not know the repercussions a missing emperor would have upon their lives. They were told of the impending storm, and the fury that was soon to come. The suspense of this created pandemonium in the streets.

The Senate had done its job well. Parlock was pleased.

20

Gromulus' steed galloped hard across the plains, carrying the two closer to the northern reaches of Nador. Gromulus had taken for granted the power of the Sword of Ellsar, Antiok, and was now truly realizing its importance. It pushed in his mind, leading them in the direction of Fayorn. Gromulus felt it odd, strange that a sword could affect him so. As the pair rode, he reflected on the night in the crypt.

Gromulus could only now realize the burdens that his friend, Fayorn, must have suffered due to Antiok. *I hope I never have to hold that sword again.* He remembered how it made him feel. Euphoric, and sad. Angry and blissful and overwhelmed. All emotions capable of a man were intensified. *No wonder Fayorn cast it away.* Gromulus could not wait to rid himself of Antiok. He attempted to take his mind off the sword and pushed his horse harder.

The land began to open wide and Gromulus and Lorylle could see as far as their eyes would allow them. They were in the great, wide-open expanse of the lands of northern Nador. The sun was bright and the soil was fertile. Roads were simple and hardly traveled. Behind the pair was the purple darkness of the great storm taking its time to deal its wrath upon Cosh. The storms now coated most of the empire; only the northern towns along Denok Forest remained unscathed. Gromulus felt as if it was pursuing only him, as if wanting to claim his head. They pressed hard the last couple of days, without stopping or hardly speaking, and were now quite a distance from the storm's fury. Gromulus knew it was coming.

Coming for me.

The air was crisp and cool. The sky that hung overhead was a radiant blue and Gromulus felt a little refreshed under the normalcy. He had heard that the skies over Aronia were even more grand and hoped that he would stay alive long enough to see them.

He pushed Ageeaus even faster.

After riding well into their second day, Gromulus slowed his horse to a trot as they approached a stream, which connected to a larger river that flowed all the way back to Cosh. In their haste, the two had not spoken much since their escape from the crypt. Now they would have their chance.

The stream was shallow and clear. The water ran softly, as if in no rush to find its destination. Gromulus stopped the horse at the edge; both he and Lorylle dismounting. All three needed to rest. The large beast began drinking the cool water immediately. Gromulus dipped a silver cup into the water and handed it to Lorylle.

"Thank you," she spoke softly. Her wide, hazel eyes beckoned him. He, again, realized how beautiful she was. He could not stop looking at her. Her skin was tender and smooth.

Gromulus only smiled and nodded in response. For some time, the two stood at the bank, admiring the open lands. The tall grass seemed to dance as it wisped back and forth in the wind, the open meadows a churning ocean of bliss.

Gromulus undid a snap and removed his red senatorial garments. He took off his cloak and robes, leaving only his black tunic and dark pants. The medallion was still around his neck and glistened in the afternoon sun. It swayed as he moved, a constant reminder of the perils he faced. Gromulus held his royal garments out and then let them drop into the river. Lazily, they floated away. He watched as they slowly washed out of sight. *It is done. I am no longer the man I once was.*

Following that, he reached into his boot. As if trying to forget, he threw the dagger into the stream as well, the memory of Lorylle's assassination attempt forgiven, yet remembered.

The expression on Lorylle's face was perplexed.

Gromulus noticed. "Do not worry, Lorylle," he said, "I have no need for politician clothing any longer. Emperor Makheb has terminated me from my office. I may not understand, but that is my order. I am no longer in servitude of the Senate."

She could tell this saddened him, but the man was keeping his emotions to himself. Lorylle asked, "You are no longer a consul?"

"Quite the opposite, actually. I am a fugitive. My company will not be safe, Lorylle. It may have been a mistake bringing you. If you continue to ride with me, I am afraid your life will be in grave danger."

"Danger? Do you think I would have been better off staying?" Before he could respond, she continued. "Master Veris . . . I mean . . . Gromulus, do you understand what happened?"

"I am not sure—"

"Your estate was being torched when I sought after you. Everyone was being slaughtered."

Gromulus glared at her. "By whom?"

"Imperial soldiers." Lorylle began to weep, her hands shaking. "Fryre, your stable boy . . . I saw him . . . I saw him murdered. He was trying to protect the livestock and a soldier—" she began crying, unable to continue.

Gromulus himself wiped a tear from his face. Fryre had only been a youth, hardly seventeen years old. Quickly, he regained his composure. "It seems the Senate has made its first move. It is happening fast." *Much too fast.*

Lorylle, her eyes wet, spoke, "I do not understand, Master Veris. Why would our own soldiers do such a thing?"

"They think I am the enemy. They will be after us. I foiled Parlock's plan. . . . Well, you did . . . by stopping Risard from killing me. No doubt, Parlock will be angry. He knows I am a threat. They will hunt me to no end."

They stared at one another for a while. Then, she said, "My lord, why do they hunt you? What could such a good man have done to anger them like this?"

"The soldiers, and soon the public, will believe I am to blame for Makheb's disappearance. I was the last to see him."

"What do you mean? The rumors are true?"

"What rumors?"

Lorylle responded, "Risard mentioned a rumor amongst the officers. He said there had been problems in Ogata with the emperor."

That was fast, Gromulus thought. "No doubt they will tell the public shortly. Soon, everyone in every town in Nador will demand for my head."

Little did Gromulus truly realize, the whispers had grown to shouts in the past two days, and word had spread quickly. Riders were dispatched and towns locked down. The search for Consul Veris was everywhere.

Lorylle looked at the medallion around Gromulus' neck. She had not seen it before. It made her curious because she selected his wardrobe daily. "Master, I do not recognize that pendant. Did you purchase it in Ogata?"

Curiously, he looked at her, and then remembered the medallion. He grasped it in his fingers, holding it close so she could see it better. "The alloy is . . . strange. No, I did not buy it. Someone gave it to me."

Lorylle was facitnated with the unfamiliar object. "Who gave it to you? It is one of the strangest things I have ever seen." Something about her voice trembled uncontrollably when she said this.

Gromulus hesitated his reply. "It . . . it was Emperor Makheb who gave it to me, Lorylle."

"Makheb?" she was bewildered. "But, I thought you said you did not—"

"I know I did, my darling," he cut her off. "And I am sorry for not being honest with you before. The truth is, I was supposed to keep everything a secret."

"I see," Lorylle uttered faintly.

Gromulus stepped closer to her, and in a soothing voice, said, "But I do not want to hide things from you anymore . . . if I can help it."

She smiled slightly, silently accepting his apology, her own fingers brushing the medallion. "Its symbol is odd. What is it?"

He shook his head. "That, I do not know. What I do know is that I am to bring this to King Kedorlaomer."

"King Kedor? We must travel all the way to Ellsar? Why?" She was anxious. The journey to northern Aronia would be far and nearly impossible.

"Yes. I was ordered to present it to him. As to why . . . I suppose that is not for me to know."

"Ordered? Who would order a consul to do such an impossible task?"

"Our emperor—Makheb did."

Lorylle then asked, "Master, why would the emperor give you such an order? You and I, alone, cannot travel through Denok Forest."

"I cannot begin to reason that question. He said he trusted me . . . that I was the only man who could carry out this mission."

"Perhaps he is right."

"I am but a senator. I told him that, yet he did not waver. The emperor commanded me to take this to King Kedorlaomer, and I shall obey his command."

"Let us pretend we can make it through Denok Forest, and into the mountains of Ellsar. Let us say we actually find the king . . . what then are we to do?"

"Emperor Makheb only told me that the king will understand, and that he will know what to do."

"None of this makes sense." Lorylle sighed with exhaustion. "Life, only a few days ago, was good."

Gromulus felt her misery. He carried the weight of the future of Nador on his shoulders. Before this mess, he had soaked in the comforts of the empire, only to now find himself on the run from it.

"He said there are three threats. The Senate is one of them, and Makheb was right. They *are* power hungry. Parlock and the others are pompous. They are spoiled by their luxuries and egotistical about their power. I knew it would one day get the better of Parlock, but I never foresaw this."

"The Senate has turned?" she questioned.

"On its ruler, yes. And on Makheb's greatest supporters. He informed me that Praetors Wallis and Jacard were murdered recently in Crevail and that the military might even stand with the conspirators." He wondered something, then continued, "Makheb told me the Senate will attempt to take my life."

'. . . *beheaded on the Capitol steps*,' he thought.

Gromulus went on, "I confronted Parlock, and this is all true. He only allowed me to leave the Senate building, I believe, for the fun of it. I guess he was sure Risard would kill me, and he would have, had it not been for Antiok . . . and you."

Lorylle batted her eyes and blushed slightly. "But Makheb is all power-ful. Why does he not stop this madness? Everyone loves our emperor. He gave us freedom."

"Yes, most do love him. This will work in the Senate's favor. They will not admit their true feelings—that they hate Makheb. No, they will conceal that fact. Their real goal is to expand. The politicians and generals will seek glory and riches."

"Greedy men."

"The world is full of them, Lorylle. However, their plan is not our biggest concern."

"Three threats to our empire, right?"

Gromulus did not respond immediately. Instead, he looked over his shoulder to the south. After gathering his thoughts, he answered, "Yes. Makheb did not seem very concerned about the takeover. Little would actually change upon his removal. The Senate would never, and could never, enslave the populace of Nador. No, that would not last. Nadorians learned that lesson during the wars. The politicians need the people. They need a thriving economy and strong military. More importantly, they need the people's support. Therefore, the government in the hands of the Senate would not drastically change the people's lives."

Lorylle commented, "The emperor *did* create the Senate. If things will not change, then he is only seeking to keep his power."

"Perhaps, but if Makheb comes back, the people will follow him. He is Nador's rightful ruler and everyone loves him. No, the Senate will appease the people. In any case, policy *will* change."

"What are the other threats of which he spoke?"

Gromulus replied, "The second he mentioned was . . . Ramunak."

Upon that word, Lorylle froze. Her hands grew clammy and her eyes wide. "Please do not say *his* name—"

The city was massive. It was much larger than the imperial Ogata, yet less modern. Either way, Baalek stood as a symbol to the power of Ramunak.

Baalek was a cultural hub to various species in the Endlands. The Troxen were the most noticeable beasts within the city's walls, somewhat due to their importance, but mostly because of their size. They were intimidating and had a thundering presence.

When the Troxen walked solitary, the ground thumped. When they walked in groups, the ground rumbled. And when the Troxen marched, the ground beneath them quaked.

The Troxen were a fearsome sight. Unlike in Nador, the Troxen were allowed to carry their arms in the streets of Baalek. When in Nador, the Troxen had to mind their manners, yet in the Endlands, they did as they pleased. Their voices were deep, and they bellowed out words loud enough to be heard throughout the streets of Baalek. They spoke loudly, commanding attention as lesser beasts quickly moved out of their way. The Troxen were capable of traveling long distances, needing no transportation but their feet. They were nearly impenetrable in battle and, for the most part, dominated the Endlands.

The Troxen were also a valuable commodity, in themselves, to the economy of Baalek, as well as throughout the vast expanse of the Endlands. The mighty Troxen were twice the height of a Man, and ten times the weight. Their hides were thick—grey skinned and wrinkled—and they feared nothing.

Nothing, that is, except the loss of trade. Rumors of Nador halting commerce were spreading, and the Troxen had yet to verify it with the Imperial Senate. They had heard there were problems within the empire of Men, and it made them nervous.

Trade with Baalek was equally important as with Nador. Although only a city, it consumed resources on an immense scale. The Troxen bartered their goods from their own civilization, as well as from the human empire. They were the connection that kept the lands of beast and the lands of Men civil. The Troxen knew that the impending trade crisis with Nador would hurt them.

The Troxen civilization was far north of Baalek, on the northern edge of the Endlands, where the desert landscape steadily changed and became the glaciers of the White Mountains. In their homeland, Murtall, production was minimal; the Troxen depended heavily on trade. Trade with the two powerful regions—Baalek, ruled by Ramunak, and Makheb's empire, Nador—kept the Troxen mighty. It also kept them off the warpath.

The Troxen knew, all too well, that the road to war usually started with the lack of basic necessities in life. Many years prior, their kind had to rely on the capturing or buying of human slaves from Ume, and selling them to the head master of the arena, Kuldeynar. Now, they did not need to do so.

Normal trade was good to the Troxen; but lately, they felt something strange as the many hundreds did their business on the streets of Baalek. Only a few days prior, Ramunak had gone against his word and cast six Troxen into the arena. It had been an outrage, and word had immediately been sent back to the Troxen king. His own son was in Baalek at the moment, attempting to get answers.

The Bloodpaws also had their place in Baalek's society. Unlike Troxen, who stayed only long enough to barter their goods and services, Bloodpaws made the city of Baalek their home. There were thousands of them, many more than the few hundred Troxen. They lived either within the city's walls, or outside in camps.

Being under Ramunak's authority, they served his will without question. And they did not respond kindly to the large Troxen foreigners impending on their homeland.

The two species had their quarrels. Many centuries earlier, the two cultures had clashed, leaving them in hatred of one another. It was always tense when a new herd of Troxen entered Baalek. The Bloodpaws had the responsibility to protect the city, and part of that protection was securing the local economy.

This put their kind in a vicarious situation. As much as they would have loved to slaughter each and every Troxen, they behaved civilly, for Ramunak would have their heads if trade ceased. However, lately there had been talk that the Troxen were no longer needed in Baalek, and they were gleeful when their mighty ruler allowed them the splendor of watching six of their foes die by the blade of Lionhead.

They had indeed enjoyed that.

The Troxen and Bloodpaws were of the highest level in Baalek, but many lesser creatures and civilizations resided there, as well. The Osa'har were one of them. They looked nearly identical to the race of Men, with some exceptions. Their faces were pushed in. They had flat noses and a wide space between their eyes. The complexion of the Osa'har was twisted and warped. Hideous scars decorated their faces. Their skin was like mangled leather.

Their kind wore long robes to protect their skin from the sun. The Osa'har were the majority of the population in Baalek, many thousands making their residence there. Although they were submissive to the Blood-paws and slaves to their god-ruler, the Osa'har were important to Ramunak.

Despite being slaves, and often treated harshly, there was a warrior class amongst the Osa'har. Legendary swordsmen, the Dakari also served in Ramunak's legions. Mostly used as assassins and scouts, they served their purpose in war as well. The Dakari, these privileged few, were revered throughout the desert. They were the fittest of their kind, brave soldiers of fortune.

Of the other creatures throughout the city, Gorgots and Tranaks were the backbone of Baalek. The Tranaks were responsible for the management of the city, which included keeping relations civil between the Troxen and Osa'har, who directly competed for trade. Each civilization's greed caused them to desire more—to exclusively handle trade in Baalek—and the Tranaks presided over such disputes. The Tranaks were slow moving, yet extremely intelligent.

The Gorgots were responsible for the upkeep of the massive city. They were small, only two-thirds the height of Man, yet still vicious in their own rights. They had six legs and many small clusters of what looked like bone that protruded from their flesh, providing them defense if needed.

The labyrinths inside the pyramid were vast, endless. They spider-webbed throughout the interior of the flat-topped pyramid, which was a catacomb of horrors. The corridors stretched far into the hollow reaches of Ramunak's lair, a wide assortment of elaborate rooms filled with wicked beings. Dark hallways led to darker passageways. Few torches burned, attached to walls, yet they seemed to cast more shadow than they did light. The large, grey stone walls were hollow, and footsteps echoed as one traveled its complex hallways, which were cold and damp. Small insects and other slimy creepers of the night made their residence inside the pyramid, along with Ramunak's minions. Furry creatures scurried the passageways, hiding in corners. They crept and clicked in the recesses of the underground. Moans and growls and sniffles haunted the stale corridors. It was musty and putrid within the pyramid—and smelled of death.

At the end of a certain hallway, many levels deep, was another passage.

This one was short, and at its end was a single door. A skull was carved into it. Inside was a large, wide-open assembly room, where the meeting was taking place.

The chamber inside was extensive. The ceilings were high and the walls far apart. The entire room was made of stone and carefully molded pillars kept the room steady. Twenty torches lit the room, and light was present. They flickered and flashed, casting shadows on the walls. The shadows seemed to dance, as if a sacred ritual, and were not consistent with the flames. It was as if the shadows on the walls had spirits of their own.

These shadows bowed to Ramunak.

The great ruler sat upon his metallic throne at the far end of the room, a great stone wall behind him. Attached to the wall were four torches that glimmered dimly, surrounding a large tapestry. The material was crimson red, with gold trim tassels on the corners. In the middle of the tapestry was an emblem. It was circular, and its design was peculiar. Its long, abstracted flails dressed the design with exuberance, reaching out from the center in unison. The symbol had a way of seducing the viewer, and far from coincidentally, it was the same icon fastened around Gromulus' neck.

Two columns stood as if sentry to Ramunak, one on each side of his throne. Around them were wound strands of cloth, much like Ramunak's robes. They rippled, seeming to climb up the columns, twirling around them.

Ramunak sat with his hands on the arms of his throne. His seat was elevated atop a platform, four steps high off the floor. His raised throne overlooked the entire chamber.

He was motionless. His robes were not. The ruler of the Endlands sat and listened, curious to the proceedings before him. His eyes were black and unwavering.

His robes were red, with long strands of gold and purple that draped from the ends. There were hordes of strands. They slithered and coiled, intertwining themselves throughout his throne. Ramunak's veil was as colorful as the rest of his wardrobe, and combined with his hood, they concealed his expression. The grey flesh of his hands, and the matching skin around his coal eyes, were all that were visible.

Ramunak tilted his head, entertained.

He allowed General Taius to conduct the meeting.

Taius, former general of all armies of Valeecia, stood slightly in front of Ramunak, down two steps, and looked intently at his audience. The past Valeecian general, once distinguished and honorable, now stood proudly near his cloaked leader.

The general had short hair. It was turning grey, but he still contained in him a raw aggression of men only half his age. His face was weathered and he had the eyes of a warrior. Taius was tall, and his shoulders were square. He was the epitome of a war leader.

In his hand, Taius held a metal helmet. It had dulled over the years, for he had worn it for quite some time. It was spiked on top, and the general shifted it in his arm, making it more comfortable. His other hand was empty, and an outstretched finger was pointing at the rabble before him.

Taius stood as if to guard the great Ramunak, although the lord of the night needed no protection. Taius wore an armored breastplate, which was as dull as his helmet. The light from the torches seemed to make his armor ripple—or perhaps it was Ramunak. On his chest was the symbol he had worn for many years. His armor bore the crest of what once represented Valeecia, but had been confiscated and assimilated by Nador—the serpenti.

Taius stood sentry between his ruler and five Troxen.

They stood in a semi-circle, facing Ramunak's throne.

Although a fierce lot, Ramunak did not fear them. He could sense their apprehension. The Troxen were angry because of his actions, yet they kept calm. Under his veil, Ramunak grinned. If these Troxen were not convincing, he would throw them in the dungeons with the thirteen others he held captive. Ramunak would let his greatest gladiator ever, Lionhead, have his way with them. His champion would most certainly take pleasure in their deaths.

It was true; Lionhead did hold the Troxen in contempt. Lionhead held all, except perhaps Ramunak, in low regard. He sat across the dark chamber, in the corner, obscured by the lack of light. Lionhead sat, rested back slightly in his lounge, the shadows making it impossible to see his expression as he watched.

Lionhead was larger than Ramunak. Mostly feline, his face and body also had some features of a Man. He stood on two legs, and had two arms. However, he could run and pounce from all fours if necessary. He had a large mane and a snout that protruded from his face. His eyes were yellow; small specks of black were his pupils. His head was three times the size of a human's, and his torso was human-like, albeit covered in golden fur. Patches of white blended in spots, as well.

Lionhead was horrific. More beast than anything, he was the perfect killer, both vicious and graceful. During combat, his instincts controlled him.

Now, Lionhead sat tense in his lounge, staring fixedly at the five Troxen who were seeking council with Ramunak. His furry hand flexed, and it calmed him. His sharp claws scratched deep into the wood. He was anxious. If Ramunak would allow it, he would slaughter these five Troxen. He would tear them limb from limb. Lionhead hoped Ramunak would allow him to do so. He growled under his breath and watched on.

The five Troxen stood, huddling together and looking around curiously at their surroundings.

The paintings on the walls rocked back and forth on their hooks.

The torches flared occasionally, attempting to seize them.

Even the cold stone walls seemed to move.

If it had been any other beast, or Man for that matter, they would have surely died of angst. Troxen, though, were intimidated by few. The ceilings were tall in the chamber, yet their heads still came close to touching it. They were enormous, towering over every creature in the room, except the seated Lionhead behind them. They were not quite his height, but their frames were three times his size. Their heads were hefty boned, their skulls thick. Each had protruding horns that jetted from the sides of their long faces, pointing in varying directions.

Their overall size was unimaginable. True, there were larger beasts in the world, but the Troxen still dominated the grounds they traveled. Able to cast a horse in the air with a single swipe, they were strong, yet also refined in the use of weaponry. Their hides were thick, much like the mammoths they sometimes rode when carrying masses of goods to barter. Only a razor sharp blade stood the chance of penetrating their hides.

Now, the five stood helpless, looking up at Ramunak, the one who would determine their fate, as well as the fate of their thirteen friends who were held captive. Adding to their woes, they had to surrender their weapons before the meeting, making them anxious about being unarmed. It mattered only slightly, though. Troxen did not need weapons to win a fight.

Taius led the debate. The requisition was simple. The Troxen wanted their thirteen comrades released immediately. They also wanted the bodies of the six killed in the arena. They deserved a proper Troxen burial.

General Taius laughed aloud, "*Ha!* What leverage do you think you have, Troxen? Your pleas are as if from beggars to the ears of the majestic Ramunak." Taius cocked his head and added, "If it were my choice, I would cast the five of you into the arena with your comrades. I would usher you in front of the crowds . . . and let Lionhead have his way with you!"

Instantly the Troxen began grumbling obscenities. One looked over his shoulder, at the seated Lionhead.

Lionhead grinned at him.

Taius raised his hand slightly, and the Troxen began to settle down. "However, the deity—Ramunak—in his glorious mercy, has agreed to hear your words. Speak swiftly, though, for his mercy will not extend far."

One of the Troxen stepped forward. He was younger than the rest, yet the chosen spokesman.

Ock-nar began, his voice deep and grumbling, booming as it filled the chamber. "*Grmm grmmm.* Why have you included Troxen in your games, Ramunak?"

Taius looked back, but the ruler said nothing. The general then turned back to Ock-nar, motioning for the beast to go on.

Ock-nar continued, growing steadily irritated, and it reverberated in his tone, "We may not understand, but we demand you cease your butchering at once!"

At this demand, the other creatures in the room came out from their shadows from behind Ramunak's throne. Gorgots snickered in the background. A few Bloodpaws yipped. Ramunak sat still.

Taius responded, "You have no authority to demand *anything* from Ramunak. He, alone, controls these lands."

"Only this region. *Grumm grmm.* These lands are vast." Ock-nar looked up at Ramunak, "Baalek you may control, but you have no leverage over the Troxen nation."

Gorgots stared.

Bloodpaws yapped, laughing and shrieking.

There were ten Bloodpaws in the room, standing guard. They spread out, their claws clacking the ground, and surrounded the five Troxen. They each held a sharp spear in one hand, and a small shield in the other.

"Troxen scum!" one shouted. "Do not speeeak to our leader as if he owes you anything. Your words will only quicken your death."

Another two Bloodpaws taunted the large beings. One acted as if he was going to thrust his spear into them. The Troxen leapt back and more Bloodpaws laughed.

Taius cleared his throat loudly, causing the Bloodpaws to turn their attention to him. Then, they moved back a step, holding their tongues as the general responded, "Again, I must warn you . . . do not anger Ramunak. What exactly do you seek?"

"We offer a trade," replied Ock-nar. "*Grmm grmm.* A sacrifice to Ramunak. We have long provided trade to Baalek. However, if you wish for trade to cease, we shall make this our last commerce. *Grmm grumm.* Heed these words. . . . Our king . . . our nation, will never stand for this."

Taius spat on the floor. "Careful of your tongue, or I shall have it cut out!"

The Bloodpaws shifted anxiously.

Lionhead readied to pounce.

Ock-nar took a deep breath, calming himself. "*Grumm.* Our deal is simple. Release our fellow brethren, all thirteen, as well as the bodies of those who Lionhead killed, and we shall provide homage to *your* ruler."

Taius grinned at this, "*Our* ruler, eh? Perhaps you are blind, Troxen. Ramunak rules all. What is this homage you pay?"

Ock-nar responded, "Three hundred human slaves. Do with them as you will."

Upon hearing this, Ramunak tilted his head. Human slaves were harder to acquire over the years. Without the risk of war, it would be easy. However, Nador was mighty now, and the once steady flow of new flesh from the east had dwindled.

Taius spoke, "These slaves . . . you took them from Nador?"

Ock-nar nodded, almost gleefully.

Taius chuckled mockingly, "You think that will come without notice?"

Ock-nar replied, "We do not care. *Grmm. Grummm.* We only seek to save our own. The three hundred humans shall provide far more entertainment for the masses than the thirteen of our own. *Grmm.* Accept this request and we will leave Baalek. Slaughter the humans if you wish, we care not."

Taius eyed him carefully. His voice filled with confidence and arrogance, he spoke, "Tell your leader, Trag-lak, that your kind is no longer welcome in Baalek. We will trade no more. If your kind trod on our land, our Bloodpaws will—"

Before he could finish, the Bloodpaws frenzied. They could not help themselves. They were in bloodlust, jaunting and jeering and taunting the Troxen even more. "Leeeave, Troxen! Baalek is ours . . . you are weeeak!"

Ock-nar stood his ground, bravely. "Without us, your economy will fail. *Grmm grmmm.*"

Taius went on, "Believe the delusions of your leader, if you wish, Troxen. The Osa'har will handle commerce in Baalek."

Ock-nar grunted at this.

Taius continued, "If our trade suffers, then we will take what we need. Besides . . . rumor has it that Nador will soon exclude you from her markets. Your nation is doomed."

"If that is true, it will only be temporary," Ock-nar admitted.

"You are wrong, Troxen. Soon, your civilization will crumble. There will be a great sacrifice—a cleansing."

Ock-nar was now enraged. He had a temper and could hardly contain himself. Before entering Ramunak's pyramid that night, he and the four others had already committed themselves to the possibility of death. If Ramunak would not accept the deal, they would each fight. A Troxen's wrath had no bounds, and Ock-nar felt that the time was fast approaching.

Ock-nar shouted, "Ramunak! *Grmm. Grmm.* You do not control us. Our culture will exist far past your rule here, just as we have for many ages. We do not fear you. Take our lives, if you wish, and you shall war the entire

Troxen nation—and break upon our shields."

At this bold statement, Bloodpaws and Gorgots began screaming obscenities.

They all spoke at once.

"Troxen scum!"

"You are dead!"

The Gorgots shrieked. Bloodpaws heckled. Their spears were close.

Even Lionhead, still seated across the room, began to tense. A wrong move and he would pounce.

The entire room was in upheaval. Behind Ramunak's throne, lurking in the shadows, appeared other oddities. Strange two-faced women, their faces protruding from the same head, stood behind the throne. They showed their fangs, snarling as if possessed. High priests peered around the throne's corner as well. One of them stretched his powdery face much too close to his ruler, and a strand of Ramunak's robe lashed out at him. It pulled him close. It tightened around the priest's neck in a flash. Instantly, as if alive, ten more pieces of the ruler's strange clothing grabbed the high priest of Baalek. He was tossed across the room, landing against the back wall.

A two-faced woman cackled with laughter.

Another high priest clicked his teeth.

Taius looked to his seated god-king. Ramunak nearly salivated at the thought of more sacrifices. It was never enough for him. He wanted more. Ramunak nodded his head to Taius. He would accept the trade, yet he did not care for the grievances of the Troxen. He would allow them to leave the city, though.

He had bigger plans.

"The great Ramunak will honor this trade," stated Taius with a disappointed look on his face. "Present your homage. Then, take your weak Troxen comrades and walk out of Baalek in dishonor. From this day forward, your kind is no longer welcome here. Do not show your faces or you shall be slain."

Lorylle asked, "Master Veris, what could possibly be worse than *him*? What is the third threat of which Makheb spoke?"

"He did not say. Makheb only told me that I would find out soon enough," Gromulus paused. "I sense it is something unimaginable."

Lorylle turned her head slowly, away from Gromulus. A rush went through her, a surge of fear.

Her eyes flashed with blackness.

21

Gromulus had to say it. "Lorylle . . . back at my estate . . . the other night—why would you want to kill *me?*" It had weighed him down for the extent of their journey thus far and now the question had finally been asked. He tried to make eye contact, but she looked away.

Lorylle, choking on her words, said, "I am so sorry, master . . . I . . . I was not myself. I could never harm you." She began sobbing.

Gromulus realized how much he cared for her. He reached for Lorylle, pulling her close and embracing her. The breeze blew gently as they held one another.

Finally, she admitted, "It was the nightmares."

"The nightmares?"

"Yes. Since I could remember. In the dark, alone at night, is usually when they would come." She paused, stumbling through her next words, "This time . . . it was different. It was the first time my dreams crossed into my waking world."

Gromulus tried to relax his tone. He realized this was painful for her. "Tell me about these nightmares. Have you had them for a long time?"

She nodded.

"Are they always the same?"

Lorylle paused, thinking. "No, not always. But, they are always dark and . . . gloomy, and have many similarities. The *feeling* is always the same, though."

"How do they make you feel?"

"Cold and hollow inside."

Gromulus continued, "And you felt this same feeling when you tried to—?"

Lorylle nodded. "It was more powerful. I could not control my body, or my mind. It was as if I was not awake. I was in a dream, but I could see what was happening. I shouted and cried for myself to stop. I suppose I won, because I dropped the knife before it was too late."

Gromulus waited for a moment, pondering his next line of questions.

"You say you have had these dreams for a while? Since you were a child?"

"As early as I can recall, I have dreamt of darkness."

The birds flew overhead, unaware and uncaring as to the business of Men. In the distance, four deer frolicked in the tall grass, aware of the couple's presence, but unafraid. The trickle of flowing water of the stream and the gentle breeze made Gromulus wish he could stay there forever. *I could build a house and fish from this river, and grow vegetables on my land. I could hunt these plains and happily live out the rest of my days.* Then, he swatted away the dream. *No, first I must complete my task.* Gromulus realized how much he wanted Lorylle. He looked at her as she gazed down the stream. She was humming softly, a beautiful tune.

He asked, "Where did you learn that one?"

Lorylle blushed. "It was sung to me when I was very young. It calms me."

Gromulus forced a smile. "I can barely remember my own childhood."

"Why is that?"

"It was . . . cut short."

Lorylle seemed to understand. "You mean you were forced to grow up fast?"

The young man stared off for a moment; his eyes looked east, "Something like that."

Lorylle stepped closer to him. "I had to grow up quickly myself." Her face showed sadness.

Gromulus, feeling depressed, asked, "Did anything bad happen to you?"

Lorylle shrugged her shoulders. "I suppose that is a matter of opinion. Everyone has his or her own horrors in life. As for my own, they were what they were."

"Perhaps the nature of your nightmares has something to do with your childhood?"

"Most likely," she was quick to reply.

"Tell me, Lorylle. I want to know more about you."

Lorylle looked at him oddly. "What would you like to know?"

The man thought for a moment, and voiced his answer, "Well, I guess you could start by telling me of your early days. Where were you born?"

She did not immediately respond. Instead, she stared west.

Gromulus pushed harder, "Lorylle?"

The girl shuddered, and then composed herself. "Baalek. I was born in Baalek."

Gromulus did not expect to hear that answer, but could tell she was not joking. "Baalek?" He was curious—mystified. "You were born in the Endlands?"

"Yes."

"Yet . . . you are human. I did not know humans existed there."

Lorylle returned, "Many of our kind live there. However, they are not free. Mostly, humans serve as slaves . . . taken by the Troxen before the wars."

Gromulus knew the Troxen had been notorious for taking human slaves, but that had long since ceased. "The Troxen do not speak of that issue. On the other hand, they do tell tales of many beasts that roam the Endlands."

"Many foul creatures exist there."

"Tell me what they are like."

Lorylle continued, "Bloodpaws are the enforcers in Baalek. They rule with an iron fist. They are brutal . . . much worse than the Troxen."

"Yes, I have heard mention of them. What do they look like?"

"Well . . . they are strange. Almost a combination of a man . . . and a hyena."

Gromulus had no response.

Lorylle went on, "Other beasts roam there, too. They are all wicked and bloodthirsty. Death looms on the streets of Baalek. There is no law there. No reason. Only death. Beasts rule there. Men and women, like us, stand no chance. They can only suffer the penalties and hope to be left alone. There is, though, another species much like our own that seems to live in relative freedom."

"Who are they?"

"They call themselves, Osa'har."

"Osa'har?"

"Yes. They look like you and me, yet different. Their skin is darker, for one. Deep auburn, most likely from the sun's reflection off the sands. They speak differently. They are similar to you and me, but their faces are—"

"Are what?" asked Gromulus curiously.

"Deformed almost—like leather. Scratches and ridges cover their faces. Rough, like the bark of a tree. Their noses are flat and their eyes are wider apart."

"Interesting," was all Gromulus could say.

"Mostly, they keep to themselves. But, like all other beasts, they answer to *him*. The Troxen seem to only tolerate *his* control, but all other creatures are . . . *his*. The Osa'har are no exception. They trade goods from regions that the Troxen do not. Occasionally, they are thrown into the arena, yet they do not seem to care. They worship strange gods and conduct odd practices."

"Such as?"

"In the Osa'harian culture, sacrifice is important. I suppose all beasts love the games in Baalek, and the sacrifices to *him*. On the other hand, the Osa'har have made it part of their religion."

Much like Ungorans, thought Gromulus.

Lorylle explained, "Although not nearly as powerful and important as Bloodpaws, even the Osa'har serve a role in Baalek. Therefore, they are allowed some freedoms. They are fierce warriors, as well, although nothing like the Bloodpaws. Only the elite may serve in *his* legions. They are called the Dakari."

Gromulus asked, "You said these Osa'har believe sacrifice is important—"

Lorylle cringed at the thought of her next words, "All Osa'har offer their first born as a sacrifice."

This sickened Gromulus.

"The Dakari sacrifice themselves as well, although they are more extreme. They are never forced to fight in the arena. They go willingly to their deaths."

Gromulus pondered something. If Lorylle was indeed from Baalek, then perhaps she was aware of what had happened to General Taius and his two legions that had disappeared into the Endlands five years prior. Finally, he asked her.

Lorylle stood up straighter. "I do not know the details, but my best guess is that those men turned."

"You believe they abandoned their duties to Makheb?"

"I do not know, but there is a strong chance they turned to *his* side. *His* influence is powerful." She speculated, "I believe Taius used his legions to bargain with once he realized they would be slaughtered. Like I said, though, I do not know for sure. I moved from Baalek long before the end of the wars."

Gromulus was shocked. Taius seemed so honorable, as did his men. *Is this really true? Could that many men have really turned? What power can make a soldier choose the side of wickedness?* Gromulus looked to the west, picturing in his mind the brutalities of the great arena, Kuldeynar. He had of course never seen it with his own eyes, but had heard of brutality from the Troxen merchants. Gromulus felt both sadness and anger towards the soldiers. He was confused even more. *If Ramunak holds this much influence, then . . . what are Nador's chances? What can Men do against such evil?*

"Is everything alright?" Lorylle asked. She reached out and held his hand in her own. "What is on your mind?"

Gromulus spoke softly, "They are coming for me. If I stay in Nador, they will eventually capture and kill me."

"I do not want you to die," whispered Lorylle.

"And I do not want harm to come to you. Maybe it is best you go back to Cosh. If we are caught together . . . I cannot imagine what they will do to you."

Lorylle looked at him and said, "I am with you until the end. If you are a fugitive, so am I."

Gromulus looked at her. He reached his hand out and pulled her close. They both stood there for quite some time, both knowing they loved each other but too afraid to confess it.

At last, Gromulus let go of the girl and walked over to Ageeaus. He lifted the saddlebag flap up and pulled out a flask of whiskey he had packed. He uncorked the snapjaw flask and drank from it. He wiped his mouth with the back of his free hand, feeling refreshed.

Gromulus walked towards Lorylle again and offered the flask to her. She gratefully accepted and drank from it. "Thank you," she stated after taking a drink, "I needed that."

"Tell me, Lorylle . . . how did you come to be born in the Endlands? No one ventures west. That is, no one in his or her right mind."

"There are more humans than you think in the Endlands."

"Tell me about them."

"They came from the old Kingdom of Ume, mostly. Many generations of humans have grown up to only know the Endlands."

"They have been there for generations, you say?" he questioned, not completely believing her.

"Yes, long before the Barbarian Wars started."

"You are being serious?"

Lorylle nodded her head, handing the flask back to him, "Ume, having bordered the Endlands, was where most of the humans came from."

"You mean people actually left Ume . . . to live in the Endlands?"

"Not of their own volition. No, we are talking about human slaves, Veris . . ." she shook her head, "Gromulus."

He let it go, knowing that it might take her a while to get used to the name. "Why did the people of Ume allow that?"

"They were scared, much like the Seronans were of the Ungorans. Also, it did not help that their king was involved."

"Briom was involved? How so?"

"He received much gold for the exchange."

"He sold his own people to be slaves in the Endlands?" Gromulus could not believe what he was hearing.

Lorylle sighed, "Yes, to the Troxen mostly. Briom was made rich by selling them his own people."

"How do you know this? I am . . . was, a senior senator and I have never heard of this."

"It was not long after the wars began. Briom needed gold to support his armies if he was going to fight the Ungorans. He made a deal with the Troxen and they took almost a thousand poor souls from their villages. My father was one of them."

"So, your father was from Ume?"

She nodded, "He was a fisherman. He spent much of his time on the great rivers that run through the countryside."

"And it was the Troxen who took him?"

She hesitated, "They sold my father to . . . *him,* along with many others."

"So he became a slave?"

"Somewhat. He had certain skills that granted him relative freedom. He was allowed to wander the streets of Baalek freely, but yes, he was still a slave."

"What skills did he have?"

"He could fight. My father was a great warrior and fought for three years in the arena of Baalek. Eventually, *he* granted my father freedom. Of course, if caught trying to leave Baalek, my father would have been killed."

Gromulus nodded. He then asked, "What of your mother?"

Lorylle grimaced and then replied, "My mother, I am ashamed to say, was a whore. She was in the last group sent to the Endlands and forced to be a slave, as well. She was young, and probably had no real chance at a normal life. My mother was destined for failure."

"I am sorry," was all Gromulus could say.

"It is what it is. I have learned to deal with it over time. Everything happens in life for a reason, I suppose."

"I have an old friend who believes that way, as well."

"And you do not?"

"I believe our fates are in our own hands." He paused, and then asked, "Did you ever know your mother?"

"No," Lorylle said. "She carried me until birth and then gave me to my father. She did not want me. Although, I can understand. At least my father was able to care for me when I was young."

"What happened to her?"

"She was reportedly found dead a week later, but I do not know the true nature of her death. I only knew my father."

"Was he good to you?"

Lorylle smiled, "Yes, he was. I recall only wonderful times with him, although as time passes, I remember him less and less. Despite being born in such a wretched city, my childhood was decent."

"What of your father, now?" he asked.

The girl shook her head, and looked down. He had struck a nerve, and waited patiently for a reply. After a moment, she answered, "As far as I know, he got into a disagreement with another gladiator that day. Words must have been exchanged—my father came home angry. I was only seven at the time, but I remember him always being a fearless man. Yet, that day, he was scared. He kissed me goodbye and went to fight in the arena."

Gromulus knew in his mind what was coming. He held her hand tighter, showing his concern.

She continued, "I awoke the next morning to the voice of an Osa'harian woman telling me my father was dead."

"I am sorry, my darling."

"It was no man who killed my father. No, it was something else. . . . A monster."

"A monster?" he echoed.

"Those in Baalek call him . . . Lionhead. He is the champion of the arena and answers only to—"

"Ramunak," Gromulus finished for her.

Lorylle nodded her head.

Gromulus stepped back and thought for a moment. *I have heard that name, Lionhead.* Then, he continued, "What became of you then?"

The woman shifted her position and looked away. She was remembering. "That was when the nightmares began. For two days I remained in our shabby home. Nobody came to check on me. No one seemed to care. But, finally, a man did come."

"Oh?"

"His name was Sulchek. He found me, hungry and tired. He ended up raising me himself. I think my father would have approved of him. He was a good man."

"You said the nightmares began at this time?"

"Yes, I believe so. The dreams have always haunted me. Especially then, for I was young. Sulchek was always caring, but he could not help me with my nightmares. They overwhelmed me. I was not eating . . . slowly dying. Perhaps that would have been best."

"No, Lorylle, of course not."

She shrugged her shoulders. "Sulchek was a smart man. He knew what needed to be done. So one night he and I secretly left Baalek, and the Endlands."

"Where did you go? To Ume?"

"No, by that point the wars were underway and Sulchek did not want to go to Ume. The swamps in Valeecia were too treacherous and Serona much too far away. Instead, he took me to Aronia."

"Aronia?"

"Of course, this was when the forest was still safe. We went to the kingdom of the north to get away." She smiled. "Aronia is beautiful. Have you ever seen it?"

"No, I have not. Hopefully we will make it there."

"We will. You should bear witness with your own eyes the splendor of Aronia."

Gromulus smiled. "That would be nice."

"The people there are good," the girl continued. "We settled in the town of Isthor. It is much like Cosh is to Nador. Isthor is Aronia's business center, and that was where I spent the remainder of my childhood."

Gromulus nodded, "I know of Isthor. The man I seek, Fayorn, has told me much about Aronia. He is from Ellsar . . . but given you lived in Aronia, I am sure you know that."

"Fayorn? We seek him?" This excited Lorylle. "I have heard of Fayorn and what he means to Aronia. I never had the chance to travel as far north as Ellsar, but I hear the city is flawless. Isthor is an interesting and beautiful town itself. It is a simple place, just as the Aronians like it."

Gromulus asked, "Did you go to school there? I have heard Aronian schools are advanced, and you are well educated."

"I did. I received a wonderful education, although my studies were eventually cut short. I would have preferred the chance to further my learning, but Aronians do not fancy science very much. . . . That is what I really like."

"I am fond of science, as well," returned Gromulus. "It is a shame that they fear it so much. It keeps them from progressing. However, Fayorn would say because of that, they are better off. Look at our own empire, which puts much effort on science. Nador is crumbling beneath us while Aronia stands tall." Gromulus sighed. "Perhaps they are right."

"Perhaps," was her only response.

"So what did Sulchek do while you were in school?"

"He worked in the fields at first. He finally secured a job at the university in Isthor. He taught there for a few years. That is, until we were driven out."

"Driven out? What do you mean?"

"As I grew older, I began to realize that Aronians had problems of their own. The Ungoran menace was finally threatening them, although they handled the problem swiftly. The White Knights of Ellsar drove them away again and again. After they accomplished this, the beasts began causing trouble for them. It was the Troxen."

"I remember hearing the stories," said Gromulus, "about how the Aronians drove beasts from their lands. Fayorn would preach it to me like it was their doctrine. I think they are wrong, though. The Troxen have proven to suit Nador well. Our relations had a bad start, that is all."

"The Troxen were harsh to the Aronians. Those massive beasts were harder to drive away than the Ungorans. King Kedor had no choice but to remove all beasts from his lands."

"Yes, but also anyone else not of his culture. I have always wondered the true reason as to why Kedorlaomer does not allow other species, or other cultures, into his kingdom. I suppose it is part of his ideology." Gromulus then added, "Despite my own opinions, I know they have done well without them. However, I cannot imagine an economy without formakha or the necessary trade with the Troxen."

"In Aronia, they are self-sufficient and hard-working. Either way, we were told to leave because Sulchek was teaching science, which was not acceptable to their belief system."

"What did Sulchek say about that?"

"There was nothing much he could say about it. He never agreed with Aronian ways, but what could he do? We were made to leave because of the panic that erupted in the kingdom due to the invading creatures of the Endlands. The king drove all the Troxen away. Afterwards, he made all humans who were not Aronians leave."

"So the two of you left?"

Lorylle nodded, "Sulchek treasured science, probably much more than I do now. It seemed he was always up to some new experiment. He never shared his work with me. But, the rumors began to spread of sorcery in Aronia. The king was against such unruly practices and he had my adopted father exposed, along with a number of others like him. We were forced to leave."

"That is horrible," said Gromulus.

"No, not really. I respect the king of Aronia. He was only trying to protect his people. One day, a man approached us and asked us to leave the kingdom. We were provided with a horse and enough rations to make it through the forest to Ume. Like I said, Aronians are good-hearted people."

"I do not understand," added Gromulus, "how can a supposedly good king banish people who are only wishing to progress their understanding of the world around them?"

Lorylle stepped closer. "That is how things are in Aronia. Instead of worrying about it, I accepted my fate. It was not very bad. Sulchek took me down through Denok Forest and into the Umite lands, but we stayed away from any of the combat that was going on at the time. We settled in at a small village on the northern outskirts that had already been liberated of Ungorans, and there we stayed until the wars were over. After that, we eventually made our way down to Cosh to help rebuild and pursue a more fruitful life." Lorylle could tell it bothered Gromulus that Kedor had driven her out. "If Kedor had not removed us from his lands . . . I never would have met you."

"I suppose I do not live an Aronian lifestyle, so it is hard for me to understand."

"The banishment was nonviolent . . . done with gentleness. Kedor *is* a just ruler, Gromulus."

"Yet he only cares for his own."

"I can see how you might think that. But, you have to understand it might not be easy being a king. He may simply have been afraid. He is still a good man."

Gromulus nodded, "He did help out at the Siege of Cosh. Without Kedorlaomer and his White Knights, the Troxen might have wreaked havoc on Valeecian lines. He did help save the day. And the king did have Agee-aus presented to me after the Ungorans were defeated."

Lorylle only smiled.

Gromulus then asked, "So, the two of you eventually went to Cosh?"

"Yes, although Sulchek told me the city had changed. I suppose almost two decades of war will do that. We moved into a small place near the market district. It was not much, but it suited us fine. He tried getting a job at the university as I went to school."

"Did he end up teaching there?"

"Yes, but only for a short time. Not long after, Sulchek moved away, leaving me in Cosh."

"Why?"

"I do not know. He came to me one night and told me he was planning on leaving. I cried and cried, but something was odd about him . . . he was different."

"Did he tell you where he was going?"

"He did."

"Where?"

"Back to Baalek. He put me under the tutelage of the academy and left that very night. I was heart-broken."

"I can imagine you would be."

"But, not long after I graduated from the academy . . . I then met you."

Gromulus smiled.

❧❧❧❧❧❧

Findyk waded in the tall grass, unable to be seen. He could see, in the distance, that Consul Veris was alive and well. This relieved him. The Walfyre noticed Veris did have an unexpected guest with him, but it mattered not. He breathed a sigh of relief. All he cared for was the safety of Consul Veris.

Findyk watched as the man and the woman relaxed next to a stream. The two appeared to be sharing a moment together. Findyk chose to remain hidden and reveal himself later.

Corbidon crouched on the branch of a tree. High up, he could see everything he needed. Across a field, he witnessed the Walfyre, who had unknowingly led him to Veris and the female. Corbidon knew where they were headed. He figured their purpose was to ride into Whelmore, which was the only nearby town, and seek aid. He deduced that, from there, the two travelers would attempt to enter the forest and flee Nador. He quietly jumped down from the tree and left the scene. That evening he would report his finding to General Thad.

22

The rain had stopped and the purple skies were now behind them as Tornach and Kelnum headed northwest. The storm seemed to follow the two, albeit slowly, as the pair traveled the long road to Chybum. Finally, the sun showed itself again, peering frightfully from the swollen clouds, as the men continued. The road to Chybum was at last taking them out of the corrupted lands of old Ungora. Now, Tornach could see an endless sea of lush countryside. The hills ahead rolled in the distance, as far as the eye could see.

Tornach's usual, relaxed demeanor was broken. A few times during their travels the barbarian jumped from the carriage to walk alongside. They were early into the journey and already Tornach was restless. He wondered if he had made the wrong decision in going with Kelnum. He did not want company. He only desired to go back to his time of solitude, a life of constant wandering, where no one could interrupt his isolation. A life where he could be alone with his thoughts. Already he pondered slipping away as Kelnum drove them forward, keeping the four horses at a steady pace.

Tornach decided to wait.

Every town in which Tornach made his presence had ended the same as it had in Crevail. However, Crevail had been worse than usual. Usually, Tornach would end up in a fight against great odds. Most of the time, one of two things would happen. He either would spend a few nights in jail or be driven out. Either way, Tornach was not wanted. As villagers of Crevail desired his head, Tornach grew cynical about the people of Nador in general. He began to resent those he fought to save. He did not understand how they could treat a war veteran, such as himself, with such animosity. In Crevail, this feeling was amplified. The town was in his homeland, not theirs. The lands of old Ungora belonged to his people, not them.

Tornach sat restless as Kelnum and he traveled. He nursed his wounds, both mentally and physically. He tried not to be bitter, but he was sick of the world around him. He had made the journey back to his homeland with a sense of hope, and found that he despised the new world of Men. The barbarian would much rather have braved Denok Forest, and the malice within, than deal with mankind. Tornach was an outsider and knew he did not belong in modern society.

He had kept quiet during his first day of travel. His head hurt and his pride stung. What happened the day before, in Crevail, still clouded his mind. He pondered his life, still not finding the answers. He missed his friends from the past. The ones who mattered. The ones who once gave him hope. He only had a few friends left from the wars, and it had been many years since the man had enjoyed their company. He thought quietly to himself for some time.

Finally, Tornach sobered up and was ready for conversation. He may have refused to accept his surroundings and accept the world around him; however, he would give Kelnum a chance. The man had helped him and he deserved the courtesy of a friendly discussion.

"Kelnum, can we stop here?" Tornach asked politely.

"Of course." Kelnum pulled the reins. The four horses that towed the buggy stopped. "What seems to be the problem, young sir?" he asked. "The road to Chybum is long and we have only traveled for a short time."

"Kelnum, my thoughts have taken their toll on me. Despite that we have only been traveling for a short time, I am in need of rest." As an afterthought, "I do apologize for my silence thus far. May we eat? I feel I have not eaten in ages."

Kelnum, although wanting to make better time, was in need of a break, himself. After rummaging through a bag for a moment, he pulled out a double helping of smoked fish. It made Tornach nearly drool. Tornach loved smoked fish. All his time growing up near the sea had caused him to be fond of seafood. He licked his lips.

Kelnum reached again inside his bag, pulling out even more food—cheese, bread and olives. The two travelers had a feast in front of them. They both moved to the back of the open carriage, sitting on the end of it. They situated themselves amongst the goods Kelnum was carrying to Chybum.

The two ate quietly, as if old friends.

As they ate, Tornach looked around him, at the landscape and scenery. They had traveled out of the desolate and unsightly lands of old Ungora. Few traveled on the road they followed. Only the occasional merchant or tradesman traveled this route. This day, the road was empty.

The meat was dry, but it was good. Tornach chewed slowly, savoring its flavor. The nourishment was much needed. He spoke again. "Old man, over the past day I have heard ya'h speak, but did not comprehend ya'h words. In my own self-pity, I did not listen."

Kelnum nodded. "Yes, I could tell you have not been paying attention."

"I meant no disrespect. I cannot seem ta get the memories of my former people . . . my friends, out of my head."

Kelnum did not say anything.

Tornach continued, "Ya'h have told me that ya'h desire ta go ta Chybum."

Kelnum nodded. "That is correct, young Tornach. I travel there quite often."

"For trade?"

"Yes. My normal route takes me from Cosh to Crevail, and then to Chybum. Then back to Cosh again, and then I repeat the process."

"This is how ya'h make a living?"

Kelnum replied, "Buying and selling is my business. Not long ago, I moved to Crevail. Soon after, I sought opportunity in the mercantile industry. It has proven to be quite lucrative. I spend most of my time traveling these roads."

Much like me, thought Tornach. *Except he has a place he calls home.* Then, Tornach asked, "However, ya'h still have not given me a reason. Why are we going ta Chybum?"

Kelnum smiled. "Primarily, because the people in Crevail would have killed you."

"Perhaps."

"I know you are capable of defending yourself, Tornach. Like I said before, I have heard the stories of your abilities, and of your bravery. I only wanted someone with your reputation to have opportunity."

"Reputation? What is the reputation of an Ungoran in Nador?"

"In my book, you are a valiant warrior who helped save these people. Someone as honorable as you should get another chance. Your death on the streets of Crevail would have been disheartening. As for Chybum . . . there is much opportunity there for a man such as you."

A slight silence followed. The two continued eating. Finally, Tornach spoke again, "What does Chybum really have ta offer me? What makes it different than any other town in the empire?"

"Chybum will be much more accepting of you."

Tornach asked, "I have heard of the types that wander Chybum's streets. I am not sure they will take kindly ta me."

"Why not?" questioned Kelnum.

"Because I am Ungoran. Does Chybum not sit on the edge of Denok Forest?"

"Yes," answered Kelnum.

"The Denoktorn threaten them, do they not?"

"Yes, but they are only a nuisance to the empire. There is not much to worry about the Denoktorn . . . no, not in Chybum. Other border towns may suffer, but Chybum does not."

"Aye, but they will know I am Ungoran."

Kelnum attempted to change the subject. "Young Tornach, you speak with haste. You worry too much. It is nice to travel these long roads with a companion. You should enjoy the ride rather than fret our journey's end."

The Ungoran still needed to know more. He pressed the issue of Chybum. "I ask again, what does Chybum have ta offer someone . . . like me?"

Kelnum spoke of good becomings in Chybum. In his opinion, the border town was Tornach's 'promised land.' It was his opportunity. Tornach, however, disagreed. The two sat together, eating, and discussed their lives.

Then, Kelnum told Tornach about an upcoming tournament in Chybum. He felt that Tornach might enjoy the combat—and the money.

But Tornach frowned at the prospect.

Time passed as they continued eating and Kelnum spoke again, "Young Tornach . . . you look as if you have a burden resting upon your back, in that sack you carry. I sense many scars of many worlds."

Tornach did not respond.

Kelnum finally asked, "You are being quiet. Have I offended you?"

"Of course not," replied Tornach, "Ya'h have been most generous."

"You should enjoy the ride. This trip is a grand one. Just look around," Kelnum said dramatically, pointing at the scenery around them. "The trees are green and the birds are singing. Life could be worse, you know."

"I know," grumbled Tornach.

"Might I ask what is on your mind, young sir?"

It took Tornach some time to answer the question. He looked ahead, at the never-ending road. Finally, he spoke, "Ya'h are kind, Kelnum. No one has been as kind as ya'h have . . . not in many years. No one seems ta care. But, ya'h are different . . . and I thank ya'h for ya'h generosity."

Kelnum nodded.

Tornach continued, "The short time I was in Crevail is still dwelling on me. It has made me think, reflecting on my own life. I think of the past, mostly. I think of where I was raised and what I have become. I am a product of a violent culture."

"You cannot help where you were born."

"True. But, today has me thinking, not of old Ungora, but of the empire."

"The empire?"

"Aye, Nador. I might be a product of Ungora, but those people . . . they are a product of an evil empire."

Kelnum turned his head, looking at Tornach. "Why do you say this empire is evil, Tornach?"

"Because it is," replied Tornach flatly.

"The empire has given us all more opportunities than we ever had before the wars. The economy is strong. I was not important before the wars, yet I have made a name for myself, and a fairly good living, as well, since the formation of Nador. Everyone has opportunity in Nador."

"Not me," said Tornach.

"Young sir, there is indeed opportunity for you in Nador."

"I mean no disrespect . . . but ya'h are blind. The empire is the worst thing that could have happened ta the people of our world. Ya'h might think ya'h have a voice, but it falls on deaf ears. Politicians are easily swayed by much more important things than us."

"Such as?"

"Money—greed—power. I have purposely wandered away from civilization. It has become wicked . . . perhaps even more wicked than my own people." Tornach paused. "Kelnum, if ya'h could only see life through my eyes for a single day. If ya'h could only recall the memories I hold . . . only then would ya'h understand."

"Please, tell me. The road to Chybum is long."

Tornach took a deep breath. "When I was young, I always knew my people's ways were wrong. Even at a young age, the ways of the Ungorans disturbed me, although that does not mean I did not succumb ta my own wickedness from time-ta-time."

"What problems do you speak of?"

"Mostly, the violence of my people, not only towards other kingdoms, but ta our own, as well. I hated the sacrifices. The killing of our own people disgusted me. The Ungoran king, Alarik, found glory in making examples of his own people. He loved ta find reason ta torture and maim his own subjects. The people, for the most part, loved the brutality."

"Why?"

"Something unexplainable happened ta my people many years ago that made them . . . change."

"What made them change?"

"I am not exactly sure. I am still trying ta figure that out."

Kelnum nodded.

Tornach continued, "King Alarik was brutal, ruthless. Many suffered under his rule. He even found a reason ta kill my own mother."

"What?" exclaimed Kelnum. "He killed your mother?" He was appalled.

"After he found out my mother was Seronan by birth, yes, he had her killed."

"So your mother was a Seronan. And he had her killed solely because of this fact?"

Tornach shook his head and furthered his explanation, "She also spoke out against the king publicly. He found out about it. And being a foreigner did not help her cause." Tornach gritted his teeth, and went on, "I was a young boy at the time, only fifteen years of age. The loss of my mother hurt. I swear ta ya'h, Kelnum, I have felt no greater anger in my life."

"*Hm*... yes, that *is* understandable," he said sympathetically. "I cannot imagine your pain." A grimace was upon Kelnum's face.

"Her death made me realize how bad times really were in Ungora. By then, the raids of my people were causing much suffering on both Serona and Ume. Her death made me see how blind my people were. Blind ta the destruction ... and the genocide. Most of all, my mother's death made me realize she was right. Everything my mother taught me about the world around me became true.

"This is why I despise ya'h empire so much. We fought ta protect against tyranny, and yet I sense oppression plaguing our world once again. The people of Ungora were blind, and the people of Nador are blind, as well; I see them uncaring—their harsh words—their wicked ways."

"I am beginning to understand, I think. What happened to you after her death?"

"I had ta accept a tough childhood. Life from that point became hard. I found myself on the streets of Crevail. I had nobody, and no place ta go. I slept in alleys and scrounged for food, not much different than I do now."

"Old habits die hard, I suppose," said Kelnum.

"True. I simply survived. I fought with the local boys. We brawled and rumbled. At first, I lost most of these fights, as I was always greatly out-numbered. Even then, I think I was hated."

"So you were beat up often? *You* lost?" Kelnum was in disbelief.

"Aye, for awhile. Finally, I learned ta fight."

Kelnum grinned.

"One day in particular, I got inta a bloody fight. I cannot recall his name, but he and four of his friends challenged me. By all the gods that look down upon us, I bested every one of them. I not only bested them, I beat all four ta bloody pulps." Tornach laughed.

"It sounds like you *did* learn to fight," agreed Kelnum.

"Yeah, and after that I was accepted. I guess I proved myself. Ya'h see, in Ungoran culture, violence was important. The tougher ya'h were, the more respected ya'h became. I began ta hang out with the same boys I used ta fight with. We ran together. We were bound together, sharing the same battles with other boys in the area. We were tough, not ta be reckoned with."

"It seemed you needed friends."

"No, not friends. At the time, I thought they were my friends. Now I know what real friends are. We simply had the same goals. We used one another ta get what we wanted, and for protection. We were ruthless, taking from others whatever we wanted. We were petty street urchins, but we thought we were tough. We would run into sleeping households and steal things. We beat up beggars. We stole food and fought for fun. But those times, Kelnum, I look on with sad eyes."

"I am sure it is hard for you."

"Aye, but my youth also taught me ta be what I am today."

"And what do you consider yourself today?"

"A warrior," responded Tornach.

Kelnum smiled at this. "Yes, a warrior of legend," he said proudly.

"No . . . a warrior forgotten," corrected Tornach.

"Well, by some, yes."

"By most. The wars helped, but before I met Gromulus, I struggled ta control my rage. It guided me. It made me feel warm at night. I wanted revenge. I wanted ta take my revenge on the man who caused my pain." As an afterthought he said, "As I have grown older I have learned ta harness that anger."

"And that was King Alarik," Kelnum said definitively.

"Aye. I wanted ta pain him, just as he did me. One night, after many mugs of og ale, I announced my plan ta my mates. Drunk, I stood up in front of them and told them of my plan."

"You knew they would follow you because you were their leader, right?"

"I thought they would."

"What was this plan for? For revenge—to kill the king?"

Tornach laughed. "Nah, my plan was . . . I wanted ta steal his axe."

"What? You wanted to steal his axe?" Kelnum looked again at his passenger humorously. He stared for a moment and then turned his eyes back to the road. "Was it really *that* important to him?"

"It was. The axe was Alarik's prized possession. It never left his side. He always wore it on his back, as if wielding it gave him supernatural powers. In some ways, Kelnum, I believe there was something significant about his axe."

"How so?" asked Kelnum, still smiling at such ridiculousness.

"He was the Ungoran leader before, but once he acquired the axe, things became different. His hold on Ungora grew stronger and he became more evil. It was then, that the lands of Ungora dried up and became un-inhabitable."

"Where did he get this axe?"

"I am not sure, but the king flaunted it. He was obsessed with the axe."

"And you wanted to steal it? Why?"

"Ta take away from him the only thing he really cared about."

"And he only cared about an axe?"

"Aye."

"What happened when you told your friends?"

"My friends . . . they turned on me, Kelnum. They turned me in. I tried fighting, but the ones who came ta get me were grown men and I was still a youth. They took me ta Alarik's castle. I was jailed, beaten and tortured. Yet, after I served my time, I was released."

"I would say you got lucky. They could have killed you, Tornach."

"I suppose. They cast me back out onta the streets. They banished me from the kingdom. They gave me only a few days ta leave Ungora."

"Where did you go?"

"Where could I go? I could not stay in Ungora, or they would have taken my head for disobedience. I could not flee to Ume or Serona, they would have lynched me the moment I stepped foot on their lands."

"What did you do?"

"I went into Denok Forest."

"You did? Alone?" asked Kelnum in surprise.

"Aye. Back then, the forest was not as dangerous as it is now."

"And you lived there?"

Tornach swallowed the last bit of his food, following it with a swig of water from Kelnum's water pouch. "Aye, I stayed there for over a year. I faced death many times in Denok Forest."

"But the forest had not yet changed?"

"Right, but dreadful creatures still roamed its expanse. The forest was beautiful, but still no place for a man ta be. Even an Ungoran."

"What happened next . . . after your year in the wild?"

"Like you said, Kelnum, old habits die hard. I was once again inspired by my plan . . . ta steal Alarik's axe." Tornach grinned comically. "I went back inta the lands of Ungora and stole it."

Kelnum looked at him once more, wide eyed. "You went back into Ungora and stole King Alarik's axe?"

"Aye," said Tornach proudly.

"Is that what you carry in your sack?"

"Along with my supplies, yes. I used ta flaunt it in battle, during the wars, but now I keep it concealed."

"Why?"

"I guess the obsession has changed hands. I feel this strange need ta keep it."

Kelnum felt for the warrior, but it was an honor for him to be able to sit next to Tornach and have the man tell his story. Kelnum was only now beginning to realize the barbarian's pain. Life certainly was not easy for the Ungoran. Kelnum knew Tornach was a good man, and hoped he could help the man's future.

The two travelers sat back on the seat of the carriage and began pushing onward.

Silence followed.

23

The following morning the two woke early. Gromulus prepared a small breakfast, for they were hungry and needed their strength. After eating, they sat quietly, resting before the journey ahead of them. Gromulus still did not know exactly where they were headed, but he had faith in Antiok. The sword was in his head, controlling his direction. He felt it could read, not his thoughts, but his feelings. He trusted Antiok because he trusted his old friend, Fayorn. Even though the warrior had cast away his sword, for reasons unknown to Gromulus, he felt the bond between the Aronian and his sword.

They both sat without a word. She said it first. "What is wrong?"

Gromulus replied with a smile, "Nothing, my darling, just trying to make sense of things."

Gromulus had already explained his meeting with the great emperor of Nador and the pitfalls that followed. He explained how the Senate was taking over and that Makheb had left for the Endlands. When he mentioned the western frontier, her attention grew sharp. He could tell she had been pondering something.

"Master Veris . . . I have been wondering—"

"What is it that you brood over?"

"You speak of making sense of things . . . and if I may?" She was hesitant.

"Go on," he replied smoothly.

"I was wondering about your name . . . Veris . . . or, *um,* Gromulus. Why did you choose to hide your real identity? What is the purpose you sought in doing so?"

Gromulus looked away. "It is hard for me to explain."

"Please try. I need to know."

"Well . . . it is confusing for me, but after I witnessed Fayorn cast Antiok aside on the battlefield . . . after our last victory together . . . I began thinking about things."

"What did you think about?" she asked. "What happened to Fayorn?"

"Fayorn rode off, without farewell. I never saw him again after that. I will never forget the last time I saw the man . . . the sadness in him. . . . That memory will scar my life forever."

"*Oh*, I see. Was it then you realized that you wanted a different life?"

"Well, I suppose. I have always known my life was for a more important cause than being a warlord, but yes, that moment affected me greatly."

"What did you do after Fayorn left?"

"Tornach and I joined in the celebrations after the victory. After that, the two of us kept together, but the wars were over and we both had no real purpose."

Lorylle nodded, urging him to continue.

Gromulus said, "With the wars ended, Nador needed leaders more than warriors. With Tornach . . . well, it seemed our bond was only in battle. I knew I was better suited to help the empire in other ways. Tornach, however, could only do one thing."

"And what is that?"

"Fight. He was a warrior . . . and only a warrior. After the wars, he became a lost soul," Gromulus said. "I could feel myself becoming like him."

"How long did the two of you stay together?"

"Not long. We rode without cause, and never with a specific destination. We were without direction. The entire time he and I rode together, I could not stop thinking of Fayorn."

"Why? Were you worried about what became of him?"

"No, I knew he would be fine. I contemplated what his life consisted of and compared it to my own life. I decided I needed direction. One day I promised myself that I would not end up like Tornach. We said our farewells and I traveled south, to the old lands of Valeecia. Soon after, I began my government service, and eventually became a consul."

"You progressed rapidly," she stated.

"I did. Although, sometimes it feels as if I had help in doing so."

"Well, I am glad you did. Let me ask, though. . . . You said you did not want to end up like Tornach. What do you mean by that?"

"Lost. If you knew Tornach, you would understand. He is his own worst enemy. I did not want that sort of life."

Lorylle nodded her head, attempting to understand.

Gromulus continued, "I was quickly becoming lost, myself. I had no purpose. So, I sat with Tornach one night and told him my thoughts. I talked about Fayorn and how I envied him for renouncing the bloodshed. I knew in my heart that if I kept traveling with Tornach, my life would find battle over and over again . . . a battle with no enemies."

"What does that mean, a battle with no enemies?"

"Again, if you knew Tornach, you would understand. Anyways, I told him that it was time to part ways."

"How did he take it . . . the two of you parting ways?"

"Hard, I think. I felt bad, but I did what I felt needed to be done. I decided to walk away from that life the day I saw Fayorn discard his sword, and until now, my life as Consul Veris has suited me well."

"Why did you not serve the empire as yourself?"

"It would have been different. You see, I never wanted to be a general, like Taius. I did not want the people to know me as Gromulus the Seronan warlord, but only as a simple person who wanted to help. I did not want glory and fame after the wars, and if I went by Gromulus, I would have been expected to become a war leader again."

"Does Makheb know you are . . . Gromulus?"

"I think he does. He said things that make me believe so."

"And he brought this out in you?"

"What, my past? I guess the situation did. Makheb started it. I think the Senate and my fight with Risard made it worse."

"It sounds like being Gromulus comes with much more than simply a name."

"You are right about that, Lorylle. If you had seen death as many times as I have, you merely want to forget it all. To keep the past in the past."

"And now, you are faced with your past again? You are forced to be who you once were?"

He shook his head, almost annoyed. "I suppose."

"At what moment did you decide to become *him* again?"

"Decide? I am not sure I consciously decided. It just . . . happened."

"Tell me, how?"

"What truly brought Gromulus back was a—"

"Go on?"

"A statue," he said, embarrassed.

"A statue?" Lorylle looked at him oddly. "*Huh?* A statue made you turn back into yourself? I am afraid I do not understand."

He chuckled lightly at this. "Nor do I, Lorylle, but hear me out. Are you familiar with the statue on the north side of the Senate building, back in Cosh? The one in the center of the plaza?"

"*Oh,* yes, of course. The statue of Gromulus," her eyes widened in understanding, ". . . I mean you."

"Yes, that is the one. I headed towards my estate, and fully meant to pack my things and leave Cosh at that moment. I passed the Senate building . . . it made me angry thinking about what Parlock and the others were doing. Then, I nearly smacked right into that statue of . . . me."

Lorylle added, "That statue really does not look anything like you."

"I suppose it does not," said Gromulus, laughing again. "Anyways, I looked up at the statue of Gromulus, and finally realized why he was so important to the people."

"Why?"

"He gave them hope. He fought for what he felt was right. I stood in front of the monument, reflecting my desire to run away. To tuck my tail and leave the empire like a coward. The statue brought back the memories of my past, where goodness stood up against evil, and prevailed. I decided then and there that I would confront Parlock."

"And you became Gromulus again?"

"Well, only to myself. Lorylle, sometimes the superstition far exceeds the truth. That statue *is* Gromulus in the minds and hearts of all Nadorians. The real Gromulus . . . well . . . I have my flaws."

"I understand. The Gromulus who they made statues of is—"

"Glorified," he finished. "The statue represents the desire of people to have a hero. I, on the other hand, would be perfectly happy to remain as Veris."

Lorylle waited a few moments, and asked a question, "The statue shows you wearing a mask. Why is that?"

"I concealed my identity."

"But, why? Were you worried about people seeing your face?"

"Yes."

"Why?" she asked again, a confused look upon her face.

"Lorylle, you are full of questions." He laughed and scratched his head. "I guess . . . for instances such as this."

Lorylle only nodded. She realized he did not want to discuss the subject any further.

Gromulus spoke more seriously, "It is odd, my life. I was a leader before, and now I am to become a leader again. To be the man I once was is difficult for me. It is nearly impossible to transform back into . . . *him*."

Lorylle reflected on everything she had heard. Finally, she spoke, "I cannot imagine your burden. One man to save an empire . . . without help? Your colleagues and your empire have turned on you," she exclaimed.

"It is a burden," he agreed. "However, after handling that sword," he said, pointing to the wrapped Antiok, which was tied to his horse, "after holding Antiok . . . fighting with it . . . my burden seems not so great."

"I am sure. That sword scares me. I saw what it did to you. What sword carries with it so much power?"

"Antiok is the greatest sword in the known world."

"Is it a king's sword?"

"No, quite the opposite." Gromulus tried to relax himself. "It chooses only the most humble of men."

"*Huh?* Chooses them? How is that possible . . . for a sword to choose anything? Is it magic?"

"Maybe, but not the dark kind. Fayorn told me the story of Antiok, and how it picks its own bearer. According to him, only one man per lifetime can carry it. Legends say the sword waits many generations for the right man."

"And this sword . . . Antiok . . . can only be carried by Fayorn?"

"It would seem so."

"But you are carrying it now?"

"Yes, but you see, I have been careful to keep it wrapped. I awoke last night to have a look at it, and unwrapped it. I had to. I felt an unnecessary need to touch it—I swear Antiok called to me. And yet, as I brought my hand close, I could feel it did not want me to. My hand burned as I reached for it. It would have cast me away if I had not stopped."

Lorylle could not comprehend. She realized Gromulus could not explain it because he did not understand it himself. "But . . . you also fought with it," she commented.

"Yes," said Gromulus. He had wielded Antiok and it had saved his life. Yet, he could not imagine handling that sword again. It brought emotions out of him in that short moment of time. Emotions that he never wanted to feel again. He admired his friend all the more. "Antiok only allowed me to wield it on my promise to take it back to its rightful owner, Fayorn."

"I am sorry, master, but it is hard to understand that sword." As an afterthought, she asked, "What about Fayorn? Are the legends true? Is he really the greatest swordsman in the known world?"

Gromulus smiled. "In my mind, he is." Gromulus remembered back, years prior, to the first time he met the master swordsman and his extraordinary sword.

♦♦♦♦♦♦

Gromulus and his friend Tornach had been fighting together for nearly six months. The two had organized a small force, and had been successful defending off the merciless Ungoran raiders who attacked Serona. The two, alone, scouted in Ungoran lands, not far from Crevail. They looked for any mass buildup of soldiers, as well as anything else that would give them an edge against further attacks. They were stealthy. They tied off their horses and were traveling on foot, following the edge of a ravine.

In the distance, Tornach noticed the men first. At the base of the hill, only fifty paces away, was a group of barbarians. Tornach and Gromulus crept closer, within hearing distance, mindful not to be seen.

"Ungorans," grumbled Tornach. Over the years of his life, Tornach had grown to despise his own kind, although he still proudly proclaimed himself an Ungoran. Tornach loved his people, but hated what they had become.

Gromulus responded, "Looks like it. I count six."

"We can take 'em," said Tornach boastfully. His hand was on his sword's hilt, always ready for a fight.

"No," replied Gromulus wisely. "That is not why we are here."

Tornach knew his friend was right, but pride always got in the man's way. He continued watching as the Ungorans talked noisily amongst themselves. "It looks like a scouting party. They must be getting ready ta raid another town."

Gromulus kept watching, as well. "Wait. I see another. Seven men."

Tornach saw the other man, too. "That one there . . . is not Ungoran."

"You sure?"

Tornach looked annoyingly at his friend. "Ya'h think I would know my own kind, Grom. No, that man is not from these parts."

"Seronan then?"

"No. I cannot tell. Aronian, I think, but I am not sure."

"Why would an Aronian be in Ungoran lands?" asked Gromulus, although mostly to himself.

Tornach laughed, and then remembered they were hiding and that he needed to remain quiet. "A better question is . . . what are *we* doing in Ungoran lands?"

Gromulus smiled at this as they continued to watch.

The six Ungorans confidently surrounded the stranger. They had not drawn their weapons yet, but their hands hung dangerously close, ready. They made their way around the stranger, circling him.

The Aronian was oddly unaffected.

Tornach whispered to Gromulus, "This is going ta be a bloodbath."

"Sacrifice?"

"Aye. They will spill this man's blood and bathe in it. Poor soul."

Ungorans were notorious for their blood rage. It was a common occurrence for them to raid helpless villages and towns, as well as murder strangers caught wandering alone on their land. This poor traveler was outnumbered six to one.

Gromulus and Tornach moved in closer, careful not to be seen. Had the two brought more men, they would have possibly tried to save this Aronian's life. However, this was Ungoran business and the two had no desire to intervene. They were curious more than anything.

"Perhaps this stranger will fair well . . . if the gods be with him, and he

123

sprouts wings ta fly away," Tornach jested.

Gromulus chuckled. He kept low, behind some shrubbery, and studied the stranger. *For a man about to meet his demise, he is calm.*

The Aronian was quiet and offered no pleas. Instead, he simply kept his head lowered.

Gromulus thought, *I do not understand this man's ways.*

Aronians were unique. They were powerful people, horsemen of the highlands, lords of the glaciers. They kept secluded. Aronia rarely traded with the Men south of Denok Forest. They lived alone. They raised their own livestock and farmed their own lands. They were independent and self-sufficient. The people of the north were loyal only to one another.

King Kedor had a no-tolerance policy when it came to hostiles. Despite being peaceful, Aronian justice was righteous and swift to all who intruded on the lands, especially so, for beasts. Aronians hated beasts and witchcraft and sorcery. They detested the Ungoran's pagan ways. Aronians, under Kedor, drove all from their kingdom with a vengeance. Gromulus had heard the rumors that even the mighty Ungorans did not bother invading the north any longer.

Aronia would become the only kingdom left intact after the wars. It would be the only civilization that maintained its original customs and beliefs. Aronia would become the only sovereign nation not swallowed by the Empire of Nador.

I feel pity for this man, Gromulus thought as he looked on.

As if reading his friend's mind, Tornach said, "Hope he is quick with the blade."

The Ungoran leader was a brute named Kalak. He approached the stranger. The Aronian made no movement to ready himself for battle. It looked as if he was frozen with fear, which was understandable, considering that his future appeared certain. It was one thing to be ill prepared for battle, but Gromulus noticed it went even further. The Aronian slowly unlatched his sheathed sword from his waist. He held it out in front of him, the sword resting gently in the palms of his outstretched hands.

It was as if it was an offering.

The six Ungorans eyed him carefully. Their fingers stroked the hilts of their own sheathed swords, trying to determine the man's intentions.

Then, the Aronian did something even more bizarre. He ever-so-slowly unsheathed his sword, without menace. Gently he dropped the sheath and laid his sword on the soft ground in front of him. The Aronian stepped back ten paces and bowed his head again.

Tornach had never seen anything like it. Fighting or running to the forest would have made sense, but this Aronian was laying down his arms, and yet, did not flee. Tornach looked at Gromulus crouched next to him as if his companion could offer an explanation.

Gromulus only had one. "I suppose he is submitting himself to death. He has found himself with only two options . . . and perhaps is choosing to end his suffering quickly."

Tornach grunted, "Ya'h know submission will only extend their wrath. Ungorans torture cowards harshly."

"I know," said Gromulus as he kept watching.

"Fight, ya'h coward. Meet ya'h death with honor," exclaimed Tornach. He shook his head and added, "At least give us a good showing."

The six warriors loosely surrounded the stranger. They were large, young and agile. The thin cuts on their arms marked the men they had killed; the counting of coup on their enemies. The leader of this rabble, Kalak, had twenty such marks, giving him great honor amongst his fellow barbarians. He confidently swaggered towards the quiet man and stopped shy of the grounded sword.

The Ungoran continued to stare at the man, but the Aronian would not make eye contact. Kalak was huge. The Aronian was nothing to Kalak in stature. The barbarian leader carried a broadsword and a small metal shield. Tucked in the small of his back was a battle hatchet. The Ungoran's beard was dense and matted and his hair was long and tangled. His eyes bore into the stranger as he was angered by this Aronian's presence.

"Pilgrim," Kalak called out.

No answer.

Kalak looked at one of his men. The barbarian looked back in question and shrugged his shoulders. Kalak's temper was short, as was with most Ungorans, and he was growing angry.

"Answer me, ya'h swine! Ya'h travel on Ungoran land. Do ya'h think that goes without penalty?"

An awkward silence followed.

Finally, the stranger raised his head and with both of his hands pushed back his hood, exposing his face. He had long hair. Colorful beads were tied into his light brown hair. His beard was dark and thick, yet well tended. The Aronian's expressionless eyes met directly with the menacing Ungoran leader.

The Aronian showed no hint of emotion—no fear.

He stared into Kalak's eyes and then spoke softly, "Friend, I bring you neither threat, nor disrespect. I shall be off your lands by nightfall. Please accept my apology." Unlike the Ungoran, his voice was calm and soothing.

Kalak could not comprehend this man's demeanor. He was now getting even more impatient, but his curiosity was also getting the best of him. "It is not our custom ta let strangers walk freely about. Ya'h will die where ya'h stand. Now . . . we settle this here." The Ungoran wanted to fight.

All Ungorans did.

The stranger replied in still a soft voice, "I offer you no resistance. I can pay homage of twenty furs for my trespass."

"That will not suffice! After I bleed ya'h I will take ya'h furs anyways." The Ungoran grunted. "Pick up arms and honor ya'h trespass with ya'h death!"

"I sought no insult. I apologize if I have."

Kalak was still curious. The man before him stood composed, yet his only visible weapon lay at his feet, and the Aronian had made no move towards it. Kalak stroked his beard as he looked from the Aronian to the sword.

He tilted his head from side-to-side and then said, "Ah, I was right. An Aronian. Ya'h coward of the north. Ya'h insult us by traveling our lands and tainting our customs. I tell ya'h again, take up arms."

No response.

Kalak had one more moment of curiosity, as his eyes fell back to the sword in front of him. It lay still on the ground. In a moment, he would kill the Aronian, but for now he was amused at the man's stubbornness.

Kalak gazed at the sword.

The sword gazed back.

The sword was like no other the Ungoran had seen. It was slender, a third of the width of his own broadsword, yet approximately the same length. It was slightly curved. The hilt was ornate. Its handle was pure white, made of what looked like bone. Its pearl white hilt was glossy and contrasted by a thin, black cord wrapped around it. The most interesting part of the sword was at the end of the hilt. Embedded in it was a large, deep blue sapphire. It glimmered in the sunlight.

Kalak grinned. After he killed this man, he would present this unique sword to his king, Alarik. Surely, he would receive great rewards and honor for bringing the ruler of Ungora such a beautiful weapon, as well as this man's head. Kalak figured the weapon was of no practical use due to its thin blade, but surely, King Alarik would appreciate the gem. Either way, the Ungoran king would honor him.

Kalak continued, "If ya'h will not take up arms, then I shall take them up for ya'h. Prepare ya'hself for death."

The hefty Ungoran bent down to pick up the Aronian's strange sword. He eyed the Aronian cautiously while doing so, but the man remained still. Kalak then reached towards the hilt of the sword, at the sapphire embedded in it.

The sword twitched.

Kalak saw it. He tilted his head and then began reaching for the sword again.

This time the sword twitched harder, shifting the dirt slightly.

The Ungoran's eyes widened and he looked up at the stranger. "What magic is this? Answer me, pilgrim! Speak, or I shall cut ya'h tongue out before I bleed ya'h," declared the barbarian.

"It is not magic, I assure you. My people prohibit such craft. It is quite simply . . . well . . . my sword does not like Ungorans."

Kalak was perplexed.

One of his men, Krag, questioned aloud, "Did he just say his sword does not like Ungorans? Did my ears just hear such insanity?"

"Perhaps this traveler has been chewing siban'nac root and gotten lost," another said. The other barbarians laughed heartily.

Kalak, however, did not. He continued, "If ya'h sword does not like Ungorans, then wield it in battle!"

The stranger replied confidently, "It hates Troxen even more . . . and you want no battle with me, I assure you." A slight curve of a smile formed on his face as he eyed the Ungoran.

The sword twitched again. It moved of its own free will and this utterly baffled the Ungorans. It also bemused Gromulus and Tornach as they watched from afar. The sapphire began emitting a dark blue light as the sword grew impatient.

It convulsed and vibrated.

Everyone watching stared in disbelief.

Gromulus thought to himself, *It has to be. The legend is true. The Sword of Ellsar—Antiok.*

Kalak's men looked at him with curiosity and he felt the need to prove himself. This stranger was on their lands and was insulting Kalak in front of his warriors. He knew it was time to put an end to this man's life, otherwise his men might lose faith in him.

Kalak reached his hand out and grabbed the hilt of the strange sword.

The sapphire glowed brightly and the shock was painful.

With a loud grunt and flash of light, the fierce Ungoran warrior was thrown back from the sword violently. He was flung away, his feet leaving the ground, and landed with a deep thud a few paces from the sword. A jolt went up his arm and into his body, giving the large man excruciating pain. He immediately, by reaction, tried to get back up. His head was dizzy and his body was frozen. He attempted to stand but to no avail. He collapsed once more as the five other Ungorans stared in disbelief.

Gromulus and Tornach were also in awe.

The stranger remained still.

The sword shook. It wanted to fight.

A moment later Kalak pulled himself to a sitting position and shook his head in a daze. He looked at the stranger and then at his men. His words came out in a mumble. "Kill him, ya'h bastards," he ordered. "I want his head!"

"Yeessss! Here it is," exclaimed Tornach loudly, almost giving away their location.

The remaining five Ungorans drew their broadswords and adjusted their shields. Acting together, they simultaneously attacked from all angles.

At the same moment, Antiok began to spin. In a circle, it rotated at lightning speed. It whirled rapidly, and then stopped. Through the dirt, Antiok raced towards Fayorn, leaving a line in the sand behind it. The Aronian reached down and the sword leapt into his hand.

The five Ungorans, with their swords already drawn, closed the distance.

Fayorn raised Antiok vertically in front of him, inches from his own face. It pointed straight up. The blue sapphire sparkled and the blade glistened. Antiok had not a single imperfection. Not a scratch or a nick or a blemish infected the Sword of Ellsar.

Fayorn pivoted left and slashed at the nearest Ungoran's stomach, causing it to spill its contents onto the ground.

Fayorn stuck another Ungoran through the shoulder, and then decapitated the man.

Next, Fayorn blocked a blow and countered with two fast slices. He moved with a swiftness not known to Man. The Ungoran's arms both fell to the ground, chewed stubs left behind, spewing blood.

The other two standing Ungorans swung their heavy blades with all their might. Fayorn turned and swung Antiok in a high arc, deflecting their attacks. Then, he slashed each man twice, once across the throat and once across the belly. Both dropped their blades and died.

The entire conflict took only an instant. It was the fastest defeat Gromulus and Tornach had ever seen. Five Ungorans were dead and their bodily fluids and remains moistened the cool, black soil.

"What have we just seen?" asked Tornach, still viewing from afar. "I have never seen a man that fast with a blade."

Gromulus admired the act, although he kept his mouth quiet about the matter. They continued to watch.

Kalak sat in horror. A short distance away laid his dead comrades. They had all been raised in the same village. He had been to battle many times with these men. They had conquered greater odds in the past than one lone

Aronian, and had always ended as victors.

Now, Kalak's friends were all dead. He shook his head in disgust. His mind went to fury. He arose, the pain now numbness, and dusted himself off. He looked again at his slain men and then drew his long sword.

Fayorn stood his ground, Antiok held low, its tip facing down.

Kalak screamed, "I will kill ya'h! By the gods I shall bathe in ya'h blood!" He attacked.

The barbarian wailed and swung his sword as fast as he could. Six quick slashes and the Aronian blocked every single one with precision. The Aronian warrior's fighting style was tight and quick and aggressive.

His form is flawless, thought Gromulus, amazed by the Aronian. He had heard the tales about the man who wielded the Sword of Ellsar, and they were being proven true in front of his own eyes. The Aronian was perfect in his fighting style and he impressed Gromulus.

After his initial attack, Kalak the Ungoran quickly tried to decide what his next attack sequence would be. The man was embarrassing him, and this brought Kalak much anger.

"Ya'h bastard of the north. Come now. Let us finish this."

Fayorn circled left.

Kalak did the same.

The Ungoran continued, "By the gods I shall soak in ya'h blood this night." Kalak thrust, but Fayorn easily dodged the attack.

They circled more.

Kalak continued his verbal abuse, "Ya'h sorcerer of the north, with ya'h magical sword. I shall torture ya'h slowly for my fallen brethren." Kalak feinted a high blow and instead swung his sword at kneecap level. He missed Fayorn by a hair, but missed, nonetheless.

Fayorn smiled slightly. This was mere practice for the swordsman.

Kalak was now crazed. He was suicidal, a hell-bent savage intent on slaughtering the Aronian. He wanted to bathe in this man's blood. He wanted to drink it and feel its warmth as he honored his fallen friends. Kalak was going insane.

It was a hint of the future—a single moment in time that foretold the anguish and ultimate fate of Ungora. Soon cursed to live in Denok Forest and thirst for human blood, they would later become the dreaded Denoktorn. They would live in shadows, worship bloodthirsty gods, and forget what it was like to be human. They would become savages, heathens of the darkness. The Ungorans would become Denoktorn, and switch from rational to insane—from man to beast.

Kalak screamed, swinging his sword in a wide arc down towards Fayorn's torso, "DIE!"

Fayorn pivoted and the attack missed.

Antiok began to glow all over. The blade turned so cold it was hot. The sapphire gleamed. The Sword of Ellsar acted with Fayorn as one unit, one single entity, in contempt of Ungorans.

Fayorn's swing was faster.

The two blades collided in midair. Antiok sliced cleanly through Kalak's own sword, which splintered and fell to pieces.

Kalak looked in astonishment.

Fayorn stared, his sword twitching in his hand. *Settle down, my friend.*

He swung at Kalak's chest.

He connected.

The glowing blade sliced through the heavy armor.

Kalak fell to his knees. He choked. He coughed up blood.

Fayorn circled around behind his fallen opponent. *He deserves a soldier's death,* Fayorn thought to his sword.

Antiok agreed.

Fayorn pierced the back of Kalak's neck, driving downward sharply. Kalak spat and crumbled, dead.

Fayorn raised Antiok. It stopped shimmering and the sapphire ceased to glow. The blade had absolutely no remnant of blood on it. It was as perfect as when he unsheathed it. Not a blemish. Not a scratch. The sword was, however, aware of the presence of the two onlookers. Both sword and bearer knew of their presence from the beginning. Both were always aware of their surroundings, for sword and man did so by instinct. Perfect unity amongst a warrior and his blade. Perfect harmony in battle.

Tornach thought it was beautiful.

Gromulus thought it was useful.

Gromulus snapped back. He could not help but remember his lifelong friend, Fayorn. Memories of the man brought back a mixture of sadness and confusion, which were all wrapped up together like a cluster of snakes, intertwined and disturbing.

Then he thought more about Antiok. The Sword of Ellsar was strange. Not only in its thin-blade design, but also in its characteristics. It had personality. It called to Gromulus. It worried him. The longer he traveled, the more he wanted to rid himself of the sword. It created emotions in him that he could hardly handle. *Antiok . . . the most beautiful . . . the most perfect weapon in the world. Ah . . . what a weight to bear!*

The two traveled throughout the morning, seeking the great swordsman, Fayorn. Gromulus reflected as they rode. He thought of his own life. His past and his future. Every beat of hoof against the ground brought back the reality of both. Gromulus rode hard, fleeing his nightmares. Each step away from the life he had, he remembered the horrors of war and the bonds of friendship he had formed during such brutal times. Bonds in which he now had to trust.

As he fled with Lorylle, the storms over Nador approached from behind.

24

As the sun peaked in the late morning sky, Gromulus and Lorylle galloped to the top of a nearby bluff and looked down into a valley, at the small and isolated town of Whelmore. The town was four hundred paces from Denok Forest, humble, and sparsely populated. Gromulus nudged his Aronian steed forward, somehow knowing this small town was what he had been seeking.

Antiok.

As they headed across the open pasture, and towards the southern gate of Whelmore, Lorylle looked to her left, west, and her eyes gazed into the beginning of the barren Endlands. Her hazel eyes turned black again, only briefly, before changing back.

Gromulus slowed his horse as they neared the town's gates. He took his time, studying the place. Approximately two hundred peasants did their daily tasks and none appeared armed. The town only had four simple archer towers. Two were on each side of the southern gate, which they were now approaching, and two guarded the northern gate, which faced Denok Forest. The gate that Gromulus approached was sturdy, yet simple. It coexisted well with the town's basic outpost walls, which were made of wood.

No stone or metal here, thought Gromulus.

The warrior in him knew better than to judge this town by first glance. The town seemed to be under-guarded. This, however, went with the Aronian concepts of tactical warfare. Deception was one of their most important strategies, and Aronians used it well. If Fayorn was nearby, then the town was most likely better guarded than it appeared.

Fayorn is here. I can feel it.

Gromulus and Lorylle rode to the gate and two boys, only fifteen years old, stood guard. They were both grinning. Gromulus came within a few paces and stopped. He nodded.

The two boys looked at the horse and riders curiously, apprehensive to the strangers visiting their isolated town. Whelmore did not receive many visitors. One of the boys motioned for the two to dismount. The couple did so hesitantly.

Smart. Very smart. Getting Lorylle and I on two feet increases their odds.

The other boy raised his hand slightly, as if half attempting a wave, and wiggled his fingers.

A strange look formed on Gromulus' face.

Swisssh. Thump.

Swisssh. Thump.

Swisssh. Thump.

Three arrows, in perfect order and precision timing, hit the wall next to where he stood, missing his head by only an arm's length. Gromulus tensed and nearly reached for his swords, which were fastened to Ageeaus, but then noticed the boys laughing. He hesitated.

Lorylle clung to Gromulus' side, saying, "That is not funny."

The boys stopped laughing and became serious. One said, "Those were our archers. Try anything suspicious and you will be dead an instant later."

Gromulus believed the boy, as did Lorylle.

The other boy said, "Those were simply warnings. We Aronians are good-natured, and welcoming, but do not mistake that as a weakness."

Gromulus smiled. "Aronians hold great stature amongst the two of us." Lorylle nodded in agreement as he continued, "My . . . my wife here was born in Aronia," he lied.

The boys looked at Lorylle, studying her. Finally, one of the boys snapped back to attention and said, "What is your business in Whelmore?"

"Lad, our business here is of good nature, I can assure you. You may tell your sentries they have no need to nock their arrows, for we come to Whelmore in peace. I only seek re-acquaintance with an old friend."

"And whom might that be, good sir?"

"Perhaps you have heard of him. His name is Fayorn."

Gromulus saw the boys' eyes flicker at the mention and then they quickly proceeded to open the gates into the modest town of Whelmore. Both boys bowed without saying another word and watched as the man and woman led their horse in.

The pair entered the calm town, mostly consisting of women and children. Unlike the grand city of Ogata, or even the bustling Cosh, Whelmore was slow and quiet. The two walked cautiously in without search and without question. The residents eyed the pair, but more out of curiosity than fear. The people of Whelmore knew they were protected. Gromulus saw the guards in the towers eyeing him.

They are watching us. Aronians. They show hospitality, yet if I pose a single threat, I am dead by their arrows.

The two entered the square and walked towards a stable. Gromulus noticed something. Aloud, although not necessarily to Lorylle, he spoke, "There are no Nadorian guards posted here. The emperor promised protection to the border towns of Denok Forest. Not a single soldier here, though. If I remember correctly, the Senate ordered twenty legionaries posted here."

Lorylle mumbled something, but Gromulus did not hear. They neared a stable and he tied the reins of his horse to a post. He patted the beast's side. Once Gromulus secured Ageeaus, he reached at his saddle and grabbed the hilt of one of his swords. After all he had been through in the past week and a half, he was nervous. After going weaponless for so long, he vowed to himself not to do so again. As he was withdrawing the blade, an elderly woman approached, carrying a bucket of water. She was frumpy, with grey hair tucked back in a bun.

"That will not be necessary, sir," she said, pouring the water into the trough. Ageeaus immediately began to drink. The woman looked up and her eyes met with the strangers. She looked them up and down. "There is no violence in Whelmore, therefore you will not need to carry that. That is, unless you are Denoktorn raiders, which by the looks of you two, I would say that is not the case. And you are well protected from Denoktorn in this town, as simple as it appears." The woman smiled.

Gromulus was still hesitant. The woman sensed it, and humorously said, "Carrying that sword is useless anyways. It will only add to your labors."

Gromulus smiled back. *I am tired, I suppose. She is right; there is no threat here.* He responded, "They are not for my protection, my lady. My swords are simply dear to me and—"

"And there is no thievery in Whelmore, either," the woman interrupted.

Gromulus smiled again, understanding her point. The woman was not suggesting. She was politely telling him that he could not carry his weapons in town. *Aronians.*

Lorylle then questioned, "How many live here?"

The woman answered, patting the horse. "Two hundred and twenty-three. Sixty men." She leaned closer to Lorylle, as if to tell her a secret. "Not near enough, I might add," she said with a wink. Lorylle giggled at this and the woman went on, "Your horse is beautiful. It looks Aronian."

"Yes, he is," said Gromulus. "The boy at the gate made reference to this town being Aronian, not Nadorian. Is this true?"

"That is right, my dear. Only twenty-seven are not Aronian. Of those, twenty-three are of Umite backgrounds, the other four are Seronans. We reside in your Nador, but we are under the protection of Aronian militiamen," she said with a smile.

She said your Nador. Whelmore falls under the arm of the empire, but these people are Aronian, and those who are not, are so by choice. Gromulus returned, "Militia? Are they organized?"

"Very," nodded the woman. "Thirty-nine serve."

"Serve Fayorn?"

"Yes, do you know him?"

Gromulus nodded. "Do you know where I can find him?"

The woman pointed across the town, towards a large dwelling. Gromulus turned and looked. The woman then turned to Lorylle and began talking. Mostly, it was gossip—girl talk. This calmed Lorylle. She relaxed and allowed herself to open up as the woman began telling her about Whelmore.

The woman finished with Gromulus, "You will find your friend there. I believe he is training a few of his men right now." Then, she turned, grasped Lorylle by the arm, and walked away.

Gromulus stood for a while, staring at the building. Above the dwelling, atop the roof, flew the Aronian banner. Gromulus reached at his horse and pulled from the saddle his black cloak. He also grabbed a dark brown scarf.

He put on the cloak and wrapped the cloth around his neck. Inconspicuously, Gromulus reached under his saddle, pulled both his swords, and tucked them under his cloak. He raised the hood over his head and walked towards Fayorn's training lodge. Once at the door, Gromulus pulled the scarf up over his nose, concealing his face.

He walked inside.

"*Awww*," cried a young man, rubbing his throbbing hand. "That hurt."

Then, cracking sounds.

Whap whap whap.

Again, "*Ouch!*"

Around the youth were chuckles. The brown-haired man shook his head. He was frustrated. Both his hands were throbbing and beginning to welt. "I hate my life," Vallek mumbled. At that, the other young men in the room sustained laughing heartily.

Gromulus stood just inside the doorway and looked into the large training room. The inside had a courtyard feel to it, wide and spacious. An assortment of training weapons decorated the walls. The wooden ones, used for practice, were on the farthest wall, the metal ones on the wall nearest him. Seven stood in the center of the room, most merely adolecents.

Thriden, Baronius, Jairus, Neres and Kor stood with their backs to Gromulus, watching the other two duel. In front of them was Vallek, the man whose knuckles had turned red. He could hardly hold his training sword. Besides Jairus, all the men watching were young, less than twenty years in age, and every single one was laughing at Vallek.

Across from him stood the legendary swordsman.

Fayorn.

Fayorn noticed the presence. He had for some time. Something had been weighing on him that day, and the appearance of the masked man sparked the swordsman's curiosity. However, the training session was not over yet, and Fayorn meant to continue it.

Fayorn held his own wooden fighting sword. It was swift and brutal when connected. Already, he had thrashed Vallek four times. As the other men laughed, the brown-haired, smug Aronian youth showed his companions the swelling on his knuckles. Vallek extended his fighting stick towards the group, almost as an offering, and the group of hecklers shied from it as if it were a snake.

The men did not want to spar with Fayorn, who stood silently, waiting for them to choose. They had mocked Vallek and he now called them out. The boys looked sheepishly amongst one another. Challenged by anyone else, the Aronian militiamen would have accepted graciously. On the contrary, this challenge was different. It was not a simple youthful challenge, but it also was not a battle challenge, either. It was simply sparring with the great swordsman, Fayorn. As Vallek extended the stick with his left hand, for his right hand could no longer grip it, each of the five other young militiamen looked at him, and then over his shoulder at the awaiting Fayorn.

Fayorn's eyes were void of all expression. He fought emotionless. Fayorn kept his fighting stance with his wooden sword forward, tilted, and at the ready.

The five men looked at their teacher.

Fayorn looked through them.

Thriden, the second tallest of the bunch, was the best swordsman of the group and stepped forward to meet Fayorn. He was young and full of energy. He had taken to Fayorn's instruction and had progressed to become quite an accomplished swordsman himself. His mind spun. He did not want to spar with Fayorn, though. Thriden had only recently recovered from his own wounds from last week's lesson. Just like his friends, Thriden knew Fayorn took his practice a little too seriously.

Fayorn had trained the town's thirty-nine militiamen, himself. Of those, these six were his favorite and most promising. He was a good friend, and being almost ten years older, he was a mentor to them, as well. Normally, he was sincere and friendly. Outside of training, he was a brother of sorts. However, he was also their commander. They respected him. Fayorn taught the men swordplay, hand-to-hand combat and made sure his militia was well rounded in archery and other fighting tactics. They had to be. Approximately once a month, the Denoktorn attacked from the forest.

Like an older brother, Fayorn taught these six compassionately and patiently. However, he taught all other forms of fighting much differently than he did swordplay. He was serious with a sword. Fayorn was well known for pushing his men hard when learning how to handle a blade.

Each of the militiamen, especially these six, realized why Fayorn did so. He was a well-rounded warrior, but swords were his expertise. They had heard the stories as they grew up. In the southern lands of Nador, men such as Makheb, Taius and Gromulus were the heroes of the Barbarian Wars. However, Aronians had their own hero. Although their king was always their most important, Aronians held in high regard their greatest swordsman ever, Fayorn.

Each of the militiamen had suffered from the Barbarian Wars, as did the entire known world. Although they were too young to have fought in them, only by a few years, the youths still understood death all too well. Each took his training seriously, for his duties were to protect the innocent town of Whelmore and her Aronian residents.

Yet, as Thriden looked at Fayorn, he remembered that sparring with the warrior usually resulted in much pain.

Each of the men was thinking the same thing as Thriden stepped forward and took the wooden training sword in his right hand. He looked down at Vallek's throbbing hand and sighed. Thriden then looked at his friend, Kor, and remembered back a week. Fayorn had been in a foul mood that day. Kor, the smallest, yet strongest of the group of six, had tried to feint to the left and trick Fayorn. His reward was a rap across the face.

Kor still carried the red mark across his cheek.

Still, Thriden had taken the challenge. Whether out of courage, or fear of disappointing Fayorn, even he did not know. Truth was the blonde-haired man of nineteen was simply accepting his fate. The men did not realize that Fayorn was also teaching them another important lesson at the same time—to overcome one's fears.

With as much pride as he could muster, Thriden stepped towards Fayorn's wrath. He was the best of his friends with swordplay, slightly better than his elder, Jairus, who served second in command under Fayorn. Although Jairus, his head shaved to honor his great king, was better rounded than Thriden, he still could not best Thriden with a sword. Jairus was learning to lead men. Thriden was learning to be a master swordsman. Knowing he was the best, perhaps Thriden thought the challenge was his duty.

Thriden clutched the fighting stick tightly and stepped forward fast, lunging. Fayorn twisted and his wooden sword swiped his opponent's shoulder. Had it been a real sword, it would have cut a nasty gash into the younger warrior.

Fayorn, his voice calm, said, "Keep it simple. Master the basics. Relax your grip."

Thriden took a few steps back, recovered, and slowed his breathing. He relaxed his grip on his sword, understanding he could move it faster and less rigidly if he did so. He shook off the mistake. Thriden then swung his training sword a few times to loosen up and stepped forward again.

Fayorn grinned. He continued his instruction, as the two circled, "A good counter does not mean you are on the defensive. Instead, think of a counter as an attack. It is not a retreat, but a well-intended assault."

The two clashed three more times and continued circling.

"During your counter, you are not necessarily blocking. Defend by attacking," commanded Fayorn.

Gromulus stood in the doorway. Under his scarf, a smile formed on his face. *Fayorn taught me that,* he thought.

Thriden stepped forward fast. He was quick and agile and youthful. His footwork was fast progressing and he was a serious swordsman. The fighting sticks clashed in rapid bursts. At the blink of an eye, Thriden was on the ground, holding his side.

Fayorn stepped back, still talking. "Better. But do not anticipate your opponent. Do not ever believe you can guess his next move."

Baronius, the tallest of the militia youth, stepped forward. He was a smart man, barely sixteen years of age, and had a genuine heart. He was the youngest in the group; therefore, he was teased most often, yet loved and respected like a brother.

Baronius asked, "Do you simply wait for the opponent to attack, and hope you are fast enough?" He was a solid warrior, but he was young and lacked confidence at times. That confidence would one day grow to make the man great. However, now he was confused. A sword was not his weapon of choice; he preferred a spear and shield.

Fayorn answered, his eyes not leaving Thriden, who was standing back up boldly, "No, do not react to your opponent's attack, either."

Thriden stabbed forward twice, each missing Fayorn's midsection. Then, he slashed across, hoping to catch Fayorn, but the master blocked it and smacked Thriden in the opposite shoulder.

"*Ouch,*" he cried out.

Fayorn said, "See, I defended your own attack by attacking, myself." Then, to the group watching he said, "You have to sense your opponent's next move. *Feel* it before he does. Do not guess. Do not think. Reach into your opponent's soul. Defeat him there, and you will defeat him on the battlefield."

Thriden and Fayorn sparred a few more times. Fayorn was in a strange mood, and acknowledged to himself that he was probably taking out his frustrations on Thriden. He lightened a little and they had a solid sparring session.

Once they ended, the two bowed to one another in respect. The others were impressed. They noticed Thriden's skills had improved. They did not envy his punishment, but did respect his courage. The six were like brothers.

Gromulus also enjoyed the session—so much, that he began clapping his hands loudly. Slowly at first. The sound thudded, alerting the men.

Everyone turned as Gromulus began walking into the room. He said, "Not bad. Not bad at all. However, is it really fair for the supposed greatest swordsman in the world to fight someone so young and with so little experience? Perhaps the great swordsman is getting old, *eh?*"

The six militiamen quickly understood this stranger was mocking their teacher. Instantly Thriden ran towards the wall of weapons. He grabbed two swords and flung one to Jairus and one to Neres. Kor withdrew a dagger from his waistband. Vallek and Baronius both grabbed long spears. The six men spread out.

Jairus called the man out. "You speak to our teacher with disrespect."

"Do I?" asked Gromulus, still approaching.

Vallek called out, "Lift your cloak. What weapons do you hide?"

Gromulus flung his black cloak off and tossed it aside. In his hands were his swords. Identical and elegant. Short and practical. Gromulus kept his scarf over his face. He said, "Besides . . . wooden fighting sticks? Really? I mean, you trained men with real swords during the wars, Fayorn."

"Do not speak to him like that," bellowed Baronius, defending the man who always defended him.

Gromulus continued, "I am only saying . . . perhaps you have gone soft," his attention still on Fayorn.

Jairus took posture. "You take another step forward, and I will take your life."

Gromulus stopped. His swords held down.

Jairus furthered, "Now, drop your swords, or I will run you through."

"I did not give that order," said a firm voice behind Jairus. The six militiamen turned towards their leader. Fayorn spoke more, "It is me whom this man mocks. Let him face me if he so desires."

The militiamen backed away, interested and excited. Fayorn continued speaking, now to the concealed Gromulus. "Where did you get those swords?"

"I killed the man to whom they belonged, and took them." Gromulus swung them in circles. "What do you think?"

"If this is true you must be quite the accomplished warrior. Is it your desire to challenge me?"

"Perhaps."

"Well, might I have the pleasure of the man's name who killed Gromulus of Serona?"

"My name . . . is Veris."

"Well, Veris, I hope you know what you are getting yourself into. The man you claim to have killed was a good friend of mine."

With that said, Fayorn glanced at Neres. His militiaman tossed a sword to him.

Fayorn raised it and engaged. The two clanged metal. They twisted and spun and danced gracefully in a perfect sword ritual. A true clash of warriors. The six militiamen watched in astonishment as Fayorn and this masked man dueled.

They went on for some time, both exhibiting great swordsmanship. Then, they each stepped back, adding more tension in the air.

Fayorn spoke, "Your style is distinct." He looked at Thriden now, who proceeded to throw his own sword in the air. Fayorn caught it. Now, Fayorn and the man dueled with two swords each.

They fought beautifully.

Then it happened.

Fayorn thrusted his swords straight. He twisted both wrists and connected with his opponent's own swords. They fell from Gromulus' hands. Fayorn swept the man's leg and he fell. Fayorn placed both of his swords at Gromulus' neck, whose face still remained concealed.

The militiamen anxiously awaited the man's death.

Instead, Fayorn dropped both of his own swords and broke out in a hearty laugh. He reached down and extended his arm, helping Gromulus to his feet.

"How's it going, Grom?"

Gromulus began laughing, as well. He pulled down his scarf, exposing his face. The two men hugged and patted one another on the backs.

Gromulus replied, "You knew it was me all along."

"I could not imagine anyone taking those swords from you," said Fayorn, picking up his old friend's blades and dusting them off. He admired the craftsmanship.

"You just did," replied Gromulus.

Fayorn laughed at this. He was humble in his victory. "*Aw,* you are simply out of practice, Grom."

"How do you know I do not practice?"

"I can tell," teased Fayorn.

The two men embraced again and Fayorn introduced the great Seronan leader to his men.

Fayorn and Gromulus walked side-by-side down the road, heading towards Fayorn's home. They were both smiling. The two already began joking with one another and were genuinely grateful to see each other.

Gromulus asked, "Were you even trying?"

"What do you mean?"

"You know what I mean, Fayorn. Did I even have a chance?"

"Sure you did."

"That means no." Gromulus laughed.

It did not bother him. It was not such a bad thing to be beaten by Fayorn in sword fighting. Gromulus had always been fascinated with his friend's skills. He admired them as much as he admired Fayorn, himself. He could not imagine having to truly fight the man. He was glad they were friends.

"You have gotten, well, even more perfect over the years," said Gromulus.

Fayorn humbly replied, "Well, I do train hard."

"And still modest, it seems. Damn Aronians," Gromulus teased. The two walked slowly, catching up on old times.

They made their way to the stables. Ageeaus stood, eating fresh hay, his tail swishing. Fayorn walked up to the beautiful horse and patted its flanks. "You still have him, *eh?*"

"Yes, of course. He is magnificent," smiled Gromulus, the sun shining on his face. "Your king presented him to me, if you remember."

Then Lorylle walked up. She, too, had a smile on her face. It was as if both Lorylle and Gromulus had finally relaxed. They finally found safety and were calm in their new environment. For the moment, they let go of their tensions and were simply enjoying their time.

Gromulus turned, placing his hand on her shoulder as he made introductions. "Fayorn, this is Lorylle."

Fayorn turned from the horse to greet her. When his eyes met her, a strange look crept upon his face. He looked at her oddly and spoke, his voice cracking, "Do . . . do I know you?"

Lorylle, in turn, made a strange face herself, but only for a moment. Instantly, "No, I do not think so. I have heard many of the legends about you. Ver . . . I mean, Gromulus, speaks highly of you."

The warrior shook his head quickly, and snapped back to his friendly self. "Well, look at that. I forgot my manners. It is a pleasure to meet you." Fayorn took her hand and kissed it. Lorylle giggled and Gromulus rolled his eyes.

Always one with the ladies, thought Gromulus.

Fayorn continued, "Welcome to Whelmore."

"Thank you," Lorylle replied. "It is a quaint little town. Very peaceful here."

Fayorn smiled even wider, although he could not help but think she was familiar to him. "Yes, it *is* peaceful here. We do not see many people, which suits us just fine. Whelmore is at the edge of the empire. We are far north of Cosh, which is where Grom here tells me you two came from. To the north is Denok Forest, as you can see," he said, pointing to the ominous woods. "And the Endlands," he said, pointing west, "begin just that way. We do not venture there, though."

"It seems this town is completely self-sufficient," responded Gromulus, his eyes watching as the residents traded their goods around him.

Fayorn nodded. "Yes. You know us Aronians, we like being self-reliant. Anyways, we only see a handful of people here. An occasional trader or hunter. Very rare, though."

Lorylle asked, "What about Denoktorn? I heard they trouble the towns that border the forest."

"Yes, we have our problems," said Fayorn, looking at Gromulus while saying it. "We have to protect ourselves here."

The three began walking. Gromulus was on the right, leading his horse, and Fayorn in the middle, leading them through town.

Fayorn continued to speak, "At first, this town suffered much vengeance from the Denoktorn. The empire promised the people here protection . . . but that protection never came. When I first arrived, on my way back to Aronia, there were five hundred people residing here. Then, it was a respectable sized town. Now, only two hundred and twenty-three remain."

"Where did those people go?" asked Gromulus.

"Taken or killed. By the Denoktorn."

Lorylle asked, "I do not understand. This town still exists under Nadorian protection, does it not?"

Fayorn answered, "Officially, yes. Since I arrived in this town, however, I have yet to see a soldier presence, though it does not matter. We actually prefer it that way."

Gromulus chimed in, "Yes, but that is beside the point. The Senate signed those orders long ago. Troops were to be posted here."

Fayorn laughed. "There are no real empirical assets in Whelmore.

Mostly, we just raise our livestock and tend to our gardens. There is no gold to mine and I am afraid we are not the best loggers. We prefer going it alone."

Just like an Aronian, thought Gromulus. "Either way, it is a matter that should be looked into."

Fayorn said nothing more of the matter and the three kept walking.

Time passed and the sun was past its zenith in the cloudless sky, the same azure sky that would soon fill with the storms and ravish Whelmore. The town had seen another day as the sun gave signs of retiring. There was no promise as to if the following day the sun would appear again, or be hidden behind the approaching storm.

Rounding a bend in the road, the three came to Fayorn's house. It was quaint and modest, just as Fayorn's personality. The burq wood made the frame for the house. Stone covered the outside, and layers of sod filled the gaps. Fayorn's home was secluded in the far side of town, which in turn, told more of Fayorn's character.

He loved his people, but demanded his privacy.

Fayorn called out towards the house as Gromulus tied his horse. Gromulus could feel Antiok beckoning him from under the wrapped cloak. He touched the cloth material and felt the sword underneath. It vibrated, knowing Fayorn was near.

No, not yet.

From the front door walked out a beautiful woman. Her golden hair fell well past the middle of her back. Her welcoming cerulean eyes peered at her surroundings outside, brightening at the sight of visitors. The woman walked to her husband, kissed his cheek, and turned for her introduction.

Fayorn's eyes connected with his wife's. He then turned to their guests, "This is my wife, Kali."

Kali approached the two travelers and exchanged hugs, showing her remarkable affection for complete strangers. It was a testament to her personality. She trusted her husband, and any friends of his were friends of hers.

"Kali, this is Lorylle," Fayorn said, looking at the woman as he smiled. "And this is Gromulus. He is my friend I told you about . . . from the wars—"

146

"I think he needs no further introduction," Kali said sternly to her husband. She turned to look at Gromulus, ceasing her jest with her husband. "Gromulus, for many years, I have heard stories of you. Fayorn has never spoken an ill word about you. It is wonderful to finally meet you." Kali was genuine with her words. She looked at the pair, who appeared worn and tired. She was curious of the reason as to why Gromulus had chosen to visit so abruptly and unannounced. She knew it was too soon to ask and decided not to worry about it. She stood by her husband's side as the four acquainted themselves.

"How long have you known Gromulus?" Kali asked Lorylle.

Lorylle smiled. "A little over a year," she said sheepishly.

Then Kali turned, "I love your horse, Gromulus. He is beautiful." She patted the horse's neck and continued, "He is from Aronia by the looks of him," she stated, admiring the stallion's pitch-black tone.

Fayorn said, "My wife loves horses."

Gromulus answered, "Yes, he is. His name is Ageeaus."

Kali asked, "Where did you get him?"

"He was presented to me after the Siege of Cosh . . . by your king, actually."

"*Oh,* Kedor gave him to you," exclaimed Kali. She thought for a moment about the king of Aronia. Kali smiled. She recalled the stories her husband had told her about his childhood—growing up with Kedor. "You know, Kedor and Fayorn were closest friends growing up."

"Yes, ma'am, I have heard such. Fayorn has spoken kindly about him since I can remember. His reputation is wholesome," Gromulus then added, "And he has a fine choice of stallions."

The sun disappeared from the horizon. Kali had ushered everyone inside her home, and with the help of Lorylle, she prepared a mighty feast for the famished travelers. Their tone and their appearance had let Kali know that they were in desperate need of a warm meal. Therefore, she prepared her finest meal for these guests—these friends.

25

The two warriors sat at the table, by firelight, and talked as old friends should. The women had excused themselves and the two men were alone. Bellies full, the men rested in comfort. The meal had been delicious and plentiful, and Gromulus had needed that. He had not eaten a leisurely meal in nearly two weeks and it relaxed him. Kali had prepared four roasted hens with fresh bazak leaves and seasoned vegetables, which were handpicked that same day.

Gromulus and Fayorn sat talking.

There is a certain aura about him, thought Gromulus. *Always has been. Goodness is what it is. Pureness.* Fayorn was different than Gromulus remembered, though. He was not the same man he had known during the wars. *He seems happy now.* The solemn, expressionless face from the past was no longer. *Of course, I have been happy, too, these last few years,* thought Gromulus sadly. *Or was I?*

Fayorn laughed and joked as the two men conversed.

Fayorn was well known in Whelmore. As they walked the streets earlier, Gromulus had noticed the smiles and greetings from most everyone they passed. The people liked him. He was a symbol to the people of Whelmore, and they knew him well. During the wars he was different, though. Quiet. Fayorn tended to keep to himself, confiding mostly in Tornach during those times.

A few moments of silence passed, and Gromulus spoke, "It seems you have found a life for yourself here in Whelmore. The people . . . I can tell they appreciate you. They love you, Fayorn. It is visible on their faces."

"I suppose so," replied Fayorn, modestly.

"I can relate. I am well received where I come from."

Fayorn smiled. "It is a good feeling to know you belong somewhere, is it not? So, you reside in Cosh now?"

Not knowing exactly what to say just yet, the former senator replied, "That is right."

"Have you lived there all this time?"

Gromulus said, "No. After the wars, Tornach and I wandered together for a while. After we parted ways, I went to the old lands of Serona, and eventually made my way to Valeecia. Tornach headed north, far into his homeland . . . or what was left of it."

Fayorn smiled at the mention of Tornach. He took a moment, remembering his old friend. "Have you seen him since?"

Gromulus looked down. "Tornach? No, I am afraid I have not. We have not remained in contact over the years."

Fayorn pondered, "I often think about him. I wonder how he is."

Gromulus sighed. "My guess, he is dead. That man always had a nose for trouble."

Fayorn only nodded. Then, "What brings you to Whelmore? Do not tell me it is accident that you came here. How did you know I lived in this forgotten town?"

Gromulus said, "Well, it was mostly a guess," he lied. "I suppose luck was on my side."

Fayorn eyed him suspiciously.

After a lull of silence, Gromulus decided that it was time he told his old friend about why he was on the run. Fayorn was a smart man, and knew very well that he had not come just for a surprise visit. "I am in trouble, old friend. Severe trouble. I need your advice. The empire hunts me—"

Fayorn nodded slightly, almost as if he had expected such words to come forth from his friend's mouth.

Gromulus took time to explain everything. From his time as a consul, to his meeting with Makheb, the trouble with the ethithu in the swamps and their strange behavior, the formakha that aided him, Findyk, and his confrontation with the senators. He failed to mention Lorylle's attempt at his life, but told in detail about his struggle with Risard. While doing so, he also did not mention Antiok. As he spoke, Fayorn remained quiet, listening to his friend's problems.

Finally, Fayorn stated, "So, you came here."

It was more a statement than a question and Gromulus could only nod.

Fayorn continued, "You were lucky, old friend. Nadorian soldiers are highly trained, and by what I saw with your swordplay today . . ." he trailed off.

Gromulus sheepishly nodded, "Yes, I had help. Lorylle hit Risard over the head, preventing him from taking my life," he admitted.

At this, Fayorn laughed. He could not help himself. "*Ah, if only Tornach could be here . . .* he would never let you forget that." Gromulus sat quietly, taking the jest goodheartedly. Fayorn continued, "Let me ask you this. . . . Why do you care so much for your emperor? You always have. If the emperor formed the Senate, and for the most part, they control policy, what then is the problem?"

"They wish to expand Nador. They will swell her borders. Possibly into the Endlands, and even into Aronia."

Gromulus hoped this would prompt some emotion from his friend, but it did not. Instead, Fayorn chuckled. "Into the Endlands, *eh?* Would that be so bad? What is there that is so precious, I wonder. And, as for an invasion of Aronia . . ." Fayorn laughed again. "If you remember, the Ungorans tried it. We drove them away as we did all manner of beasts."

"This is different. Nador's military power is strong. The people will support this."

"Like I asked, why do you care?"

"The people of Nador will suffer by this new leadership. The Senate is selfish, and thirsts for power and glory."

"Yes, it is possible. However, perhaps it was time for the emperor to go. You say he ventured into the Endlands, to meet this . . . Ramunak?"

Gromulus nodded, but felt cold inside as he did so.

"Like Kedor has always said, there is something strange about Emperor Makheb. Something about him that cannot be trusted."

Gromulus grew irritated. "What do you know, Fayorn? You reap the benefits of this empire, as well. You remain in Nador—not Aronia."

"Calm down, my friend. I live here because these people need me."

"And I am on this undertaking because my people need me."

Fayorn only stared. "I will not argue with you about politics. You support the empire, I do not. You care for its glory, I do not. However, you are my friend. . . . What is it you seek from me? What sort of advice can I give a senator?"

Gromulus shrugged his shoulders. He did not want to tell Fayorn about his promise to Antiok. "Help, I guess. I must travel through Denok Forest and into Aronia."

Fayorn's smile faded. "Into the forest? Alone? *Hmm.*"

Gromulus then experienced a tingle beneath his garb. *The medallion.* He felt his chest by reflex, fingertips tracing the outline beneath his tunic. *I must show Fayorn,* he thought. *Lorylle did not understand, but Fayorn will.*

His mind boiled about, the urgency of his mission pressing him. Gromulus then had a moment of doubt.

What if it is only my mind playing tricks on me? Is the medallion calling to me, as Antiok once did to Fayorn? Fayorn would understand. Yes, he will understand.

Gromulus took a deep breath, thinking a moment about his old colleagues in Cosh. Their deception.

I trust Fayorn. He could never succumb to Ramunak's influence like the others. "I have something to show you."

Gromulus then reached into his tunic and pulled out the eccentric medallion. The man removed it from his neck and held it out for his friend to see. He sighed and said, "I must give this to your king."

Fayorn eyed the piece, but did not say anything. His eyes gave away nothing. Then, he asked sarcastically, "You have to bring that pretty little necklace to Kedor? What then?"

Gromulus had expected a different reaction. Irritated, he said, "Kedorlaomer should know the answer, I suppose."

Gromulus' mind raced. *Is it the medallion, or I? How can nobody see its importance? It is causing me to go mad.* "Have you spoken to him?" he asked.

Fayorn's expression changed, only slightly, though. "No. I have not seen Kedor since the end of the wars. We communicated by letter for about a year, but the forest became unsafe, and the riders stopped coming."

It happened in the swamps . . . and now again. What mystery surrounds this medallion?

Gromulus acted saddened by this. He knew Fayorn and Kedor were great friends, like brothers. "So, you have been isolated from your people for five years . . . well, actually more like eight, *huh?*"

Is it the medallion, or I?

"That is right. But, a handful of my people are here, in Whelmore . . . including Kali."

Is it Veris, or Gromulus?

"She is a remarkable woman. It is good to finally have met her."

Is it Makheb, or—?

"We were both lucky," said Fayorn, realizing Gromulus' thoughts were elsewhere. He looked his old friend directly in the eyes, trying to get his attention. "She made it safely through the forest immediately after the wars. Had she waited, she would still be in Aronia and we would be apart."

Gromulus suddenly realized his thoughts were wandering. He blinked his eyes, sitting up in his chair, too. Bewildered by his thoughts, and unsure of his own sanity, he asked, "Is the forest truly that deadly? I know the roads are impassible, overgrown and dangerous; trade *was* my business as a senior senator. Merchants would rarely venture into the forest. Many who tried were never heard from again. But still, I do wonder if the stories are true . . . about the forest."

Fayorn added, "It is such a shame. Trade between Aronia and Nador would be good for both. Unfortunately, it *is* true. The Denoktorn do not allow entrance into the forest. They are deadly . . . and Whelmore does not receive any help from the empire." Fayorn seemed irritated, yet concealed his blame well. Here was a lifelong friend whom he had not seen in many years, who supported the empire blindly—at least in Fayorn's opinion. He chose not to be angry.

Gromulus replied, "I do not understand that issue myself. Why are no legionaries posted here? A town the size of Whelmore . . . at least a dozen or two are needed."

Fayorn looked at his friend from the past, and smiled. He chuckled as he spoke, "You are the politician, not me. I do not have that answer . . . you should." He continued chuckling.

This irritated the former senator. Gromulus had once visited a few border towns. One, Chybum, about a year prior. In Chybum, there was a soldier presence, however light. The residents complained, angrily, to the then Consul Veris. They wanted protection. Now, Chybum's security was better, but by no means far progressed. In such a wide empire, progress took time.

Gromulus said, "Yes, that was my duty. Perhaps my emperor dismissed me . . . because I no longer suit the empire. The people should live well under the empire's great arms, not in fear of a forest."

"A forest filled with Ungorans."

"Ungorans are no more. They changed long ago. They became beast-like . . . something else. They are primitive. Nador could crush them. The Denoktorn are no longer a threat."

Fayorn responded, "Bold words. The Denoktorn are . . . possessed. But, behind that blank stare is still an Ungoran." Before Gromulus could speak, Fayorn leaned forward, across the table. The firelight made his brown eyes flicker. "They are wicked in their ways—the Denoktorn. If they ever show the will, they could cause harsh times for Nador, as well as Aronia."

Gromulus sat back in his chair, taking it all in. Like most Nadorians, he had become naïve. Safety was a thing that was relative to where one lived. A resident of the mighty Ogata, or the grand city of Cosh, or even Crevail and Chybum felt safe when they slept at night. Arrogantly, they viewed the Denoktorn much like the ethithu of the swamps.

However, Fayorn saw it differently. He witnessed the Denoktorn first-hand many times. He had spilled their blood, just as he had spilled Ungoran blood years before.

Gromulus now realized that Fayorn might know more than himself.

Fayorn continued, "After our first winter season in Whelmore, when the ground became fertile and the sun warm again, the Denoktorn attacked. It was a small band, only six. We could tell something was different about them . . . like I said . . . possessed. They fought differently. They were still barbaric and without organization, but they were more bloodthirsty than I had ever seen from the Ungorans. The six that attacked were enraged. I witnessed three of them kill a young girl—I believe she was Seronan."

Gromulus stared, unable to speak.

Fayorn's face was grim. "Before I could kill them, the Denoktorn slashed and ripped that girl apart. Ungorans were at least soldierly, for the most part. No, these changed Ungorans are different." He paused. "As time passed, I realized they are not necessarily hard to defend against. It seems the Denoktorn are not truly capable of rationalization or reason. They attack on instinct, much like an animal."

"Yes, and does that not make them but a mere nuisance?"

"They are more than that. They are not like formakha slaves."

Gromulus thought back to the barge. Then, he said, "More like ethithu? The villagers of the south keep the populations low by—"

"No!" Fayorn pounded his right fist on the table. "The Denoktorn are still Ungorans. They are the *same* people. I have seen young ones, which means they are breeding. The Ungorans were bloodthirsty heathens—barbarians. Yet, they still had reason behind their atrocities. These Denoktorn seem to have no cause."

"There is no excuse you can make about Ungorans. Not to me. You and I have both seen the brutality of their culture. We have seen it firsthand, if you forget, Fayorn. Did you not spill their blood for the same good reason as me?"

Fayorn, realizing Gromulus was on the defensive, calmed his tone. "My friend, right or wrong is not the point I am making. Yes, we fought on the side of goodness during the wars. I will grant you that. It was important to stand up and fight them. However, there are two problems."

"What are they?"

Fayorn stated, "First, what we, the people of the other four kingdoms, did to cause their hostilities. Second, the simple fact that Nador has yet to accomplish the original goal."

Gromulus pondered this. "Are you saying that the old kingdoms made the Ungorans do what they did? That is preposterous. No, Ungorans are wicked."

"Gromulus, do you not recall their crops drying up? Their cattle dying? The rains stopped falling over their lands, and on the occasion they did, it rained red. Some say it was blood. The ground became dead, spoiled. How many times did they ask for aid?"

"I . . . I do not recall much of that time, so I do not remember. However, I have heard what you say is true. In the latter years, King Briom and King Nyrusus refused aid to Ungora when asked. While they bathed in gold, the Ungoran people starved."

"That is my point."

"Yes, but Ungorans did not only steal food. They slaughtered many people. Many of *my* people."

"As we did theirs. They were not always as bloodthirsty as they became. Something heinous entered their souls. Then, once driven into the forest, they became . . . hollow."

Gromulus thought this out. "What do you think we should do? The wars are over. . . . What is done is done."

"Yes, that is why I think Nador should enter the forest with legions, and rid this world of the Denoktorn before they become worse. Finish the task that was set, and defeat the Ungorans."

"How could they become worse?"

Fayorn said, "Their numbers. As I said before, they are breeding. Also, if anything could take power over them, they would still be a threat, despite your beliefs that Nador is invulnerable."

"Nador is mighty, but I do agree with you, although I did not realize the importance until now. Makheb, too, spoke of them."

"Yes, Grom . . . the Ungorans are still a threat."

Meanwhile, a day's ride from the gates of Chybum, the two men rode. Tornach sat next to Kelnum, and relaxed for the first time during their journey. They were in central Nador, traveling the old lands of Ume. The wind blew and the land around them was now a soft green. Tornach forced himself to take a few deep breaths, taking in the fresh air and trying to appreciate the beauty around him. He was grateful for his new companion, Kelnum.

The two rode up a hill, and once they reached the peak, they could see far into the distance. Ahead of them were fertile grounds and small farms that made up much of the old Umite territory. Behind them, the storm could still be seen on the horizon.

Tornach noticed a large cloud of dust ahead of them. He mentioned it to Kelnum, while pointing. However, Kelnum shrugged it off as nothing more than Nadorian soldiers doing routine exercises. Tornach, who trusted no one, made sure his sword was accessible. The two continued riding towards the troops.

At this point in their journey, he opened up to Kelnum. He was candid, telling old stories from the past. Kelnum, who was taking him to an unknown future, sat silently next to the barbarian, listening intently. Tornach talked about old friends, especially Fayorn and the mysterious sword the man carried.

"It was strange," said Tornach. "As well as disturbing. Antiok, that is. Being close ta that sword always gave me an eerie feeling."

"Really? A sword?" Kelnum smiled. "How could a sword bother you so?"

Tornach returned the smile. "I know it sounds odd, Kelnum, and I am afraid I cannot completely explain." He paused for a moment. "In the hands of Fayorn, ya'h cannot have a better pair by ya'h side during battle, but when I got close ta Antiok, it would cause the oddest of emotions. Ya'h can feel sad and happy all at once. The closer ya'h stand, the stronger the feeling is."

"Hmm . . . that is strange." His smile fell and his face scrunched up in confusion.

"I know. What is even stranger is that the closer ya'h get ta Antiok, the more ya'h can feel its power. Ya'h can actually feel its personality."

"That makes no sense," said Kelnum, baffled.

"The Sword of Ellsar is truly a sight to behold. In combat, it is a glorious sight, the speed and precision it holds, but alone with the sword, however, is a different thing."

"Huh? What does that mean? Is the sword as frightful as being alone in the swamps at night?"

"Ha, again, Kelnum, I know it sounds odd, but when Antiok and Fayorn are apart, one can sense the sword is unhappy. I could always tell Antiok did not care for me. Fayorn did, but his sword did not."

"You sound as if this bothers you, Tornach"

The Ungoran nodded. "Aye, it did. But not as much now."

"I do not know, Tornach. How can a sword not like you . . . or anyone for that matter? A sword is just a piece of metal."

"The truth is, Kelnum, I am not sure what Antiok is made of, but this sword likes no one other than Fayorn. It is alive, ya'h see. The sword is cursed in my book."

"Do you hear yourself, Tornach? A cursed sword. That is farfetched. How could you be sure it was cursed? Did you ever try and hold it?"

Tornach laughed. "I have tried, old man, and it would not let me."

"What do you mean?"

"Well, there is a story behind that, Kelnum." He paused a short while, clearly collecting his thoughts.

"Come on Tornach, tell your story."

"Shortly after meeting Fayorn, Gromulus and I took him back ta a small village in Serona we used as a base camp. We introduced him ta the militia. The men were polite, because he was my guest. I think, though, that they did not really like Fayorn at first."

"Why is that? Was it because he was Aronian?"

"Perhaps. His demeanor is . . . quiet. Anyways, that night I convinced him ta let me touch the sword. He kept warning me, but I did not understand. Finally, he stood up and stated he was tired, and going to get some sleep."

Kelnum nodded again.

Tornach continued, "I asked him one more time . . . ta let me touch Antiok. Then, Kelnum, Fayorn did the strangest thing. He unsheathed Antiok and slowly pushed its tip down inta a tabletop, inside the pub we were at. The sword pushed inta the wood table with ease. There was Antiok, sticking straight up from the table, with my men and me staring in disbelief. Then, Fayorn said goodnight and left for the evening."

"Leaving his sword?"

"Aye, he left his sword."

"What if someone would have stolen it?"

"That is just it, Kelnum. We could never have taken it." Tornach took a swig of water from the snapjaw canteen and continued his story. "I could not hold my curiosity for long. I reached for the hilt and I could feel it did not want me ta try, but I did anyways," said Tornach, gleefully. "I put my hand around the hilt, and guess what?"

"What?"

"The next thing I knew, I was on my backside and could not get up. I blinked a few times and I saw a few of the men who stood close with their hands over their ears. I guess the sword made a sound when it tossed me aside."

"I am afraid, my friend, I do not understand."

"Nor do I, Kelnum. But when ya'h touch Antiok, it hurts. I have had open gashes and have even been struck by arrows, and ya'h know, I think touching that sword hurt worse. It drove me crazy. I reached for it again and again, and each time it knocked me ta the ground."

Kelnum started to laugh out loud. "Why would you keep reaching for it if you knew what would happen?"

Tornach shrugged his shoulders and the constant smirk on his face left. "Because, Kelnum, it bothered me. I could not comprehend, and cannot ta this day, why the sword was the way it was. I am a warrior, and I wanted the weapon, but Antiok would not have me."

Kelnum nodded his head. He could see why this would cause some conflict, although he still had trouble understanding.

Tornach's face brightened again, "Finally, I made up a game, though. My men and I began drinking and daring one another ta touch the sword. Over and over we did it, until everyone went ta bed."

"That is ridiculous," he looked at Tornach with a smile. "Why would you and your men do such a thing?"

"Because it was fun," said Tornach, grinning. "It knocked every man in that bar ta his back at least two times. At one point, we were touching it seven men at a time. Same effect, though. It was fun. My men had seen so much blood in recent weeks that they needed a small amount of entertainment. Finally, when everyone else had gone ta bed, I stayed up even later. I sat in a chair, looking at Antiok. I did not try ta touch it anymore. Instead, I just stared at it. Its only care was Fayorn. I sat all night, the sword keeping me awake. I was baffled, and I suppose I still am. I had never seen anything magical and I must admit, I would rather stand up against ten Ungorans than be near that sword again. Ya'h know what the most unbelievable part was, Kelnum?"

"No, what?"

"I swear ta this day, and on the grave of my mother, that damn sword laughed at me that night."

"*Hmm* . . . Yes, Tornach, that is almost unbelievable."

Tornach continued, "The next morning I awoke still in the same chair.

Fayorn walked inta the pub, smiled at me, and withdrew Antiok from the table. I think he knew what my men and I did that night, and I think it amused him. For someone so serious, Fayorn also has a sense of humor."

Kelnum laughed at the thought of Tornach's stubbornness causing him to fly through the air. He seemed like the type of man who would not leave something like this alone. "It is indeed strange about that sword."

"Ya'h know what I think, Kelnum?"

"What is that?"

"Antiok is alive . . . is what I think."

The conversation halted. Kelnum stopped the carriage. In front of the travelers, where two major roads intersected, was a line of Nadorian soldiers, traveling south. They marched, the ground rumbling as the columns of legionaries, all in full armor, passed Tornach and Kelnum. They carried all their battle necessities, and wore their spiked helmets, as if headed to battle. As far as Tornach knew, Nador had no enemies.

Kelnum had an uneasy look upon his face. Tornach wondered what he was thinking.

The barbarian grasped his sword, ready if needed.

The progression of soldiers took quite some time. They kicked up dust as they moved, singing marching songs. Their cadence kept the formations locked and passed the time. The six hundred or so soldiers chanted in unison. The sight of them exhilarated Tornach. The thought of war made the hair on the back of his neck stand up. The legionaries chanted:

> 'We are Nador . . . Nador . . . Nadorian,
> We are proud . . . proud . . . until the end
> We are the Fifty-Seventh Infantry,
> We pin Ungorans to the trees
> With our sabers, happily,
> And hear our women scream, OOOiiiEE!
> We are Nador . . . Nador . . . Nadorian'

Their singing was boisterous and yet soothing to Tornach. He also knew that this was no training exercise. Troops were being moved. Something was going on. Tornach peered at the flags the men carried. They were indeed the Fifty-Seventh Infantry and the symbol on the flag told him they were from Fairmeadow.

As the formation came to an end, Kelnum whipped his horse and crossed the intersection. The two were skeptical as to what they had just seen.

Tornach finally asked, "Kelnum, are we at war? I have been away for some time. Did something happen in my absence? Does this have something ta do with the death of those two praetors?"

Kelnum looked uneasy. Keeping his voice low, he said, "Tornach, I do not know. There are undeniably some things happening in the empire right now. I know a few magistrates in Cosh and a captain stationed in Chybum. I trade whiskey with them for information. Each of them has recently mentioned rumors that the emperor of Nador is missing. Nobody has seen or heard from Makheb in over a week. They spoke of these strange storms, and what they said ended up coming true. These storms are devastating morale in Nador. I am worried."

"Why?"

"Something is not right in the empire."

Tornach could tell this was bothering the man and wanted to calm him. He changed the subject back to the past. "Forget the troops, Kelnum. There is nothing we can do about it now. As soon as we arrive in Chybum, we will figure this out. Now . . . if I may ask, ya'h have listened long enough ta my ramblings. I am curious about ya'h own past. Tell me of ya'hself, Kelnum. Where are ya'h from? What was ya'h life like during the wars?" Tornach was genuinely curious.

"Well, Tornach, I am afraid my story is not quite as exciting as yours. I was born in Cosh and lived in the city for most of my youth. I was the son of a blacksmith. If you ever have any questions about smithing, you just let me know," he said comically. "I was to carry on my father's business, but my dream was to own a farm for myself. The wars changed that dream, though. The closest I ever got was bartering produce."

Tornach listened.

Kelnum kept talking, "I fought in the wars. I was in the infantry out of Cosh. It was the first time I traveled outside of the lands of Ume. My company, in particular, was in charge of burning Ungoran villages after our troops went through." As soon as Kelnum said these last words, he wished he had not.

Tornach's smile faded fast. The man next to him was one of the ones responsible for the complete obliteration of old Ungora—his homeland.

Kelnum changed the subject quickly, to make Tornach forget what he had just said. "*Uh* . . . but . . . *ah,* but what about you Tornach, what did you accomplish during the wars?"

Tornach was still thinking of his homeland burning, but the more he thought about it, the more he realized it did not matter. Ungora was no longer. It did not matter who did what during the wars. The enemy was defeated. They had won.

Kelnum thought Tornach was upset. He could read the man's face and he was thinking of Ungora. "Listen, Tornach, I was only doing what I was ordered to do."

"*Huh?*" Tornach snapped out of his thought. "*Oh* . . . no, Kelnum, I know it was only orders, they *were* the enemy, after all."

"Alright, well, tell me more of your times in the wars."

"Well, the Barbarian Wars were the best time of my life. I had everything I wanted. I found that the battlefield excited me, and I was good on it. I was involved in most of the major campaigns towards the end of the wars. Gromulus and I personally created the Seronan resistance. I had respect. I had love."

Kelnum nodded. "Yes, and you were at the Siege of Cosh, as was I. Those few days will never leave my mind. Even when I close my eyes, I can still see the horrors."

"I know what ya'h mean. I killed twelve Ungorans that last day," Tornach paused a moment for effect. "And *six* Troxen."

Kelnum turned and looked at Tornach. His eyebrows raised in astonishment.

Tornach added, "I was respected back then. People cheered my name. I did my part and people loved me for it."

"And now it is different?"

"Aye. People forget too easily what good deeds I did. The people have forgotten what I sacrificed, fighting my own kind. My legacy is of the past, Kelnum. I am blamed for my people's ways, even though I fought against them. Now, my people are long-since driven inta the cursed forest. They have become savages. They have eaten much raw flesh. Either that, or something in the forest is affecting them."

Kelnum noted, "The wars seemed to have been good to you. As far as your reputation, if only people took the time to get to know you as I have, they would feel different about you. The world of Men is consumed with what they see and hear and rush to judgment. The people of Nador are too obsessed with their own greed to take any time for, what to them, is a petty issue."

"Wise words, old man." Tornach smiled. "I never want pity, but I was a war hero. I should be treated with the respect of a soldier. I have led men and held them as they died on the field. I would have gladly given my life ta save any one of theirs. Why am I still in exile?"

There was no answer. Only the silence of the two men as they rode. Both veterans did not understand the way the world worked. Kelnum accepted the fact. Tornach never would.

The two talked a while longer. They laughed and spoke of old times. Tornach had many stories to tell Kelnum, and Kelnum listened to every word. The two shared a bond from the wars of old. Each had been able to tell his side.

Tornach's spirits were high as the two drew ever closer to the outskirts of Chybum.

26

The room was silent as the two men sat still, both pondering their pasts. Both were wondering about their futures, as well. Then Fayorn spoke, "There is one thing you must realize . . . and that is, under your Emperor Makheb's rule, the threat that affected the world for so many years still remains. He was premature in his victory, as were every man, woman and child in what is now Nador."

"Perhaps you are right. You were not at the festivities. Neither was your king, nor his White Knights."

"No, my king left in a rage that day. He saw Makheb, the true Makheb, and left. He understands what Makheb represents."

On guard and with tension in his voice, Gromulus questioned, "And just what does Makheb represent?"

His face solemn, Fayorn whispered. "The end of mankind."

Instantly Gromulus responded, "You are wrong. You Aronians are all the same. Your vision is narrow, my friend."

"Narrow, *eh?* My king left that day the only ruler with his kingdom intact. All four of the southern kingdoms are now gone, morphed into the empire's so called greater glory." Fayorn paused. "Makheb changed the people of our world."

"For the better," Gromulus stated.

"I believe differently."

Gromulus waited a moment, and then asked, "You say Kedorlaomer saw Makheb? Did he see his face?"

"Yes," responded the warrior.

"I have, as well. What does your king say he is?"

Fayorn regretfully said, "My king has kept that to himself. Even my queen does not know. Regardless, I trust Kedor. He must have solid reason not to trust your emperor."

"Then why would Emperor Makheb order me to present this medallion—" he said, holding it again in his fingers, "—to Kedorlaomer?"

"That, I do not know."

Gromulus was frustrated. It was as if the entire fate of the world rested upon his shoulders, which according to Makheb might be true. Now, even one of his best friends did not seem as supportive as he hoped.

Fayorn noticed and chuckled. "Grom, old buddy, do not fret. You only ask my opinion. The question you should ask is whether I care or not."

"Do you?"

"I pray for a good life for everyone in this world. I hope each and every person can have peace in his or her life. However, the answer is no. I do not care for your empire. If it falls, it falls. It makes no matter to me. It is not in my hands. I only wish to live out my days and have many children and perhaps even grandchildren."

"Where is your passion, Fayorn?"

"My passion is to three things—my god, my family and my kingdom. Aronia matters, Grom, not Nador."

"But . . . you were so great! The best warrior upon whom I have ever laid my eyes. You could help save this empire from becoming—"

Fayorn interrupted, "Becoming what? Nador is doomed. She was never built to last. Why has your emperor not rid us of the Denoktorn? What about the two Valeecian legions that were sent into the Endlands? Why, in five years, has your emperor not sought an answer to why they were never heard from again? And, if there is indeed a takeover, why has your emperor left you alone with this burden? Where has your great god-king run off to?" he said mockingly.

Gromulus could not answer and Fayorn continued, "Perhaps they are right, those who lead this takeover. Perhaps your emperor has dulled your senses with luxuries. While the people of Nador fatten themselves with overindulgence, the great empire slips out of the hands of the one who formed it."

Gromulus defended his emperor, "No, Makheb united the people under a single government. He made the laws equal, and fair."

"Yes, but you are still making an excuse for an emperor who will not show the public his face. You said you met him. You saw his face. Ask yourself who or what he really is. Is there not something completely odd about him? Is it only Aronians who see this? Your leader conceals himself under robes and a mask." Fayorn remembered that Gromulus did the same during the wars, and decided not to further it. "I personally do not believe he is human."

He is not, thought Gromulus. "That does not matter to Nadorians, though. We have been quite successful in our dealings with other creatures besides Men. Relations with the Troxen have done our economy well."

At the mention of Troxen, Fayorn's lip quivered.

Gromulus continued, "The Walfyres provide us many things, as well. And of course, without Makheb's formakha workers, Nador would have no wheels. They are the core of Nador's power and might. That, and of course, our legions. Tens of thousands of soldiers."

Fayorn did not want to ruin the evening. Although the discussion was tense, and the two had different ideologies about life, they were still friends. "Well Grom, I am not sure I can provide an answer to this mess. What is good for an Aronian may not be good for a Nadorian."

Gromulus replied, "You chastise Makheb, but these conspirators will bring turmoil. Like I said before, there was mention of expansion."

Fayorn nodded. "As expected by politicians and generals."

"North . . . into Aronia is a possibility," said Gromulus.

Fayorn only smiled. "And like I said, Aronians do not worry about that. The armies of Nador would never even see the outline of Ellsar," he said confidently. "However, Makheb has never threatened us. Although my king, as well as myself, despises your emperor, we do recognize that he has grieved us none. His and Kedor's affairs have not crossed, which is good. Instead, Makheb has simply ignored Aronians as we have ignored him. We live peacefully that way, I think. Denok Forest is perhaps a gift from above. It separates two cultures that desperately need separating."

"Are we not all Men? Do we not share the same features? The same needs?"

Fayorn answered, "Yes, but different beliefs. I am not sure how I can help you, for I do not know what you are asking of me. Personally, I do not care for Makheb, and I do not place much effort on him, either. I live my life. I follow Aronian ways. I only bow to my god, and defend my kingdom. Logically, it makes sense that you defend your emperor, though."

"Of course it does. Emperor Makheb keeps this empire standing. The politicians and greedy elite will destroy Nador if we do nothing," said Gromulus.

Fayorn leaned in close once more. "Grom, you say the empire is falling . . . I say the empire never had a chance. You say you can save her, and I say she has already failed. Nador was doomed from the beginning. I can only hope people will not get hurt, and that you are successful in your task."

"Aronians are indeed wonderful people. I do know that you care, Fayorn . . . that your king cares . . . and that his people care. Despite all this, let me ask you one question, as my friend."

Fayorn smiled. "Ask and you will receive."

"Do you not serve your king? Do you not understand my commitment to my emperor?"

Fayorn nodded. "Yes, Grom, I do understand. All too well, I understand."

Gromulus went on, "I am under orders to deliver this medallion to Kedorlaomer, and I will carry out my orders until I either accomplish this task, or die. I know you well, Fayorn. You would do the same if Kedorlaomer ordered you."

"Without a doubt." Then, Fayorn added, "These storms foretell of hard times to come. I am sorry I cannot join you in this quest; I truly am. But this fight is not for me. I can, however, supply you and point you in the right direction. My men have experience in the forest and will show you the best path."

This disappointed Gromulus. He had secretly hoped Fayorn would join him. *Like it used to be.* Yet, he understood his friend's position. Much like himself, the greatest swordsman in the known world wanted his real identity masked forever.

What have I brought upon him? Antiok. Maybe he does not truly want it. I have endangered a man who will be made responsible.

Then, as the pressure of his undertaking weighed heavy, he realized he might have put Fayorn in danger. "I am sorry to have come here. Soldiers will be looking for me."

"No worries. We shall point them in the wrong direction." Fayorn sounded certain.

Gromulus was concerned, nevertheless. Fayorn was underestimating the brutality of the Nadorian military. "I will leave first thing in the morning. I regret putting your people . . . your own wife, in danger."

Fayorn smiled. "You are in my thoughts and prayers. Take with you the constant reminder that there are some things in life that are not within your control."

Gromulus only nodded. He had always had a hard time with that. He felt he could control the destiny of Nador, even the entire world, if he tried hard enough. Fayorn's advice pained him, because deep within, he feared it to be true.

Fayorn added, "Be sure to tell Kedor you spoke to me and please give my regards—and to Niralyn, as well. I miss them. You will serve them well."

What does that mean? Gromulus then spoke, "You are the one who serves him, not I. You are his chosen protector, his friend."

Fayorn corrected the man, "His friend, indeed. He is the best of friends. However, I do not protect Kedor. He needs no protection. He is as bold a leader as any."

"True. I have seen him in battle firsthand. I shall correct what I said. You are the much-honored protector of Aronia, as the legends say."

Fayorn responded, "Still wrong. I serve my king, yes. I do his bidding without question, because he is my king. In serving him, I serve my kingdom. Kedor is also a servant—to Aronia. He leads. Unlike your emperor, who rules, Kedor allows no man to take a knee before him."

Gromulus thought that odd. "I know he cares for Aronia, but he is still a king. Noble men should be respected properly."

"Kedor is noble because it is *he* who bows to his people. The people serve our god. Our king serves our people. I serve our king."

"I think I understand," said Gromulus, although not really sure if he did or not. "Yet, the legends say otherwise. Are you saying you protect no one?"

"That . . . is not completely true. I serve my king's will, but I do protect one."

"Whom?"

"The high protector of Ellsar is sworn to always defend one. That has been so for many generations."

"Whom do you protect?" Gromulus repeated.

Fayorn did not answer.

Niralyn sat by firelight, alone. Her form cast a shadow into the dark chambers. She sat with her king's sword gently across her lap. She wiped the blade with a silk rag, softly polishing it. Niralyn was careful, for it was sharp. When she was finished, the blade gleamed. Then, she did the same to his helmet and armor. She took meticulous care in doing so, taking pride in preparing her husband for his departure.

The recent news bothered her. Things were odd now. She had feelings, strange feelings. The dreams had not stopped. She had dreamt of Ramunak every night, and now that her husband was leaving for the western borders of Aronia, she felt alone. She worried for her husband and concealed it for her kingdom. She was majestic, a true queen.

Finally, Niralyn rose. She rested the armor on a table, subsequently taking her husband's indigo cloak and hanging it from a hook. Her fingers brushed the outline of his helmet, which bore many years of warfare. Lastly, she propped his spear next to his shield. Niralyn stood back and admired his battle dress. She was proud of her husband. As soft and gentle of a man as he was, she had also heard his soldiers' respects to their king. He was a true warrior. Kedor believed that a true king should lead his men into battle, not direct them from behind. He would never commit his kingdom to war unless he was willing to lead the charge.

Niralyn was afraid.

The two warriors kept talking.

Fayorn said, "Loyalty to our god, duty to kingdom—and honor our people. That is all I have. That is all I live for. As for the Troxen, they do not matter. Nador—it does not matter. These are the ways of Aronia. For generations, we have lived this. We care about others, but take no part in their affairs."

Gromulus asked, "But what of your own contribution, Fayorn? What of your involvement in the Barbarian Wars?"

Fayorn responded, "Have you asked Tornach that same question?"

"That is not an answer."

Fayorn smiled, acknowledging Gromulus' response. "My own involvement was not for reasons the same as you. Grom, you and Tornach fought for your own personal reasons, whatever they may have been. I did not."

This concerned Gromulus. "You acted as if you cared."

"I did, dear friend; and I still do care. You view Aronian ways all wrong. They are not as selfish as you perceive. We care for all humanity. We pray for them. Before the wars, Aronia sent masses of food to Ungora. We fed their people for many years."

"Really? But they attacked your people, too?"

"Towards the end of the wars, they did. They attempted to raid our border towns, but to no avail. We drove them away. Besides, the southern kingdoms were better suited for raiding . . . closer . . . more abundance of goods. However, our king still tried to provide food to the starving Ungorans even after this."

"That is incredible."

"My point being, do not view Aronian ways as if we do not care. We care for all. Yet, do not think that my own duties, serving by your side, were my own doing. What we did was fulfilling. We did a good thing, Grom, we really did, though I served not the dream of an empire, but because my king ordered me to."

"Why?"

"Much like I cannot answer why your own ruler sent you on this near impossible mission. Kedor had his reasons. And yet, our armies did not march."

"You are wrong," responded Gromulus. "Kedorlaomer led his riders that last day. He drove the Troxen away from battle. Without his intervention, the tides of combat might very well have changed. I was there—as were you."

"True, but Kedor did not march his masses. Those were but a few of our forces."

"Yet he still joined."

"Kedor does feel good about the defeat of the Ungorans that day, as well as the Troxen. You fail to see the point. Kedor did not ride his knights into battle to save the southern kingdoms, or to create an empire. He did it for Aronia."

"What do you mean?"

Fayorn sighed. "You may not understand, but do not begrudge me for not joining your cause. You are my friend, and I stood by your side proudly. Yet, I do not entertain your beliefs. I am Aronian. I am loyal. It is all I have. I serve my king and I serve my people. I honor my god by serving them."

"Yes, you have told me about your friendship with Kedorlaomer. If you hold him in high regard, I do as well. I do not mean to question your beliefs. I only do not understand them."

Fayorn replied, "Nor do I yours. Your empire is immense. It is an ever-growing fire and is fueled by the feuds of Men and beast."

Gromulus then asked, "Why do Aronians hold everyone else in contempt? Or, at least they appear to."

"We can only count on one thing—ourselves. Much like battle, Grom. I trusted only the men to my sides. I honored them. I was loyal to them."

"Yes," said Gromulus enthusiastically.

Fayorn kept speaking, "It is on that feeling of brotherhood that you are lost in your ideology."

Gromulus shrugged his shoulders.

Fayorn continued, "Look at your empire, not as a senator, but as a commoner. Look at it as I do. Look at it as Tornach would."

"Nador is glorious," replied Gromulus, although his voice was not convincing.

"The world does not work the way you see it, Grom. Your empire will fail. It does not put effort on the individual, only the collective. Eventually people suffer from that philosophy, and Nador will crumble," Fayorn stated definitively.

"What do you mean?" Gromulus was perplexed.

"Gromulus—let me ask you a question. What were your ruler's intentions? Why did Makheb form the empire?"

Gromulus' reply was simple, "To unite the people against oppression."

Fayorn asked, "Do you know this without a doubt? Why take Rhoaden's crown; and Briom and Nyrusus? Why, instead of helping, did he demand their crowns? And why drive Alarik and the Ungorans into the forest? And why anger Kedor—it was my king who prevented a dismal outcome that day!" Fayorn sounded irritated.

"I do not know these answers. You should be the one who knows why Makheb angered Kedor, not I."

"Kedor is a good judge of character—the most righteous man I know. He saw something wicked in Makheb."

Gromulus frowned. "Makheb is like a god."

The Aronian only smiled at this.

Gromulus added, "He holds the key to our future, Fayorn."

"Yes, Grom, he does . . . but not how you think."

❧❧▲▲◢◢

The arid desert was endless. Makheb, the legendary emperor of Nador, rode proudly atop his colorful serpenti. The plethora of colors of the beast contrasted with the golden mist of sand that blew across the Endlands. Each grain whipped at his veiled face and battled his robes.

Makheb's mount was affected, as well; it hissed and flithered its tongue in annoyance at the sand-filled winds. Makheb's serpenti pushed farther, with persistence, into the abyss of heat and into the unknown.

Makheb knew the beast's anguish, and made it labor that much harder. He needed to reach Baalek soon.

Even though it had been not much longer than a week, time was lost to Makheb. Travel in the Endlands was different than in the world of Men. It was slower, more dangerous; and seemed to pull at the will of a man. Makheb was no different. He remained focused on his objective.

In the distance, the emperor was able to see an outline of a village. Despite the fact the sands were calming, he almost missed it. Makheb pulled the reins of his serpenti, redirecting it, and the beast moved towards the desert town in the distance. As he drew closer, he saw an isolated cluster of buildings and huts. There was activity in the village, and Makheb rode un-fearfully towards it.

He realized it was an Osa'harian settlement. Makheb wondered how they survived alone in the desert, under these conditions. He rode in, the serpenti underneath him irritable. He needed water for his mount, and the bottom of his own flask had been dry for some time.

Once Makheb's serpenti saw the water hole in the middle of the village, its motivation increased. The two entered the town; it had no gates or walls.

A few buildings were in the center. The streets of the town were simple, yet wide enough to conduct business. Makheb stopped his serpenti in the town square, and the villagers stared in awe. He looked around from atop his beast at the Osa'harian traders who occupied this village. Only their kind would live this far into the unknown. The Osa'har followed only the rules of their religion—which was Ramunak.

Makheb saw there were several traders going about their daily routines throughout the streets. Tents of goods were filled, and merchants and buyers bartered with one another in the strange desert dialect of the Osa'har. Across the village, Makheb could make out large shipments of mined metals being purchased. On the east side of the village, a small group of human slaves were strung and chained together.

The business in the Endlands was much different than the business conducted in Nador. In the human empire, people traded not only for need, but for their own greed, as well. In the Endlands, trade was for a greater purpose. These Osa'harians bartered for the simple, common goal—to survive another day under the sweltering sun and vengeful sands of the Endlands—and to serve the will of their lord, Ramunak.

The serpenti's scales flexed and pushed, the villagers making way for the large beast. It found the water hole, still and stagnant, and drank from it. It whipped its tongue, lapping up the mucky water. Then it spit water onto its dry and burnt scales. The Endlands were no place for a serpenti. Makheb was surprised it had survived this long.

After the beast finished drinking, Makheb kicked its sides. The beast tightened and released as it pushed on through the village. He passed a long corridor of mud-brick buildings on his right, and tents, which flapped in the wind, to his left. Despite the winds, the smell of the air that surrounded the village was stale.

Makheb passed through the center of the village and noticed more workers and laborers occupied the streets. They came from under their tents and from the darkness of their buildings. The Osa'har stared at him strangely.

The traders and merchants, peasants and workers were crowding around Makheb and his serpenti. They were careful not to get in the way of the giant snake, but were still dangerously close. The serpenti had an urge to reach out and attack one, but it was not sure if its rider would punish it.

Quick jabbers and broken dialect raced through the village. The Osa'har muttered inaudible commands in their native tongue. Makheb was not the least bit worried, though; he knew he could handle it if they turned on him. He was cautious, but decided that the Osa'harian villagers were of no true threat.

Makheb was not prepared for what came next.

Hundreds of villagers lined the streets, each dressed in long robes, their distorted faces staring up at Makheb.

In a single fluid motion, the Osa'har fell to their knees, showing homage and praise to the mounted Makheb.

They chanted, "RAAAAMMUNAAK . . . RAAAAMMUNAAAK . . . RAAAAMMUNAAK . . . RAAAAMMUNAAAK!"

The Osa'harians repeated their worship, over and over again. They bowed to Makheb. They bowed to whom they believed was their god-ruler. They did not understand who was under the veil; they only assumed it was their ruler. Hundreds of the savages humbled themselves to the presence of Makheb—praising who they believed was Ramunak.

They sustained their mantra as Makheb rode his serpenti out of the village. They continued on, until he covered some distance and could no longer hear their voices.

In Baalek, deep within the reaches of the horrid Endlands, the city was in uproar. A strange, mystical aura had surrounded the city, and the residents wanted bloodshed. They gathered in masses.

Gorgots and Tranaks jeered.

Various other species shouted.

The Bloodpaws stood around the temple base, armed and growling at the chaos, keeping relative order. Their sharp axes, which were extremely long, were held at the ready.

In the back of the crowd stood the humans. They had long been taken from their homes and had long since changed. Now, only expressionless looks were upon their faces. They would have preferred to stay in their huts, but the sacrifices were mandatory.

Many others stood near the humans. The Osa'har gathered in large groups, hands raised to the sky, giving praise to their deity. Ritualistic verses were recited in unison, monotone, yet distinctive. They joined all the other beasts in a collective of pagan celebration. If there was only one thing that the desert dwelling races had in common, it was their lust for blood and carnage.

Then, Ramunak appeared high atop the pyramid. Taius stood next to his side. Six high priests, deformed and wicked, stood behind the pair and twenty Bloodpaws guarded them. Upon Ramunak's entrance, atop the flat top of the pyramid, the crowd below cheered and called his name.

A strange yellow light swirled around Baalek. It flew like a bird over the dirty streets, up around the pyramid, and then high in the air. Ramunak held his hands high and the light became stationary. Ramunak's robes danced with glee. They twisted and swirled in all directions, feeding on his energy.

The crowd chanted, "Ra-mu-nak! Ra-mu-nak! Ra-mu-nak!"

Their god-emperor lowered his hands.

Taius nodded at a Bloodpaw sergeant, who barked orders at his men. On the ground, between the crowds of beasts and the stationed guards, nearly two hundred men were led in chains. The crowd spat on them and the Bloodpaws laughed hysterically, their voices high-pitched and sinister. They heckled with sadistic intent, anxiously scratching their cleaving paws on the firm sandstone beneath them.

Then, halfway up the pyramid steps, at one of the many closed entrances, the door opened and sixty women, both old and young, were led out. They were petrified. They begged for their husbands, brothers and fathers below for help.

The men had been brought to watch.

Taius grinned under his helmet. He spoke, "This shall motivate the men to fight."

Ramunak nodded.

27

The night was late and the storms still approached from the south. Fayorn and Gromulus hugged again, perhaps for the last time, and each went to their separate rooms. They would both sleep deeply, completely unaware for the moment of the troubles that stormed both above and within Nador. Instead, all of Whelmore slept peacefully.

The next day, two boys stood at the gates of Whelmore. They had watched Gromulus and Lorylle leave on their Aronian horse, before the sun rose. No grand exits and no emotional goodbyes. Gromulus simply waved as the two boys who stood guard watched on, curious. Gromulus and Lorylle headed east. Fayorn's men had filled his saddlebags full and informed him of the best way through the forest. The two now headed towards Chybum, to gather more supplies and a little much-needed information, and seek a broken trail that supposedly would lead them through Denok Forest.

Gromulus was skeptical.

As the sun reached the highest point in the sky, the two boys were growing bored. They took their guard duty serious, and would never leave their post, yet they were bored, just the same. Instead, they found interesting games to play, such as throwing stones at nearby rabbits and carving objects out of small pieces of servium stone. One of the boys, Farak, had nearly finished his. It looked like a small creature. He showed it to his friend.

Dhar asked, "What . . . is that?"

Farak replied, "It is a Troxen, dummy. Can you not tell?"

"That is not what a Troxen looks like."

"How do you know what one looks like? You have never seen one."

"Yes, but my father fought them a long time ago. He described them to

179

me. That," he said, pointing confidently, "is not a Troxen."

The boys continued arguing, mostly out of boredom, and did not notice the approaching riders. Four mounted Nadorian soldiers rode up and stopped. Instantly, the boys took notice. The archers were dining; therefore the sentry towers were vacant, leaving the responsibility to only the boys.

Usar, a burly centurion who appeared to be about forty years of age, led the other three. His steed snorted as he looked at the small town of Whelmore. He grunted himself, unimpressed, and then looked at the two boys. They were intimidated, as they should have been. Nadorian soldiers were menacing. The sergeant spoke, "Boys . . . move aside. We are entering your town."

The boys looked curiously at one another. Farak, replied, "Why?"

Usar growled as he answered, "Because I say so, mongrel. Do not question me! We seek a fugitive and he is in your town."

The boy spoke again, "We have no fugitives here."

"Where is the traitor?" Usar looked around, and then added bluntly, "And do not lie to me."

Farak stepped closer to the horse. "I am not sure of whom you speak. Whelmore sees no visitors. I cannot remember the last time we had company here."

Usar looked down at him. Anger flashed in his eyes. "Come closer, boy."

Farak stepped even nearer, now at the soldier's right side. He trembled with fear. His pale face and wide, brown eyes stared up at the centurion.

Usar stated bluntly, "I shall ask only one more time—where is Consul Veris?"

The boy said, "Perhaps you are at the wrong town. Let me fetch Fayorn, he leads the militia here."

One of the Nadorian soldiers laughed, murmuring, "*Ha*, militia," under his breath. The centurion, Usar, turned his eyes back to the youth. Suddenly, he pulled a spear from its harness, and in a flash, impaled the boy in the chest. Farak gurgled and his body shook. The centurion withdrew the spear and the youth fell to the ground—dead.

Angrily, Usar now looked at the remaining youth, Dhar. Tears welled up in the boy's eyes, having just watched his best friend die. The boy trembled, his breathing heavy.

The soldier spoke, "You are next. Open the gate or I will take your life, as well. We are here by imperial order and I have no time for peasants, barbarians . . . or Aronians."

The boy looked up at the mounted Nadorian soldier, and muttered something under his breath. Then, young Dhar turned towards the gate. Instead of opening it, however, the boy stepped to the side and rang a small bell. It clanged loudly, warning the people within the town, and alerting the archers to take to the walls.

The soldier kicked at his horse, and closed the distance. And like the other, Usar stabbed with his spear, catching the boy directly in the neck. His men laughed as he did so.

At once an arrow hit the centurion in the leg. It stuck deep. Usar screamed. He pulled heavily on the reins of his horse, causing it to rear up. Another arrow slammed into his arm, just underneath the protective layering of his armor. The third arrow found its mark, hitting the soldier squarely in the throat. The horse threw its rider and the elite Nadorian officer fell to the ground, dead.

Quickly, the three other riders galloped away. The legionaries rode over a nearby bluff and disappeared out of sight.

The archer, who had shot the soldier, began yelling, "We are under attack! We are under attack!"

Jairus, the most senior man in the militia, ran from a nearby shop. He sprinted towards the front gate, joined by his friend and fellow militiaman, Baronius. Jairus hollered up at the archer tower, "Denoktorn? How many?"

The archer responded, "No—soldiers."

Jairus froze, staring at the man in disbelief.

Jairus and Baronius approached the front gate, turned the wheel that opened it, and looked at the three bodies. Jairus turned back to the archer tower. "Soldiers did this? Nadorian soldiers? How is this possible?" He was disgusted. Farak and Dhar were mere boys.

The archer nodded his affirmation. The two militiamen hurried to pull the boys inside the gate as other men secured them.

The gate will only slow them, thought Jairus. *It will not hold out imperial soldiers. Where is Fayorn?*

Immediately, Jairus began barking orders to the men. He was a natural leader. "More archers to the front towers. Move it! Form a line there. Prepare the northern gate and the horses, on the chance we need to take the women and children out of here."

Baronius asked, "Are there more? Why would they do this? We are a Nadorian town. Why would they kill innocent boys?" He was utterly confused and scared. He leaned Farak's lifeless body gently against a bundle of hay as the boy's mother came rushing forward, screaming. Baronius stepped back, himself crying. His hands shook.

However, his training quickly came to him and Baronius ran towards the sparring center. He rushed inside and was met by Kor and Thriden, who were gathering their weapons. Baronius grabbed a spear and a shield from the wall, and then attached a short sword at his hip.

"Where is Fayorn?" shouted Baronius.

"I do not know," replied Kor hastily, grabbing more arrows and rushing outside to the madness.

Thriden followed him, armed with his own sword and spear. "You two get into position and I will find Fayorn."

He ran out the door.

Baronius then raced back outside, following Kor to the front of the town and seeing Thriden bound towards Fayorn's home. Baronius sprinted back to the center of the town, where many had gathered. A few women, young boys and elderly men held weapons. Their weaponry was crude and the villagers were panicked.

Baronius ran past the terrified residents.

Chaos shrouded the town of Whelmore. Women screamed, men shouted and children cried as they prepared for the attack. This was not a Denoktorn raid. The people had grown accustomed to the forest raiders. This was more sinister. The empire, which was supposed to protect them, had just slaughtered two young boys.

The entire town felt *it* coming. A storm of Nador's wrath was about to crash into them as the purple tempest watched from the distance, threatening to overtake. The people of Whelmore felt the depravity of the situation. They instinctually knew this was going to be bad. Men scrambled up ladders into the two guard towers and stood atop walls, armed with bows. Of the thirty-nine in Fayorn's militia, thirty-seven had currently positioned themselves inside Whelmore's meager walls. All the other men of the village stood guard around the women and children.

They waited.

Only Thriden and Fayorn were not present.

Baronius stood thirty paces shy of the flimsy gate. His breathing was heavy and he forced himself to relax, for that was what Fayorn had taught him. Next to him was Jairus, sword in hand. Kor and Neres were to their right, another fifty paces, and had positioned themselves atop a large bale of hay. They held their bows out and their arrows nocked.

Vallek quickly approached Jairus and Baronius, his eyes blinking with anticipation.

Had the men not had a job to do, perhaps they would have succumbed to their fears. However, the responsibility bestowed upon them as protectors of the town did not warrant the young men the opportunity to crumble. Instead, the proud Aronian youths stood their ground, waiting for the attack. Whelmore was now chaotic. Panic enveloped the town. Bells rang, summoning the militia and warning the people. Residents gathered in the middle of the town while the militiamen took their positions. Everyone was armed, including the women and young children. People ran and shouted. Pandemonium was everywhere.

Thriden bound into Fayorn's home without knocking. Kali gasped at the sudden intrusion, her hands held out in question, "What is going on outside?"

Thriden panted for a moment, gasping for breath. "We . . . we are under attack. I need to find Fayorn."

"Denoktorn?"

"No—soldiers. They killed Farak and Dhar outside the gates. They are dead, Kali. Dead!"

Fayorn's wife gasped. Tears filled her eyes. She had known the boys. Kali was friends with their mothers, who no doubt, right now, were devastated.

Thriden repeated, "I need to find Fayorn. Where is he?"

183

Kali shook her head and replied, "In the second bedroom. I will get him."

Thriden nodded and stayed in the doorway.

Kali rushed up the stairs and into the bedroom. Fayorn was not there. She then ran into the second bedroom, where Gromulus and Lorylle had spent the evening, and saw her husband. Her eyes were still flooded with tears. She shook and her breathing was heavy.

In front of Kali, kneeled at the edge of the bed, was Fayorn. His long hair fell past his shoulders and hid his face. His back was to her and his head was down.

"My love—Whelmore is under attack," she cried out.

No response.

"Fayorn! What is wrong with you?" asked Kali, terrified. She walked into the room and looked over her husband's shoulder. The Sword of Ellsar rested on the bed, and Fayorn kneeled in front of it. Kali quickly brought her hand up to her face, covering her open mouth. She tried stifling her scream.

Kali and Fayorn had been married for almost ten years. Much of that time, Fayorn had been involved in the affairs of the southern hemisphere while she resided far north with her people, in Aronia. She knew of her husband's responsibilities and the legends about the man. She knew he was the chosen man to hold the Sword of Ellsar. She knew none thus far had matched his talents. She knew all of this and accepted it as any noble Aronian soldier's wife would. She never questioned it. However, Kali had never really understood, nor seen, what Antiok did to Fayorn. She did not understand the sword's affect on her partner. She placed a gentle hand on her husband's shoulder.

She could feel Antiok's presence.

"My dear, what is happening?" she almost whispered. "What is wrong with you?" Tears dripped off her delicate cheekbones.

Fayorn, still kneeling, looked up at his beautiful wife. His eyes were flooded with tears and he was sobbing himself. His hands rested in front of him, on the bed's edge, daring not to touch the sword. "Kali . . . I . . . cannot . . . handle it," said Fayorn, his voice barely above a whisper.

Kali tilted her head. She heard the bells clanging loudly outside. She heard men yell and women gasp. She turned back, looking down at Fayorn. This was not how her husband would react. She spoke up, her voice harsher this time, "Darling, Whelmore is under attack. Nadorian soldiers came," she paused, not wanting to think about it, "and killed poor Dhar and Farak. They were only doing their jobs—" she wept. Then, Kali began to cry hysterically as she heard the commotion grow louder outside as her husband kneeled in front of her, unable or unwilling to move.

Fayorn only looked up at his wife. His soft eyes pleaded with her, although he said nothing. He could only stare.

Kali continued, in a panic because of her husband's lack of response. "I do not know what is wrong with you, but we are in trouble here. We need you . . . I need you."

Fayorn only shook his head. Back and forth, back and forth. He muttered, "It cannot be. I cannot do this again."

Then Fayorn screamed.

"Do what? Fayorn . . . your men need your help. Soldiers are going to ravage this town." Kali was panicked and utterly confused. Her husband was frozen.

He responded, "The sword . . . Antiok . . . it is too much." He gasped for breath.

Kali leaned in closer, whispering in his ear. "I do not understand your burdens, or your fears, but you have to get up."

Fayorn looked back at her, lost. Tears streamed down his cheeks.

She continued whispering, "We only have a chance if you help."

He stared.

"Fayorn, your people need you!"

His eyes were helpless. All emotion dying within him.

She finished, "Fayorn . . . I love you so very much!"

He blinked. His eyes dried. The warrior's hands reached out, grasping the sword. A surge went through Fayorn's body as he convulsed, throwing his head back. He screamed again. This time it echoed throughout the house. It was a sound Kali hoped she would never have to hear again.

She took an involuntary step backwards. Her eyes were wide with anticipation.

Fayorn stood up. He was different.

"Now . . . fight," she whispered.

He looked at Kali, brushed her arm with his hand, and strode past her. Antiok was beaming.

He walked past Thriden and into the street. He saw his town burning around him. He heard his people's cries.

Thriden stumbled through his words, chasing after him. "Wh . . . what is h . . . happening?"

Fayorn did not respond. Instead, he nodded to Kali, who had just run out the doorway, urging her towards Thriden. "Get her out of here! Get everyone out of here," the warlord commanded. His voice was fierce, anger on his face.

Thriden grabbed Kali's hand and began to run off. He hesitated. Turning towards Fayorn, he questioned, "Where are you going?"

Fayorn looked to his apprentice. "To kill every last one of them."

ᕙᕦᕙᕦ

"Ya'h know Kelnum, if I may say something?"

"Go on, Tornach."

"I have not had such a conversation with anyone for quite some time. I have been traveling . . . lost, for the past few years. I have not found anyone whom I could talk with as I have talked ta ya'h . . . five or six long years. Have ya'h any friends, Kelnum?"

"Well, I have had friends all throughout my life. I remember playing childhood games with friends. I remember playing on the trodding field in my school years . . . I had many friends in those days. But I think you have more of a point to what you are saying, Tornach. What is it?"

Tornach looked around—the land more rural, more populated, as they came closer to Chybum.

"My point is . . . that I have nobody. When we reach Chybum, I still will have no one. One thing that troubles my life so, is that I have no friends anymore. I had a group of boys that I hung around as a child, but we eventually all parted ways. Kelnum, my best friends were soldiers I fought with in the wars, they became like family to me."

186

"Yes, Tornach, I can tell the past has been on your mind."

"*Ha,* ya'h are right. Well, they were family. Gromulus and I were inseparable. We were legends. We trained men ta be warriors, capable enough ta take on Ungorans. Grom and Fayorn and I . . . Kelnum, we were best friends. Through all the blood and death, we stuck together. It is odd . . . through all that pain, we found happiness. I am sure ya'h can relate."

"I do know exactly how you feel. The bonds we form in times of war are—" Kelnum stopped, rethinking his words, "—like brotherhood." He rethought his own past.

"*Hm,*" was the only answer that came from Tornach's mouth.

The two sat, each pondering his own path, the way things were in times of war. The pain of seeing a friend die. Holding a man while he takes his last breath. Promising to tell his wife and child that he will always love them. The pain that each man held on his shoulders, weighed both of them down.

The bonds that were formed.

The city of Chybum was now straight ahead. Tornach's eyes glimmered in the afternoon sun and a slight smile curved upon his face—a sign of hope.

Jairus was now standing next to Vallek and Baronius, as well as a few older men, in the center of Whelmore. They were fifty paces from the gate. All was quiet. Jairus wiped a bead of sweat from his brow. Baronius shifted his shield, making it more comfortable.

Jairus stood at the front, and asked again, "Where is Fayorn?"

Before anyone could reply, a militiaman shouted from a sentry tower. Everyone stopped talking and looked over the low gates of Whelmore. Four hundred paces from the town was the bluff where the three soldiers had fled. Now, many rode towards the gate.

The legionaries had returned. With them, they brought death.

One hundred well trained, fully armored, and mounted Nadorian soldiers rode to the top of the bluff. Shields on one arm and sharp spears held in the opposite hand, they were dressed for battle. Their armor was bulky and they wore their battle helmets. Instead of colorful plumes, the tops had metal spikes, just like the infantry that Tornach and Kelnum had seen marching on the road to Chybum.

They charged on their massive steeds.

"*Oh,* no!" exclaimed a woman standing near Jairus.

Jairus trembled. He could hardly hold his sword steady.

The whole town of Whelmore could only watch in horror as the hundred legionaries, led by the vicious General Thad, raced towards Whelmore. A cloud of dust kicked up behind the mob as they appraoched.

Terror held over the town as the militia and the rest of the citizens braced for the attack.

It came quickly.

Once the riders were close enough, the archers in the towers and on the walls began unleashing their fury. Dozens of arrows were fired, over and over again. However, because of the thick Nadorian armor, most bounced off harmlessly. Three soldiers went down. Six horses were hit, throwing their riders.

Twenty legionaries raced their steeds headfirst into the gate, slamming into it and breaking through with ease. The fragile wood splintered as the gates exploded open. The horses were wide-eyed and the soldiers enraged.

I knew it, thought Jairus as he readied himself. *It did not even slow them. What chance do we stand against soldiers?* The young man was terrified.

Neres shot one of the legionaries in the neck. The blonde youth had begun firing the moment the soldiers came bursting through the gates. He nocked another arrow and it found its target in a horse's flank. The soldier fell off and was crushed under the beast's weight. The man screamed in agony. Kor, standing next to Neres, fired simultaneously.

Even more soldiers burst through the wide-open gates. Twenty to a side, they attached ropes around the posts, which held up the archer towers, and pulled. Both towers fell, crashing to the ground. Men were hurled everywhere. Three were crushed. Others were severely injured. They moaned in agony.

The soldiers then turned their fury on the standing militia. Jairus, Baronius, Vallek and other men stood between multitudes of highly trained soldiers and the majority of Whelmore's frightened residents. They were hand-picked by Thad, the best and most seasoned of his ranks—the odds were impossible. The Whelmore militia had no chance. They had heart, but lacked the armor and skill to face such a force. They knew it in their hearts, but remarkably, kept their courage.

The militia spread out as the first wave of mounted soldiers charged at them.

"Steady boys!" shouted Jairus. "Wait for them."

The soldiers' horses smashed into the awaiting militiamen. Baronius thrust his spear, catching one of them below his chest piece. He heaved his attacker off the horse. He withdrew his spear. The young man then stepped forward, smashing his shield into the side of one of the horses, and forced its rider from it. He impaled that one in the throat. Baronius fought, all the while screaming in anger.

Jairus spun out of the way of one horse and slashed at the next. The horse reared up and its rider fell to the ground. Unfortunately, the legionary was not hurt. The man stood up, drawing his own blade. The two clashed swords.

Baronius stabbed at another group of riders, taking two from their saddles without hesitation. Fayorn's training had done the young men well, thus far. He parried with another rider with whom Vallek had dismounted.

Ten of the riders rode around the front line, towards the terrified villagers who were huddled together. They ruthlessly rode into them, slashing and stabbing at the innocent people. More militiamen smashed into them, screaming their battle cries throughout the streets.

Even more soldiers on horseback rode into town, lighting torches. They began to toss them into storefronts. The people of Whelmore fought back in primal rage and the slaughter was underway.

The melee was insane. The legionaries showed no mercy. They maimed men. They slew women and clubbed children. Everyone was fighting to the death.

Kor leapt over a bale of hay and confronted two soldiers who were on foot. He fought the two, simultaneously. He was fast, and his training was paying off.

Jairus and Vallek stood shoulder to shoulder, thrusting at another group of soldiers. They stood together, like brothers, defending the merciless raid.

Baronius ran across the plaza, attempting to save a child. He cast into a horse and rider, and all three fell to the ground. He quickly got to his feet and dodged as another soldier attacked. Baronius stepped forward, fuming with rage, and impaled the man. The legionary coughed twice and died as Baronius withdrew the spear. Blood splattered across his face as he did so. He stood for a moment, over his victim, in shock.

Killing Denoktorn was different than killing soldiers. Denoktorn were easier. Denoktorn were less human. Baronius felt a moment of remorse, but then remembered quickly that the soldiers were killing innocent people without cause. He was Aronian and would fight for his people. He would die for them if need be. As his own father had, and as his master would expect. Baronius raced forward, meeting another who was lighting a torch.

Baronius stuck him in the back and kept moving.

General Thad sat atop his horse, behind his men, just inside the gates of Whelmore. He dismounted and drew his sword. His guards, twelve of them, held their spears firmly, standing shoulder to shoulder. These men were not cavalry by trade. Fighting side-by-side, on foot, was more to their advantage. Another column formed in front of Thad's bodyguards, twenty-five in all, including the general. Twenty more soldiers were running rampant within Whelmore's insides, causing chaos.

It was a good distraction and a solid tactic. More legionaries took to the walls, fighting the Aronians who fired at them. Five were left outside to guard the horses, and chase down any who escaped. Some of his men had fallen, but that did not concern the general.

He wanted the glory of killing the senator himself.

He wanted to kill Consul Veris.

A sinister smile rested upon Thad's face. The man was brutal and enjoyed killing. He faced two men and sparred with them. The older Aronian militiamen had no chance. Thad cut them both down without hesitation. He looked upon the town as his men destroyed it. Buildings began to burn. Screams echoed Whelmore's streets. Men, women and children scurried as his soldiers laughed, taunted and killed.

Thad approached another man, this one elderly and clutching a child. He slashed at the two, slaying them easily. He stood up straight, surveying his surroundings. Thad snapped his wrist, flinging the fresh blood from his sword's blade.

Corbidon walked up behind him. In his hand was his own sword. It was short and thin and straight. Unlike Nadorian soldiers, Corbidon was lightly armored and carried no shield. Only his blade. He stepped up next to Thad.

Thad said, "You may join if you like. I hear your kind enjoy a good sacrifice. . . . Take as much blood as you desire."

Corbidon nodded and entered the madness.

Kor and Neres were fighting furiously at this point. Kor used his spear and was defending as Neres fired arrow after merciless arrow at the enemy. His aim was sure as he brought down another soldier. Neres yelled out to Kor, "We cannot win this."

"Keep fighting," was Kor's response.

"Where is Fayorn?" Neres yelled back.

Across the street, Thriden and Kali ran from an alleyway. Kali joined the frightened people who were huddled together. Thriden entered the fight. Jairus and Thriden began fighting, back to back. They were both excellent swordsmen, the best of the militia, and fought furiously to defend Whelmore. Jairus stabbed his sword underneath a legionary's armor, causing the soldier to gasp.

"We are dead," exclaimed Thriden, surveying the massacre.

Jairus agreed. "We have to get the women and children out of here."

Thriden nodded and the two killed another legionary. They pushed back from the battle, to regroup and protect the innocent. The people were panicked, soldiers all around them.

Thriden stood in front of the mob, with his sword, fending off attacks. He surpassed his training, defending against the bloodbath—as did every man.

Jairus was doing the same; he slashed at another soldier, but missed. A man next to him helped as the two finished off the Nadorian. Jairus then looked towards the front gate, where Thad stood.

"Look," gasped Jairus.

"Where is Fayorn?" asked Thriden.

Now, sixty paces away, Thad and his twenty-four seasoned soldiers marched smartly at them. This was their fight. Each man's shield protected the next, spears jettisoned from the impenetrable wall. The invincible phalanx closed the distance.

Kor and Neres joined from the side, having run down an alleyway. To protect their friends—to protect the people. Vallek approached from the left, and stood next to Thriden. Of the six, only Baronius was missing. He was closer to the gate now, only steps from the wall of soldiers. He stood bravely, knowing death was imminent.

Jairus, inspired by his friend's bravery, stepped forward a pace. He turned and looked at his friends. "We die protecting our people. *That* is the Aronian way!"

Thriden gritted his teeth, the warrior being born within him. "I am with you. For our god—for Aronia!"

They turned back just as the Nadorians were nearing Baronius. The militiaman was courageous, bracing his shield and staring down his own spear. "You may take my life, but I will take two of you with me," his teenage anger screaming out.

It was Vallek who saw it first. Behind the columns of legionaries, coming through the gate, was Fayorn. The swordsman raced atop a tan mare through the wide-open entrance of Whelmore, leading by a rope the horses of the five dead soldiers who he had just killed outside the town. He urged the steeds furiously through the open gate. Once inside, Fayorn pushed off his own horse, landed on his feet and stepped to the side as the other five beasts stampeded after the one on which he had ridden.

Unaware, they had no time to stop.

The horses' momentum was all that was needed. General Thad leapt out of the way as the six beasts stampeded past him. He watched in horror as they inadvertently crashed into the backs of his men. The legionaries were each in mid-turn as the horses fell upon them. Most were knocked down. Bones were broken. Soldiers screamed. The horses were confused and began to rear up.

They bucked and panicked.

They kicked.

The front column was forced to turn its attention away, as well. They stabbed wildly at the beasts, only adding to the problem. The horses went insane. Soldiers were scattered in the street, their lines broken. Behind them, Fayorn looked at his men who valiantly protected their own.

Jairus then understood. *Smart. He broke them up.*

Fayorn continued to view them from down the street.

Jairus was the first to run, yelling, "Now!" Twenty-five more men were not far behind. They ran forward, battle cries echoing.

Baronius was caught off guard. He was much closer to the disarray. Dust kicked up and men were shouting. He was confused. His instincts took over. Baronius madly stabbed at the nearest Nadorian. His spear stuck. He drew his sword and swiped at another. He then pushed with all his might, knocking both himself and a massive soldier to the ground. The soldier was skilled and flipped Baronius to his back. Baronius lifted his arm to stab with his sword, but the legionary grabbed his wrist and flung the youth's blade aside. He now sat atop Baronius and raised a dagger.

"NO!" screamed Jairus as he ran forward. He knew he would be too late.

The legionary looked down at his victim and grinned. Baronius, looking up from his back, took a breath.

Antiok pushed through the legionary's back and out his chest. The sword's tip was suddenly a finger length from the tip of Baronius' nose. He bellowed, pressing his head deeper into the dirt. Baronius looked up at Fayorn.

Antiok had gone through both the back and the front of the soldier's armor. It killed the man neatly. Its tip being near his face, Baronius could feel heat coming from the sword. It also seemed to cast a shallow, but distinct tone. For a moment, Baronius could not hear anything but the sound. It was in his head. It was a perfect pitch.

Then—silence.

He blinked once. Twice.

Fayorn pushed the soldier's body away and reached his arm down. Baronius took it and was on his feet quickly. He looked at Fayorn, shocked. The man held Antiok for the first time in five years. The mystical sword and the legendary warrior—reunited. Baronius felt the spiritual moment. It seemed to quiver through his body. He looked Fayorn in the eyes.

Without a word, Fayorn picked up Baronius' sword and handed it to the young man. Baronius took it, bowed his head to Fayorn in respect, and ran back into battle to help his friends.

Jairus, Thriden, Vallek, Neres, Kor and nine others smashed into the now unorganized Nadorian soldiers. They screamed like maniacs, thrashing wildly like cornered Denoktorn. Their primal instincts took over.

Fayorn then looked at the legionaries around him, and with Antiok, began executing them.

28

The day was brilliant, the skies blue over Aronia. Kedor secured the straps on his saddle and patted the brown and white stallion on the flanks. Dozens of feathers hung from its tail. The stallion's face and haunches had been painted by Niralyn, as was custom of Aronian wives.

Around Kedor, two hundred knights of Aronia were preparing themselves for travel in the same way.

The White Knights of Ellsar were legendary. Since Aronia's inception, the White Knights had been loyally protective of her borders. Only the best horsemen and warriors could serve. They rode swift steeds and carried sharp swords and deadly lances. The terrain of the highlands in Aronia suited their fast-paced fighting style. For years, the White Knights of Ellsar had protected Aronia from both Man and beast.

Kedor attached his shield to the horse's left side and his sword into a sheath under it. He carried one spear, and behind the saddle with his supplies, were three more. Each with a sharp point. Around him, his men were also dressing their horses. Along with the two hundred knights were another fifty men-at-arms. They would set up camp and escort wagons carrying the bulk of the supplies. Two hundred and fifty men in all were to travel to the border. Reports said another hundred Aronian foot soldiers would be ready upon their arrival. Three hundred and fifty defenders of the known world's last free kingdom would be ready if hostilities broke out with the Troxen. Kedor knew it was excessive, but the show of force was necessary. The Troxen had caused much damage to the kingdom years prior, and the display of power would be something that Trag-lak would respect.

Kedor looked up at his towering keep. Situated high in the Ellsa Mountains, the capital of Aronia was majestic. Its beauty still awed the king. The city rested in the base of two mountains, its walls thick. The buildings and the walls were made of servium stone, and glistened white like the mountains that surrounded them. The architecture was surreal and the streets clean. The residents went about their lives with smiles upon their faces, for life was good in Aronia. Crime was almost non-existent and the only security was to guard the city from enemies afar. Kedor stared at his magnificent Ellsar.

I would die for my kingdom . . . for my people, I would do anything.

Kedor was adjusting his stirrup when Niralyn touched him on the shoulder. He turned and said, "Do not worry, I shall not be gone long."

She only smiled, helping him secure his stirrup. Finally, she spoke, "Today, I feel sad."

Kedor smiled back. "My queen, we have been apart for much longer. It will be but less than two weeks." His attitude was positive, upbeat. It had to be. He had to lead by example.

"Yes, my love, I know this. In my heart, I know you will return. Yet still, I cannot rid my heart of sorrow today."

Kedor leaned close to his wife and whispered, "There is one thing you must always remember."

Her glassy eyes, now filled with tears, gazed into his.

He leaned in closer. "Goodness *will* prevail."

"My love, it is hard to have faith in a world where wickedness lurks in every corner."

Kedor pulled back. "Yes, but it is important to have faith."

Niralyn said, "I know. I do. I only worry for the safety of my husband, and his valiant knights. I hope this is not a trap."

"We are well-prepared if it is."

"I know. Your men would follow you to the death." She turned, looking at the knights of Ellsar, "Are you going to say anything to them?"

Kedor looked around. His men were saying their farewells to their loved ones and mounting their horses. "No, my love, that will not be necessary. They do this not for me. They do this for themselves—for their kingdom, and for their families. They need no words from me to encourge them."

❦❦❦❦❦

Jairus ordered the militiamen back towards the large group of villagers that huddled together in the middle of the street. They were fighting off soldiers who laughed as they tore at women's clothing and cut into men. Baronius and Vallek raced to them once more.

Kor and Neres ran to the side, positioning themselves to fire their arrows. They shot at the soldiers who were now climbing down from the walls to join their fellow comrades. Nine Aronian men climbed from the walls in pursuit. They joined Jairus and Thriden as they began feuding with the soldiers.

Fayorn was horrified. He had nearly forgotten the raw impiety of war. Despite his efforts, Whelmore was doomed and he knew it. He yelled for his men to get the residents out. Fayorn had to abandon his home, and that very fact devastated the man.

Then, he saw Thad.

The general was standing against a wall, looking down at a fallen woman. She was old and had a gash in her side, no doubt dying. She pleaded to the general to end her misery. She did not fear death, but begged for it. Thad only laughed and walked away.

Fayorn knew this was the man he needed to kill. Thad was responsible for his peoples' deaths and his town's destruction. Enraged, Fayorn strode rapidly through the melee, towards the general. He smashed his fist into one soldier's nose, downing him, and severed another's arm. He pushed past a third, nearing Thad. The general looked at him oddly, mesmerized.

Fayorn screamed, "FIGHT ME!"

Thad spit on the ground and raised his own sword.

The militia was in trouble. The legionaries had gathered themselves back in order and were now angry. They had lost men and hungered for revenge. The young militiamen who fought them gathered children and women and placed them on the backs of horses. More died and the youths realized they were all facing annihilation.

"Get them out of here," yelled Thriden in panic as he fought with yet another soldier. His face was bruised and his body was battered. He was wearing down. "Get everyone out of Whelmore. They have a better chance outside the walls."

Jairus nodded in agreement while boosting a woman and her son onto a frightened horse. A legionary stabbed at the beast and it bucked off the two. Jairus screamed. He charged the man—hate coursing through him.

197

He nearly took off the man's arm as he chopped at the soldier who held his hands up in defense while falling.

They all kept fighting.

Hand-to-hand, to the death.

The mass of soldiers and militia blocked any exit. Jairus hollered at Kor and Baronius. "We have to get everyone out of here. We have to save them."

Baronius nodded, looking at the fight before him. He turned to his people, some on horseback and most on foot.

"Follow me!"

He then did something radical. Baronius raised his massive shield, lowered his head, and charged. He screamed as he plowed through the soldiers. His momentum and rage scattered the troops, creating a pathway through the madness.

Jairus thought to himself, *That is why we call him the bull.* He shouted for the people to follow. They did.

Now, Whelmore's residents were beginning to escape the town. The first soldiers who stormed into Whelmore were now running freely through the streets. They blocked the northern gate, preventing exit from it. However, Fayorn's diversion had created opportunity to escape through the southern gate from which the soldiers had come.

Flocks of Aronians ran out.

Finally, the remaining survivors of Whelmore had escaped the town. They rushed out, both on horseback and foot, the militiamen aiding in their escape. Only Fayorn's younger students stayed. They stood at the entrance of town, their people fleeing behind and the soldier's toppling their homes before them. The legionaries did not pursue. Instead, they searched homes, looking for their objective—Consul Veris. They looted and pillaged as they did so.

Fayorn was staring at Thad, ready to kill him.

Then, Corbidon stepped out. He walked between the Nadorian General and Fayorn, holding his sword out in challenge. Fayorn stepped forward and the two clashed swords. It was remarkable. They twisted and spun, blocking and defending. Corbidon was good, keeping pace with the

Aronian. They watched on as a group of soldiers noticed.

Observing the clash, Thad shouted to his men, "Take his head."

The five rushed forward, swords swinging.

Now Fayorn was engaged with six. He swung at the legionaries rapidly, yelling wildly in the process. One went down. Another three soldiers joined the battle.

From the gates, Jairus saw Fayorn was alone. He yelled to his comrades, "Fayorn is in trouble!" All six ran back into the town's limits. They reached the fight, slamming into the Nadorian elites viciously.

Jairus yelled, "Fayorn, the people are safe. Let us get out of here while we still can."

Fayorn did not respond. He continued fighting.

The vivid display of his swordsmanship captivated his favored students. They saw in him, for the first time with their own eyes, the man the stories had only tried to make him out to be. He was not simply the boys' mentor and teacher anymore. He was not the humble Fayorn whom they thought they knew. He was beyond that—beyond anything the old war stories could have described of him. Fayorn was a true master of combat—not a flaw in his movement. He truly was the rightful recipient of the Sword of Ellsar—the chosen bearer of Antiok.

Jairus then realized what Fayorn was doing. The Aronian was committing himself to death. His wife and fellow Aronians were safe, and all the legendary swordsman could do was kill as many legionaries as possible. Jairus bellowed again, "Fayorn, we have to leave!"

Fayorn kept fighting. He slashed at two more soldiers and continued sparring with Corbidon. The desert dweller was fast and answered back.

Clink. Clink.

More soldiers came running. They surrounded Fayorn and his men.

Fayorn looked around. His own death did not bother him. He was gladly committing himself to that fate. However, it was his men, his favorite in the militia who caused him hesitation. They were loyal, as Aronians should be, and guilt instantly stabbed at Fayorn. *They are too young for this. I cannot be responsible for their deaths.*

Behind Corbidon stood Thad. He laughed at Fayorn's attempt at his life. He ordered his men, "Kill these last few . . . and find Consul Veris! I want his head!"

Fayorn stepped low, blocked a blow and pushed all his weight into Corbidon. Off balance, the Dakari swordsman stumbled into an assortment of stacked pottery. Fayorn turned and killed another legionary. Even more soldiers came to the aid of their general.

It was Thriden who acted. He grabbed a fallen torch from one of the dead soldier's hands. Thriden flung it into a stack of hay and it caught quickly. The fire then caught the overhang of a nearby shop and it, too, was ablaze. The soldiers backed up, continuing their taunts.

"We need to leave," pleaded Jairus.

Fayorn still kept fighting. He screamed, smashing into a soldier, bringing them both to the ground.

Kor hollered to Jairus, "He will not come. What do we do?"

Jairus had a decision to make. He stepped up behind Fayorn, grabbing the man. Baronius and Neres followed his lead, and the three pulled the swordsman away from the fight.

Fayorn began screaming. His rage filled the smoldering streets of Whelmore. He stared at Thad, who hid behind his men. "Fight me, you coward!"

An emptiness brought about by the cluster of emotions Antiok fed to him was overwhelming. "I will take all of your lives!" Fayorn continued screaming, displaying his wrath to the opposing soldiers.

In that moment, something bizarre happened. Fayorn's rage had finally become alive as the hilt of Antiok glowed blue. Several of the fighting soldiers were blinded for a moment. But when they could see again, they saw Fayorn's eyes.

His eyes matched the glowing sapphire of Antiok.

The two had become one again.

The soldiers took two steps back, not wanting any part of this man's rage. They looked at one other, confused. Fayorn did not relent in his attempts. He shook off his men who held him back. He closed the distance and the soldiers backed themselves even more. Fayorn's blue eyes pierced through every one of them. Fear riddled the legionaries—these hand-picked veterans.

Despite his screams, the militiamen finally managed to pull Fayorn away from the soldiers and out of Whelmore.

Distraught and enraged, Fayorn left his home.

Corbidon, the master Dakari warrior, watched with a simple grin as his match in swordsmanship was taken away from the battlefield. He knew this was just a taste of things to come—that he would get his chance to duel with the man another day. He was sure they would meet again.

❧❧❧❧❧❧

The swordsman's loyal students led him far enough away from the burning town. They headed east, away from the current threat. Fayorn forced himself from their grasp and dropped to his knees, the tall grass of the northern steppes concealing him from the enemy's sight entirely. The militiamen followed suit in the drop, but that is not why he collapsed to the soil.

Fayorn's body was shaking with lunacy, and he stared at the ground, unwilling to answer his men as they tried to get his attention. His mind was elsewhere, consumed by Antiok.

"Fayorn," Jairus said to him. "We have to keep moving. I know this is hard. It is for all of us. But there is no time for that right now."

The Aronian swordsman still did not reply.

Jairus put his hand on Fayorn's shoulder. "We have to go," he added softly. "The others have been sent on their way. . . . Kali will be worried about you."

"Kali. . . ." Fayorn said finally.

Her name got his attention.

"Come, sir," Neres started. "We will take you to her. All the others are regrouping over that hill. They will be awaiting your guidance."

Jairus then said, "Do not fade on us now. The others need you."

Fayorn looked at his men with compassion. They all gazed at him, eagerly waiting for him to say something.

A brief time of silence passed by, and the Aronian slowly began to calm down, gathering his wits once again. His eyes gradually ceased to glow blue, as did Antiok. Both flickered a few more times, gradually dimming until the light at last vanished. All that remained around his eyes were the tears of anguish, pouring forth the fear and anger of what had just taken place. The attack had caught everyone by surprise, and only now were they all able to think rationally about what had happened.

Whelmore was in shambles. The wake of the imperial army had proven its might. All was lost from the Nadorian onslaught but the lives of the few survivors. Even that did not seem like much amidst the fist of power that was just struck unto them.

Their lives had changed forever.

Despair engulfed Nador as the storms covered the southern regions, promising to overtake the entire empire shortly. They increased in size and fury, spreading their ashen plague ever northward. The citizens were wary, their fates in the hands of those who deceived them. Blindly, they began to call for the death of Consul Veris—the Senate's plan coming to fruition.

Fayorn and his people hurried east, from Whelmore, unsure of their destination. Attempting to flee the brutal and vicious General Thad, the Aronians marched on, into unknown fates.

The resurfacing Seronan war hero also rode east with Lorylle, towards Chybum. Distraught by his long-time friend's disdain, Gromulus realized he was alone. Unaware of the disorder in Whelmore, the urgency of his task became greater. Little did he know another long-time friend was already making himself present in the same northern settlement to which he was headed. With the burden of Antiok no longer consuming him, Gromulus urged Ageeaus faster, his mission now the only thing weighing on his mind.

In Aronia, King Kedor and his White Knights left their majestic city of Ellsar, heading to the western border and their own unsure fate. Queen Niralyn, alone in her chambers, could not sleep.

She was afraid of the dreams—afraid of Ramunak.

LEGENDS
— IN —
TIME
PLIGHT OF THE WARRIOR

What will happen to Fayorn and his people? Will Tornach find what he is looking for in Chybum? Will Gromulus and Lorylle make it out of Nador in time
to deliver Makheb's urgent message to the king of Aronia? Don't miss out on
the next installment in the *Legends in Time* series as authors Vincent Hobbes
and Jordan Benoit continue to take this fantasy tale to a new level in *Plight of
the Warrior*, due out in 2009.

ISBN: 978-0-9763510-5-4

www.legendsintimebook.com
www.myspace.com/legendsintime

VINCENT HOBBES

Here is a sample excerpt from *LIT* author Vincent Hobbes' forthcoming novel, *The Blue Bus*, which will be released in 2009.

ISBN: 978-0-9763510-3-0

For more information about this and other Hobbes End Publishing products visit: www.hobbesendpublishing.com

THE BLUE BUS

Does a homeless man know he is without a home? If he has never had one, does he truly know what he is missing? What about a man who has never really eaten—does he feel true hunger?

Do the enslaved hear the bells of liberty ringing?

How can one wish for something one has never had?

How can a person know love if he is told love does not exist?

What about family?

God?

Does a crazy man know he is *crazy*? Do the insane, who walk the dark streets—careful of the shadows—do they know it? Do they know they are stark raving mad, or is their world simply different from ours? Do they know something that we do not?

How do they perceive the 'sane'?

And, if an insane person knows he is indeed insane, why would he not change to become normal? Does he simply accept his insanity? Does he gaze into the eyes of his creator, and see himself looking back? His reflections revealing the real horror.

Do insane people walk ancient valleys and float through forest dreams?

If so, what is their reward?

Either way, they suffocate on the fate of mankind. Life, as well as death, completes this process.

People conform in such a way that they offer themselves as sacrifice to self-destruction. Sycophantic social sluts. Slaves of sex. Of war. Death. Megalomaniacs of a dying world. Pushing themselves to the edge of humanity—they bleed one another of it. Conceding their rights to those who claim to have designed them.

. . . And all in a world where everything is in bulk. A society where everything 'mega' is standard.

The Mega-burger

Mega-theater

Mega-plane

Mega-city

Mega-Life

Enter the Mega-human—where modification is everything.

Unhappy with your lips?—fill 'em full.

Unhappy with your hips?—suck 'em dry.

Only humans mutilate themselves with intent.

Living in the depths of Mildred-like lies of bliss.

Mega-plex

Mega-state

Mega-media

Mega-Death

Civilizations always succumb to their own inventions. Decay. Syndromes. Instant-fixes and one-night stands. They ignore the beautiful and brake at wrecks, staring; painfully trying to fill themselves with every horror available. Gawkers of a new society. They are junkies of adrenaline, chaos and death. Morbid fascinations, seeking anything that might shock their insensitive existence.

You can walk the streets—although I would not recommend doing so at night—and see thousands without a place. Mumbling. Lost. Veins pumping toxins bought for recreation. Hollow eyes. Drunk on cheap wine, willing to sell themselves for the next fix.

Their vacant souls, cold and empty inside. Void of emotion. They live in their dreams, and only sometimes in real life. What is real life? Yet, the crazies . . . the insane . . . they seem to trap it. Just as a bug-light attracts insects, and wipes them clean. This world, this place—it did the same.

Some spoke out. Some fought. Most did nothing.

Now, they are less. Logic brokered reason, and they became many less. Society could do such things now. The world could never stand for the crazies to gather such attention, so they limited them. By consensus. A state of mind formulated, agreed upon—and enforced. The politicians offered a solution. The people voted with thunderous applause. The Blue Bus imposed their will.

A solution to the problem?—or was it the other way around?

Yet, still, they exist.

They wander down the boulevard. We look the other way as we pass. We pretend they aren't talking to us when they obviously are. We see them in shadows and outside cities. Underground and in back-alleys.

Crazy

Insane

Mad

We pass them off as such things. Something happened to them in their childhood. Something Freudian. Or drugs. There are always the drugs. Demons, mental illness and late night talk shows. We whisper such excuses to ourselves, quite convincingly, that the insane must either not know they are insane, or enjoy their insanity.

Yet we all wonder one thing. Do they—could they—hold the answers to freedom? We dare not ask it, though. Not these days we don't.

We avert our eyes and remain silent.

We accept it—or surely the Blue Bus will come for us too.

CHAPTER 1

It raced into the night. Along the vast openness of the superhighway, its engine purred—humming a death pitch. Down the open lanes, crossing the complex city, the Blue Bus was alive.

The night was late—2 A.M. The sky was murky and a haze covered the moon. This made the streets appear even darker. It kept the people in—or perhaps it was the new curfew. Either way, it was a quiet night.

Along the highway were long rows of streetlights. Tall and looming, they ran along the center divider which separated the opposing lanes of traffic. Contrasting with the dark skies, they filled the highway with a strange, ominous orange glow.

The traffic was scarce and the Blue Bus rolled quickly. The endless row of streetlights flickered by rapidly along its left side, appearing as a single strand of light that went on for miles. The highway was relatively empty and the road's eight lanes made it easy to pass what little civilian traffic there was.

The Blue Bus was modern, fine-tuned and threatening. It was somewhat longer than an ambulance, and designed for high speeds. It had six tires. Each was wide and gripped the road for control. The Blue Bus sat upon a hefty metal frame. It was formidable—its shell solid—impenetrable. The walls were thick metal, painted blue, and aerodynamically shaped to withstand high rates of speed. Streamlined, it was designed for a purpose.

The Blue Bus always delivered on time.

Come rain or shine.

In the front cab sat the driver. It was dark inside, except for the glowing green lights that illuminated the various dials and switches. He sat alone, thick metal separating the cab from the back—the driver isolated.

He preferred it that way.

120 mph

It was cramped in the back of the Blue Bus, yet its interior was highly organized and served a purpose. Restricted, five men sat in the back.

Three large men were against the left wall. Seated in their jump seats, they felt little comfort.

Between their burly bodies were small compartments which held their gear. Combat-ready shields and helmets. Restraint harnesses. Personal neutralizing gas canisters. Handcuffs. Stun guns and other authoritarian devices at the ready. All within easy reach.

Along the front wall, their backs to the driver, were two more seats. Another two men sat patiently. They had more space between them, for their jobs required movement.

Between their seats was a cabinet. Inside its white doors were products of horror—various restraints and medical supplies. Needles. Towels to mop up any mess. Pharmaceuticals. Pokes and prods and other surgical atrocities. Above them, even more equipment.

Along the right wall was a metal gurney. Bolted to the floor, it was cold and eerie. Leather straps loosely crisscrossed it.

The gurney was highly polished and smelled of disinfectant. Sterile. The straps lay seemingly calm across it. Clearly intended to restrain, the straps were activated upon touch. Once the Subject was placed on the gurney, the straps would automatically clench. Tight. Overhead was a large lamp. It connected to a swivel. It was off.

More strange equipment, seemingly haphazard, littered the back of the Blue Bus. Machines and blinking lights and hoses. A syringe, attached to the end of a motorized arm, connected above the gurney on the right wall. It hung overhead, its metal tip sharp—waiting. A mask, with a hose connecting it to a small tank of gas, was strapped in the corner. The motion of the bus caused it to sway back and forth. It looked oddly like a mechanical snake.

The gentle rocking of the Blue Bus soothed the five men. It was dark in the back and they were calm. Quiet, too.

It always was before a raid.

130 mph

The Blue Bus continued to speed down the highway in the bleak of night. The metropolis was massive. They were close.

During daylight hours, the roads were packed solid with traffic. However, late at night, they were bare. It was dangerous to go out at night without reason. As the few cars around them traveled a furious one hundred and five, the Blue Bus passed them with ease.

140 mph

Its engine was turbocharged. It made a high-pitched, whining noise—soft and balanced. It was perfectly timed and tuned. Atop the metal roof were its lights. Flashing. Signaling all that death was on the prowl. Though the howls of its siren had yet to pierce the night.

Soon.

The Technician and the Censor sat next to one another. One, normal by all standards. The other, small and frail.

The frail one wore glasses and was pencil-thin. On his face was a slender, oil-slicked mustache, which looked more like a smudge than facial hair. The hair on his head was thick, combed back, and greasy. It appeared as if a permanent fixture. His glasses were thin, and no matter how hard he tried, they always seemed to slide down to the tip of his pointy nose. He had a smug look on his face. He was the Technician.

The man who rode next to him had blonde hair, normal build, and was clean-shaven. In his hands, he held a clipboard. He appeared to study it, slowly making marks with a bored look on his face. He was the Censor.

Both men sat quietly. Preparing.

The three Regulators sat adjacent to them, their backs along the left wall. They were massive. Their knees pulled close, they sat bored and uncomfortable. Each man's hair was cropped the same. Short. Their eyes expressionless, a lazy look about them. Thousand-yard stares. Each wore his combat suit. Fully protected, they were covered neck to toe in their blue uniforms. Atop their heads were riot helmets, their visors open.

150 mph

The driver gripped the wheel with his left hand, passing another dozen cars. He grinned at the narrow miss.

With his right hand, the driver pulled a cigarette from his lips, slowly exhaling a cloud of smoke inside the dimly lit cab. It swirled. As if in a ritualistic dance, the smoke flowed past his face and out the slightly open window. Cigarettes were illegal—*but what would they really do?* He was a driver of a Blue Bus—he was feared. Besides, most of the Blue Bus operators smoked—it was as if the basic design of the job required it.

Either way, the driver did not ultimately care. He pulled the cigarette back to his lips, slowly taking another drag. He felt the smoke in his mouth and the burn in his lungs, and it felt good.

Another cloud of smoke danced as he exhaled. He smiled at this. Then, he put the cigarette back up, holding it with his lips.

The driver took his right hand and flicked a switch near the steering wheel. It, in turn, illuminated the back of the bus in a faint red light, signaling the men in the rear to begin preparing.

Almost there.

160 mph

In the back, the Technician, Censor and three Regulators began making preparations.

The wiry Technician put aside his clipboard and sifted through a drawer. He withdrew a few vials of liquid substance and set them on a small rack. From another drawer, he produced two syringes. He pulled the orange caps from each and began concocting his remedy.

When he was finished, he organized his effects and adorned a white lab coat that hung behind him. He tightened a mask over his nose and mouth, his beady eyes staring blankly—he was now ready.

The Censor punched some final numbers into his handheld computer. Double-checking. Triple-checking. Finally satisfied, he too donned a similar mask.

The Regulators prepared, as well. Although the space offered little room, they expertly began getting ready. They still appeared bored, their eyes lifeless as they tightened their armor. They adjusted the helmets upon their heads, lowering their thick face shields. They attached belts around their waists, which held an assortment of weapons. More armaments attached across their chests. They moved in orchestra, each man graceful and fierce.

Very soon.

170 mph

The driver took a final drag from his cigarette. With his left hand still grasping the wheel, the driver reached across his face and flicked it out the window. Through his side mirror, he saw a brief shower of embers as it hit the pavement. Then it was gone.

With his hand now free, the driver reached to the middle of the dash; protruding from it was a thin, mounted computer monitor. He swiveled it towards him so he could see it better. The driver turned it on and a spectrum of touch-screen buttons appeared.

His eyes flashing from the road to the screen again, the driver expertly punched in a series of numbers. A few moments passed as he downloaded the necessary information.

The engine screamed as he passed another series of cars.

180 mph

A few more moments passed and the appropriate data finally appeared—the Subject's name lit up the screen.

The driver pushed yet another button, and from below the monitor, he tilted a second screen, this one much smaller. On it was a map of the location. It showed him his exact position and the proper route to the Subject's home. Another quick glance at the two screens and the driver concentrated back on the road ahead of him. He mashed the accelerator harder.

190 mph

The Blue Bus shifted on its suspension as it careened past another group of cars, one being a police officer's patrol vehicle. It, like the civilians, gave way to the Blue Bus—to its authority—to its glory.

He passed another car on its right at exactly the same moment it began to merge. The Blue Bus driver, with not so much as a moment's hesitation, reacted quickly. He jerked the wheel left, nearly swiping the car full of intoxicated teenagers who were oblivious to his presence. The driver stole a glace in his mirror, but the kids were already out of sight.

He smiled.

Not much of anything mattered.

One of the men inside the back pounded an angry fist on the bus' inner walls. The veracity of the knock let the driver know that his near fatal, last minute jolt of the wheel caused the three Regulators, who were standing as they got ready, to topple upon one another.

He laughed aloud. He did not fear them.

195 mph

The driver held onto his grin for a moment longer. It was as if he were afraid to let it go. It was the only thing he had left.

Besides, he thought, *they will have their fun in a few minutes—this is my time.*

CHAPTER 2

Farther down the never-ending superhighway of the metroplex, one of many in the world, the driver blasted on. He felt invincible. He no longer cared. The driver, somewhere deep in the recesses of his mind—where not even the government reprogramming and thought detection machines could reach—secretly wished for it all to be over. The driver hoped a car would veer into his lane and cause him to lose control.

Ha. The end of the whole mess of things, he thought. *I hate this life.*

Instead, he kept driving. His professionalism overcame. He exited at a sign marked: EXIT 271. He sped even faster. He checked the coordinates again. He was close. Ten minutes. Perhaps eight.

The Blue Bus now drove through the reaches of the mazelike metroplex. The streets were even darker than the highway. Flickers of red and blue flashed as the bus' lights rapidly swirled atop, warning anyone in its way. The siren remained silent.

Not yet.

The driver pushed another button and the Subject's violation and sentence became visible. He studied it carefully. It was his job to make sure the proper procedures were followed. That they went to the right place. That they collected the correct Subject.

This was something that once done, couldn't be undone.

His eyes, sharing their time with the screen and the road, read the details. He double-checked to make sure everything was in order. It was.

He then radioed headquarters. Confirming everything verbally, the driver reached up to the ceiling of the cab and grabbed a microphone. It was attached to a receiver by a small cord. He switched it on and spoke into it, allowing those who rode in the back to receive their orders.

Although routine, they listened intently. The evening's mood would be dependent upon the driver's next words. They heard the squelch of the intercom, the small speaker high in the dark corner—crackling.

The driver's monotone voice stated, "This is case number 62991A. Our directives are as follows . . ." He paused. "The Subject's name is Jerry 4492 of North Ridge residential living, sector eight. Street address—1408 Westlake Drive."

The driver pushed another button and continued, "Household is a standard, single-family residence. Accompanying him in the house are the Subject's parents. They are registered citizens. Also, they are tested and certified breeders."

The driver could almost hear their sighs.

He continued, "A bench warrant for the Subject . . . all digital forms present . . . CFR seal verified. The Subject's sentence is seizure and reprogramming." Again, he could almost feel their let-down. The driver finished, "Target house—two minutes."

The driver turned on Westlake, as directed by his GPS map. Finally, he flicked the red switch on the panel in front of him. This was his favorite part. The siren wailed loudly, promising to waken everyone within a four-block radius. Deafening, it screamed into the night. The flicker of red and blue lights seemed to intensify as well, tucking into the alcoves of the dark streets. Illuminating them. The siren howled. People woke. He could see lights in bedrooms turn on. Then porch lights.

The residents, however, were cautious to peer out. What sick curiosity they entertained as to whom the Blue Bus was after, they each secretly worried it was them. They would not leave their homes until they knew. Not when the Blue Bus came-a-calling. Instead, they would peer carefully through blinds and from behind drapes. On occasion, a child would pull back the curtains curiously, innocently, and expose the gawkers and gossipers.

When this happened, the driver always thought their expressions to be funny. He would pass and see the sheer horror on their surprised faces. They would cast the curtains closed as fast as they could and turn off the lights. They would miss the event. They would miss the fun they could have—but they would not risk being seen. Not when the Blue Bus was near.

This time, however, he saw no peering faces. They were there, to be sure, but they remained hidden. They would hide, still and silent, until they knew he was not coming for them. They would cringe in dark corners, surrounded by their pitiful fears as the Blue Bus passed. Hoping—wishing—begging for the Blue Bus to pass them by. Their minds racing with possible crimes they may have committed. Wondering if it was their time. Fear swirled in every one of them—the cowards. Self-survival instincts churning. Wanting it to be someone else. Wishing for the Blue Bus to please take someone else.

The driver finally approached. The bold numbers stood in contrast with the dark night as he read the addresses.

1400

He tilted a lever with his right hand.

1402

Spotlights turned night into day.

1404

1406

He jammed the brakes.

1408

The three Regulators leapt from the back door.

The Technician and Censor exited after them.

The driver looked at his watch. He was two minutes ahead of schedule. He lit another cigarette.

LIBERTY OR DEATH

A NOVEL BY JORDAN BENOIT

Following is a sample chapter from *LIT* author Jordan Benoit's novel, *Liberty or Death*, which marks the beginning of his new science fiction series. Due out in 2009, *LOD* will be the first book of the *Makhaira Chronicles*.

ISBN: 978-0-9763510-4-7

For more information on this title and other Hobbes End Publishing products visit:
www.hobbesendpublishing.com

He awoke with his head throbbing. He sat up slowly in the vast darkness of where he had lain. *How long was I out?* the man thought to himself. *What happened?*

Lieutenant Myron Vasilis began rising to his feet, hitting his head on an overhanging pipe in the process. He quickly rubbed his head, feeling the writhing pain the sudden unexpected collision had added to his already hurting cranium. Not being able to see anything in the pitch-blackness of the environment, he moved slightly to his right and tried standing again, this time using his hands above his head to guide him and to prevent any more unwanted head injuries.

He felt around in a pouch around his waist and pulled out a pair of black goggles. Myron slung the goggles over his shaved head and situated them over his eyes. He subsequently flipped a switch on one side to give them power and then rotated a knob on the other side, clockwise, until his eyes became aided by the night vision. He slowly turned around, looking all about the small area. Myron was deep in the ship's under works, a tightly congested system of small corridors that ran all throughout the undercarriage of the *Prowler's* hull. He remembered. He had been making routine checks on the ship's functionary gauges when a large, unannounced force collided with the ship, sending him hurling down the tight corridor. The lieutenant must have hit his head on one of the many large pipes running throughout the ship's underbelly, and had been instantly rendered unconscious. There had been, however, one other engineer in the under works with him at the time, but Private Emmanouil Aison was nowhere in sight. Myron looked around some more, quietly calling out the recruit's name, but found no answer. Eventually, he gave up.

This is all too weird, Myron thought. *What did I miss?*

Almost immediately, the naval engineer worked his way over to the gauges with which he had been working, and tried getting them back online. He pushed switch after switch on the console, rearranged wires, anything he could possibly think of to get the machine working again. It was no hope, though, and he knew it. Instinctually he had known it since he regained consciousness. Normally there would have been a light, sustained hum in the background, an ambient soothing ocean of sound waves that Myron loved so much. But they were not present. The under works were deathly quiet, and this struck a tinge of fear in the man, but he knew he needed to keep himself together and figure out the status of the current situation. The backup emergency lights were out; he needed to get to the bottom of what was going on.

Myron worked his way through the confining corridor, retracing his steps to the ladder that led back to the bridge. On his way, he kept an eye out for anyone else who might still be down in the under works, but to his surprise, he found no one. The lieutenant felt unnervingly alone in the deep recesses of the *Prowler's* hull. A small bit of claustrophobia hit him, but he forced himself to pass it off as anxiety. Myron just wanted to get out. The twenty-nine year old naval engineer had been onboard the *Prowler* for an active period of three standard years, never once taking leave to set foot off the ship in that duration. He loved this ship. He

217

knew the interior's confusing web work like it was a part of him, an extension of his personal being. He never had a desire to leave her confines before, but something rigid flashed in his mind, now—something that made him uncomfortable. There was something lodged in the back of his mind, and he could not ascertain exactly what it might be. All Myron knew was that something strange had indeed happened aboard the ship whilst he lay unconscious.

Eventually, he rounded one last corner and approached the ladder, but as he grabbed hold of the sidebars with his hands, his feet unintentionally collided with an object lying on the floor. Myron looked down inquisitively to see a small sidearm on the metal floor. It was a T-240 Licos, a small pistol that had a silent shot and bit hard into the enemy like a wolf. It was the standard-issue sidearm for any military personnel in the U.C.H. fleet, but this one in particular had more meaning to the engineer. He picked it up and saw some distinct scratch marks on the shaft—subtle, but apparent, nevertheless. Myron knew these tick marks, and to whom the pistol on which they were engraved belonged.

Emmanouil.

The lieutenant put the loaded pistol in one of his pouches on his belt, as his own Licos already accompanied his holster. He grabbed hold of the ladder once again and began climbing upward. As he drew near the top, Myron noticed that the hatch was already slightly ajar. He ever so discretely slid the hatch further open, just enough to poke his head out without making any noise.

Strange, he thought.

What he saw before him was like an eerie dream. The hatch opened to a small corner of the ship's bridge. Had everything been normal, the bridge would be crawling with crewmembers and high-ranking officers. Myron took a moment to gaze at the lifelessness of what was once an astounding sight. Papers were strewn everywhere, haphazardly mangled across desktops and the bridge floor. All lights were out, just as he witnessed in the under works of the ship. He felt quite fortunate that he had his goggles, for he often needed them when working down in the under works, and now he needed their aid more so than ever before.

Without them, he might never find his way in this abandoned abyss.

After deciding that it was clear to move in, Myron slowly crawled out of the under works and stood to his feet on the ransacked bridge. As a precaution, the lieutenant pulled his Licos from his holster and released the safety. If anything were to jump out at him, he wanted to be ready.

Myron began walking about the bridge, pistol held firmly in the palms of both hands. Although he had gone through the same military training as the rest of the navy personnel, the lieutenant had never seen a day of combat in his life. It had not been his calling. Myron Vasilis was an engineer, an expert with computers and military technology. He had been assigned to the *Prowler* at his personal request, after showing much promise at the naval academy on mankind's home planet, Gaia. He was a natural with machinery—a genius in the minds of many of his superiors. Myron thought he was well on the path to working his way up to admiral. But that had all come to a halt, now, as far as he was concerned. Lieutenant Vasilis had to remember his training as he nervously held the Licos in his now sweaty palms. This was like no situation he thought he would ever have to confront. Myron had seen the horror movies growing up. He loved watching the scary movies where one person was alone in the dark, and some frenzied monster lurked about, waiting to prey on him. But now the very thoughts of such shocking entertainment made him all the more unnerved. He felt as though he had been put smack in the middle of such a situation.

Myron had to shake such thoughts away.

Monsters were not real.

He was sure of it.

He called out, "Private Aison," quietly, unsure if he should be saying anything at all in such a situation. He stepped over the loose sheets of paper that were scattered about the floor, and then accidentally kicked a plastic coffee mug, which then went sliding across the floor until it collided with a nearby desk. The lieutenant ducked down immediately, startled by the minute noise that seemed to be amplified amidst the rest of the stillness of the area. He chastised himself for not being more careful.

What happened here? he then asked himself, as though he should be able to answer his own query. Myron stood utterly confused. Where was everybody?

Lieutenant Vasilis carefully stood upright again. He adjusted the knob on his goggles to make the greenish picture clearer. He thought he could not afford to be inadvertently running into things anymore, for it might mean the difference between survival and martyrdom. And he had no desire to sacrifice his life for the 'greater good' of the empire, for he knew his death would not have the significance to others as it might to himself—at least not yet. Myron was a man of much passion, and he knew that such passion would get him through this . . . whatever *this* was. The engineer continued his way across the bridge until he reached the main navigation terminal, directly behind the round holo-map table where the admiral would have stood to issue commands. Myron stopped for a moment to admire the extent of the area, and although it was deserted, the lieutenant realized he had never stood on this part of the bridge before. In fact, not many had. To Myron, this was hallowed ground. He dreamt that one day he would stand on a bridge like this, in command of one of the massive battleships, or even an entire fleet. But he had to place those thoughts aside for the time being. What Myron did not know yet, was exactly how much trouble he was really in.

He looked at the table through his goggles and saw nothing—no electronic maps, no plotted coordinates—nothing. The tabletop screen was blank and cold to the touch. And as he noticed this, Myron soon realized there was a bit of a draft in the large room, as well. It was as though someone had turned the A/C on full blast and forgot to turn it off. The cold was not yet intense enough to be bothersome, however, for the lieutenant was dressed in his white, heavy workman's jumpsuit.

Lieutenant Vasilis turned back around to face the navigation terminal and walked steadily over to it. Like the holo-map table, it, too, was shut off. Yet, being a man of skill with computers, he did not let himself panic. He could fix this problem. He knew he could. Myron carefully sat down on a nearby swivel chair, still trying not to make any noise. He had a deft hunch he needed to remain as inaudible as could be. He rolled the chair silently to the terminal's keyboard, set his Licos down next to the keys, and began typing dexterously. He tried code after code, anything to get the computer back online. Nothing worked. He knew a plethora of codes that could render most computers serviceable, but none of them worked at this time. It could not be an issue of being unplugged, for someone would have had to dig deep into the walls to disengage any wires, so he quickly disregarded that possibility. But what could it be, then?

Myron stopped his fingers after a while, accepting it as useless to mess with the keyboard anymore. He picked up his Licos and reared back in the chair, pondering.

Then he heard something, a light rustling. Anxious, Myron stood up from the chair with haste and turned to face the sound, pistol aimed. He began taking methodical steps over in the direction from which it had come, instinctually knowing he needed to be at full wits. The rustling came again, and the lieutenant proceeded with caution. He made his way across the bridge, almost all the way to the massive window that gave a permeated view of the cosmos beyond, when he started to be able to pinpoint exactly from where the sound was coming. He passed a series of control desks with computer terminals at his flanks, all of which would normally be manned by numerous personnel on each side. The computer screens were all off, just as he expected them to be, headsets appearing haphazardly placed on the floor and seats, as if the crewmembers had been ripped from their seats without warning. The very thought of what may have happened to his fellow crew began to sink into Myron's mind, causing his nerves to frenzy even more as he held his pistol at the ready, nearing the front of the bridge, the bow of the *Prowler*.

When standing at the forefront of the ship, the window reached from floor to ceiling, bending back at an eggshell arc as it reached for the top, and took up most of one's peripheral vision. From Myron's perspective, it appeared as if he was standing alone in the blankness of space, like there was nothing separating him from the vacuum beyond the ship's confines. Lieutenant Vasilis had had the pleasure of standing at this spot before, when inspecting some of the bridge's machinery on routine maintenance rounds. He had witnessed the grandeur of the view, the breathtaking feeling of being in deep space. Before, he had welcomed such a feeling, but now, because of his current situation, it felt much different—much more alone, and suffocating. Myron took a deep breath and stepped closer to a small, discrete hatch at the spearhead of the ship. The rustling had stopped, but he knew that this was from where it had come. He was sure of it. The engineer had worked down in the confines many times before, and knew that it would be a great place to hide in the case of an emergency. The hatch blended in perfectly with the rest of the ship's flooring. One would have to be looking for it in order to notice it. Lieutenant Vasilis crouched down with caution. He gave a light tap on the hatch with his Licos, letting whatever might be down there know that he was about to open it.

There was no response.

He took another deep breath and began opening the hatch with his left hand, keeping his pistol in his right, aimed at the opening. As the hatch door raised, it made an unwanted shrieking sound that he could not avoid. The hinges needed to be oiled, but there was nothing he could do about that right now. As the opening cleared, Myron peered into the darkness beyond. Down in the small compartment, which could only fit one person comfortably, he saw the body curled up in a fetal position, shaking frantically in terror. Using his goggles as his aid, he could see that the person was wearing a deckhand jumpsuit, much like his own, but yellow instead of his white. The white of his signified Myron was the chief engineer. However, the fact that everything appeared green through his lenses, he could not decipher this at the moment, for yellow was not the only other color jumpsuit the crewmembers wore. What he knew for sure was that this personnel was one of his.

"Private," he called out in a whisper.

A shiver accompanied the response from this deckhand. "G . . . go . . . away. . . . Ru . . . run. . . . S . . . save yourself. . . ."

Chills went down Myron's spine when he heard the panic come out from her mouth. "Private, get ahold of yourself," he ordered at first impulse.

"Th . . . they . . . they came. . . . They . . . t . . . took them . . . all. . . ."

"Who came?"

She looked up at Myron, though being dark and not having a pair of goggles of her own, all she could see amidst the blackness was the green glow illuminating from his goggles. She covered her face with her hands in reaction to what she obviously deemed as a frightening sight. "Y . . . you're one . . . one of them." She breathed heavily, as if she had been running on a treadmill for hours. "Le . . . leave me alone . . . p . . . pl . . . please. . . ."

"Private," he started calmly, trying not to show his own fear, "I am not one of *them*, whatever *they* are. I am Lieutenant Myron Vasilis."

"S . . . sir?" She moved her hands from her face, looking at the glow of his lenses once again. Although this deckhand was panic-stricken, she seemed to have enough of her wits left to ascertain that this man was indeed a member of the *Prowler's* crew . . . and not one of *them*.

"State your name, private," the lieutenant ordered, lowering his Licos, and turning the safety back on. He then replaced it in his holster. "It is dark everywhere. I cannot see a thing without these goggles, and even then, things are not crystal clear."

Her heavy breathing sustained, but gradually became less harsh as she realized this man was not going to harm her. "A . . . Adonia . . . si . . . sir. . . ."

"Private Hanna Adonia," Myron said with relief. Indeed, she was one of his. After a brief pause, he said, "Where is everyone, private? What happened here?"

"Sir, did . . . did you not see, sir?"

Only being able to recall the loud thud against the hull of the ship, then subsequently banging his head, which sent him unconscious, he knew he had missed whatever happened, and was fortunate to have been lying *safely* within the confines of the *Prowler's* underbelly.

"No, Adonia," Myron said with regret, "I believe I was unconscious. I . . ." he hesitated sheepishly, "I hit my head."

Hanna replied in a whisper, lifting her body up slowly, warily, to a standing position, "Sir, they took them, sir. They took them all! The crew, they are all gone!"

Myron asked, bemused, "Who took them?"

She could not answer. She only shook her head. It was too much for her to bear right now.

"Here, take my hand," the lieutenant then said, after realizing she was still in shock. They could talk later, once he knew they were safe.

Hanna recoiled. "No. . . . Sir, I'm not going out there, sir. They'll get me, t . . . too."

"Hanna, you can't stay in there." Myron was not used to being forceful with his deckhands. He had always been easy going with them, but that was perhaps because no one ever questioned him when he gave orders. His subordinates loved and respected their lieutenant. They were always happy to do whatever he requested of them, but that did not seem to become Hanna, now. "I know you're scared, but you're a soldier, and you need to act like one. Whatever has happened, we need to stick together, and we need to reestablish communication with the rest of the crew."

"Sir, they're all gone, sir. Did you not hear me?"

He did not want to believe her. There was no way, in his mind, that he could fathom an entire crew of ten thousand personnel simply vanishing. It was ridiculous. "Private Hanna Adonia, pull yourself together, dammit! You are getting out of that hole, and that is an order!"

Hanna sighed, not wanting to disobey orders, but at the same time, regretful of what she was about to do. With Myron's hand still offered out to her—she could see the outline of it in the dark given off by the glow of his goggles—Private Adonia took hold of him. Lieutenant Vasilis pulled her out of the maintenance compartment and both stood to their feet.

"Now," Myron said, "that wasn't so bad, was it?"

"If you don't mind me saying, sir . . . we're both dead. They'll come for us, too."

"Nonsense, private. We'll get through this. . . ." He added under his breath,

222

turning around to look at the scoured bridge again, "Whatever *this* is."

"I can't see a thing, sir."

"Just stay on me, Adonia. I'll be your eyes until we can get the lights back on."

"Sir. . . ." Hanna started as Myron began walking back to the command deck of the bridge, but then trailed off.

He stopped in his tracks and turned to face her. "What is it, private?"

"Sir, I . . . I saw them take him."

"Saw them take who?"

"Emmanouil, sir. He tried to fight back, but . . ."

"But what?" Myron uncontrollably put his hands upon her shoulders. He was shaking her and didn't even realize it.

"They're . . . they're not human, sir."

Myron pulled back. "Not human?"

"He didn't stand a chance . . . none of them did. . . . We don't, either." Tears welled in her eyes.

Lieutenant Vasilis still did not want to buy into what this terrorized deckhand was trying to tell him. "Private Aison can take care of himself. We'll find him, soon enough, okay?"

Hanna nodded her head, sobbing. She wanted to believe Myron, like he was her father telling her the boogeyman was not real, that she had only been dreaming, and everything was going to be fine. But, she knew she had not dreamt. She had seen it with her own eyes . . . what Lieutenant Vasilis could not conceive. Private Adonia was a soldier, but she could not seem to gather herself together at the moment to act like one. She shook in fear, like this was the end of her existence, and she was not ready for it.

"Arm your Licos, private," Myron ordered as he removed his from the holster at his side again. "Whatever we are up against, we can deal with it. We are soldiers, and that is what we do." He was unsure of himself as he said this, but he could not let her sense his fear. He was her superior officer, and had to make sure he set an example with morale.

"Sir. . . ."

"What now?"

"My Licos, sir." She then said uneasily, knowing very well the consequences of losing track of her sidearm. "I seem to have misplaced it, sir."

Exhaling deeply, not wanting to deal with reprimanding one of his deckhands at the moment—more interested in trying to find out exactly what was going on—Lieutenant Vasilis pulled Private Aison's pistol out from his side pouch and handed it to her. "Here, use this for now.

"And private," he paused, waiting to make sure he had her full attention, "don't misplace this one."

And also coming soon, the *Legends in Time* world is about to get a whole lot bigger with two new tales of other peoples and places that are sure to please fans of the series:

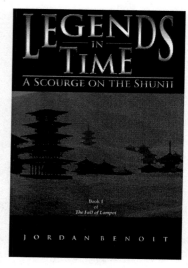

THE FALL OF LAMPOI PART 1: A SCOURGE ON THE SHUNII

by Jordan Benoit

Far from the reaches of mankind's knowledge, another vast land exists. Home to the species known as the Nal'k'har, the continent of Oka'taryn covers a great expanse of territory, much larger than the western world of Men. During a pressing time in the Empire of Lampoi, the fates of all the inhabitants rest on the shoulders of an unlikely heroine. Ayuna trains for acceptance into Lampoi's most revered order of military agents, the Ying'wuren. As a final trial, Ayuna is ordered to oversee the protection of the nation's soon-to-be emperor, Mor'dian. Little does she know, this simple task will thrust her into an epic voyage to save her world.

ISBN: 978-0-9763510-7-8

PRIDE OF THE SCARLET CROWN

by Vincent Hobbes and Jordan Benoit

In this stand-alone novel, the world of *Legends in Time* grows even more. Nilow and Wylim are brothers of a tiny race of people known as Covaks who inhabit the lush, tropic jungle terrain to the far west. The two Covak brothers uninvitingly become thrust into a world much larger than they ever realized. They must traverse through foreign lands, finding themselves in a world quite different from theirs, and take part in a crusade that will change their their lives forever.

ISBN: 978-0-9763510-6-1

www.legendsintimebook.com
www.myspace.com/legendsintime